One Bad THING

Jenny Hilborne

One Bad Thing
By Jenny Hilborne

©2018 by Jenny Hilborne

This book is a work of fiction. Names, characters, places, and incidents are a product of the author's imagination or are used fictitiously. Any resemblance to actual events, locales, or persons, living or dead, is coincidental.

Cover Design/Interior Design: www.TellTaleBookCovers.com

Published by TreasureLine Publishing

ISBN: 978-1-61752-203-1

Also available in eBook publication

PRINTED IN THE UNITED STATES OF AMERICA

To Mum. Thanks for everything.
Love you always.

Thank you to all those who provided their time, expertise, and encouragement through this book, my readers for their patience, and my family for always supporting me.

Chapter 1

Saturday, late January 2013

"I want to see you tonight."

As her warm husky voice breathed the words into his ear, Wilkes Smith leaned against the wall of the café and closed his eyes for a second, picturing his girlfriend with her long hair all messy on the pillow. She'd been on his mind since he'd crawled out of her bed early yesterday morning, before two men had involved him in a murder. He wished he could go back to her and that innocent place.

"Same here," he said, opening his eyes and casting a glance at his watch.

"I miss you."

"Same here," he said again.

"I guess that's love."

A thrill went through him, the same thrill he always got. Even though they'd spent many years together, it still made him feel like a schoolboy when he heard her say it, because he knew she meant it.

"I love you, too." The distance and dread made him feel it even more acutely.

"When will you be back?"

"I'm not sure."

"I thought you were going to call me sooner. I was worried."

"Sorry." He moved away from a group of chattering people, so he could hear her better. "I don't want you to worry."

"I can't help it."

"Remember why we're doing this," he said, desperate to unburden yet determined to keep the facts to himself now that it had all gone so horribly wrong. "I'll call you whenever I can."

"Tell me everything is okay."

"Everything is fine."

"No, it isn't. Something's wrong, I can tell." Her tone changed. She sounded frightened. "What's happened, Wilkes?"

"Nothing." He couldn't tell her he had killed a man. Murder was never part of the plan; at least it was never part of his plan. If she found out, she would despise him, and that would be even worse. Ignoring the people around him, he turned away from the café to face the street and pressed his cell phone to the other ear. "Why do you always think something is wrong?"

"I can hear it in your voice. Has something bad happened?"

Yes, he wanted to say, something very bad. "A small setback. Don't worry about it."

"I want you to come home. Now."

"No. Not without the money."

"This was a bad idea, Wilkes. We should have involved the police instead of trying to deal with it ourselves."

"Well, we can't involve them now."

"Why not?"

"I don't have time to explain. I'll call you again soon."

"I'm scared."

"Don't be." Her fear took away his capacity to deal with his own. He needed her to stay strong. "I love you. Don't ever forget it."

"I love you." Her voice dropped to a whisper. "Thank you for doing this for us."

"Of course." The validation was essential. "Everything will work out, baby," he said. He paused, not wanting to get into it, but yearning to know. "How is the boy?"

"The same."

"As long as he's not getting any worse."

"No, he's no worse, but I don't know how much longer we have."

He heard her light a cigarette and blow smoke into the air. He hated the habit and wished she would stop, though he would never tell her.

"Baby, I have to go," he said. "Please don't worry about me. I'll be fine. I'll call you again soon, I promise."

Chapter 2

A night of excessive drinking failed to calm Amelia Miller's nerves. After leaving a new cocktail bar in the city, one she'd never been to before, she ended her Friday night alone at Skin Deep, a local tattoo studio on Lombard Street in San Francisco. Upset after the bust up with her estranged husband, the fight was the first thing she remembered an hour later when she woke up in the back seat of a cab outside her Dolores Heights home.

After paying the driver, she stumbled up the front steps to her house and spent a few minutes fumbling through her pockets for her key before she managed to let herself in. She closed the door with her heel and ditched her shoes, then made her way to the kitchen, almost tripping over an old backpack she'd dumped in the hall. The place had been a mess for four months, since Oliver had taken whatever he could fit into a suitcase and moved out, but Amelia didn't care. Without anyone here, she could live how she wanted.

In the kitchen, she fed her dog, drank another couple of shots of gin, felt it travel to her brain, and passed out around midnight on the couch.

Startled awake by the sensation of falling, she sat up, sweating and shaking, then realized it had only been a dream. She wiped her face with her sleeve. It reeked of stale alcohol. For a moment she felt panicky, then tried to remember what it was she had been worrying about. She focused her eyes on the clock, watching the illuminated hand creep around the face as the early hours of Saturday morning ticked by.

The room felt colder than usual. Her head hurt as an unwelcome image filled her mind, one of her middle-aged, cheating husband with his young and pretty girlfriend. Fighting the urge to vomit, Amelia closed her eyes and leaned her head back against the cushions.

"Screw you," she whispered, picturing them both dead. It couldn't be his body or his looks, she thought, so it must be money the young woman wanted. What else would attract a beautiful blonde to a man old enough to be her father?

Now that Amelia was heading into her late thirties, with a less than healthy lifestyle and fluctuating weight, especially around the middle, this slender new woman in her husband's life made her feel old, ugly and irrelevant. To make it worse, Oliver's girlfriend was petite and sweet, the complete opposite of Amelia who, at almost six feet, was bigger than the average woman and had the build of a shot-put competitor. They'd only met once, last night, and already Amelia hated her. She hated her husband's new happiness. It wasn't fair. She hadn't changed. She was the same wild, beer-drinking, sex addict Oliver had married; only now she wasn't good enough.

Her stomach churned and she headed to the bathroom. As she sat on the toilet and waited for the dizziness to pass, she thought back to her teenage years, when she'd been about the age of Oliver's new girlfriend, and realized she had been no different. Back then, she was boozing and sleeping with older men, crashing anywhere she could as a way to escape the attention of her mother's boyfriends, and when she hit her early thirties, she moved from Ireland to the United States and started seeing a therapist, but continued to drink. It was a phase she did not foresee ending.

She flushed the toilet, washed her hands and face, then made her way into the kitchen to do as she'd been taught and have a little more of what bit her the night before.

Her skin itched beneath a bandage on her left arm. Peeling back the tape, she traced her fingers gently over the bumpy new black lines, remembering the argument over the tattoo. It was supposed to resemble a pair of wings, but it didn't look good and it was not what she wanted. Her fault, she supposed, for insisting on getting a tattoo when she was drunk.

At the back of her wooly mind, there was something else nagging.

When the phone rang, the sound of it terrified her, reminding her. She'd forgotten that she'd plugged it back into the wall socket and hugged herself tightly, waiting to see if it stopped. The machine picked it up. A man spoke. It was the same male voice she'd heard the night before. He began to leave a message.

Last night, he had asked to speak to Marcus Miller. Insisted. She remembered the conversation.

"Marcus is a friend," he explained. "He's been looking after something for me. I've been away, but I'm back now and I want to collect it."

"I don't know anyone by that name."

His tone quickly turned menacing.

"Don't mess with me, Amelia. I want to talk to Marcus."

"How do you know my name?"

"Marcus gave it to me. He also gave me your address."

"You've got the wrong person."

"I don't think so."

"Nobody with that name lives here."

"Then you better tell me where I can find him."

She'd hung up only to have him call back; convincing her it was not some sick joke.

"This is not some fucking game," he said.

She'd slammed down the phone.

Each time he called back he became more aggressive, until she'd threatened him with the police. Then it had turned truly frightening with him telling her that if she involved the police he would stab her in her bed. Those chilling words were now fixed in her brain, rattling her again.

She remembered hearing him sucking in deep breaths, trying to control his anger. It was the same way her mother used to breathe.

For reasons known only to her, instead of calling the police she'd removed the plug from the phone jack and gone out, met up with her friend, and got drunk.

"I want my money and I'm going to collect it," he was now saying into the machine. "I know you live alone, so you might want to think again about trying to cheat me."

This new message left her feeling sick in her stomach. She wiped sweaty palms down her legs and pushed her hair back behind her ears. Once again, it didn't feel like a hoax. It seemed horribly real. This man knew her. He was looking for someone with her same last name. Amelia believed her husband must be caught up in it, even wondered if it could be the real reason he left. Was he running from someone?

Crumpled on the floor by her feet lay the handyman's flier she had ripped from the front door. She smoothed it out and reread it. Last night, she had tossed it aside. Now it seemed like it might be important.

Chapter 3

Miller was her married name. As far as Amelia knew, nobody in her husband's family went by the name of Marcus.

"Miller is not an uncommon name," she said to herself. "Must be hundreds of them." It made her feel better to think it, but the caller looking for Marcus had used her first name which meant he knew her or he had been given the information.

She wondered how much money was involved and where it came from. Who was looking for it, and who had their hands on the money now? More questions like these raced through her mind as she sat brooding over the gin in the kitchen, wondering what to do.

If Marcus had once lived in her house, no evidence of it existed. Mail continued to turn up for former tenants, yet in the four years she'd lived here no bills or junk mail had ever been delivered for Marcus.

The caller said he'd been away. She began to guess where, and imagined the toxic kinds of people he might mix with. What if he sent some of them here? Money was a strong motivator and the thought of it made her shiver.

"Damn you, Oliver. What the hell are you involved in?"

She finished her drink and put the bottle away, deciding Marcus must be a relative her husband had never told her about. He hid many things from her, mostly the truth. Was it the money that brought Oliver back into the city? If money lay hidden in the house, he would most certainly come back for it.

Her dog tried to get her attention by pawing at her hand. She found a biscuit and fed him, then opened the back door for the animal to go outside.

As she stood watching him do his business, her mind started working with a little more clarity. Over the past few days, maybe longer, there'd been a number of unusual occurrences, all now indicating she might have been targeted.

First, there'd been the white car. She remembered it because it incorporated her initials before marriage: AEO, Amelia Ellis O'Malley. If not for that, she might not have noticed it, but she knew she'd seen it parked on her street at least three times in the past few days, including last night, and she had even spotted it once outside the dental office where she worked.

Then there was the odd chalk mark on the curb outside her home.

Someone was watching her. Had Oliver hired someone to follow her? Why? Was it because of the money? The idea of it made her mad. His scams and cons had nothing to do with her.

"You bastard," she said with a sigh.

The dog came inside. Amelia closed and locked the back door, then went into the living room and peered through the front window, checking the street for another sighting of the white car. This is madness, she thought. I don't know what the hell is going on.

From somewhere inside her purse, her cell phone rang. She crossed the room to get it and saw that the incoming number belonged to her best friend, Penny Chapman. She answered and tried to keep her tone even so that her friend could not tell she'd been drinking.

"Hi, Penny. What's up?"

"Where are you?"

"At home." Amelia frowned at the brusqueness, wondering why Penny sounded so upset.

"Are you okay?"

"I'm fine. Why are you asking?"

"Then I guess you forgot."

"Forgot what?" The vagueness was starting to irritate her.

"You were supposed to drive me to the airport this morning."

"Oh, shit." With a rush of regret, Amelia remembered her friend's early morning flight to New York. "Shit. I'm sorry."

"Lucky for me I haven't missed my flight."

Amelia switched the phone to her other ear, struggling to hear her friend over the noise in the background. "I forgot all about it," she said. "Forgive me?"

"I usually do."

"You should have reminded me last night."

"You were hammered. Anyway, it's my fault. I should have expected this."

The comment hurt because Amelia knew what it meant. "What you're saying is that you should have planned better and not relied upon a drunk. You're probably right." She forced a laugh. "I feel like such a shit."

"It isn't a big deal. I got a cab and I made it on time."

"I'll reimburse you for the cab fare."

"Don't worry about it. I'll call you when I get back on Tuesday."

"Tuesday." Amelia made a mental note. "I'll pick you up from the airport."

"It'll be late. I'll take a cab."

"I hate that I've upset you." Amelia apologized again. "I'm trying to make it right."

"You haven't upset me, I'm worried about you," Penny said.

"I forgot about it because someone is harassing me." Blurting it out relieved some of her guilt. "Last night, before we went out, some guy threatened me on the phone."

"Why didn't you say anything?"

"I didn't want to spoil your birthday."

"That's ridiculous. How did he threaten you? What did he say?"

Amelia told her.

"Have you called the police?"

"Not yet."

"Why are you waiting?"

"Because I think it has something to do with Oliver, and I don't want to get him into trouble."

"After everything he's done to you?"

"Despite everything, he's still my husband and I love him."

"Amelia, he's not coming back. I know from experience."

"Yeah, he was your first love, but he's my husband. It's different."

"I still love him, too," Penny said. "He's my best friend. Let me talk to him."

"No." Amelia went back to the window to stare at the street, weighing it up quickly and choosing not to mention the white car. "I don't think I'm in any danger." When she drank, she imagined things. Perhaps the vehicle belonged to a neighbor. "I'm probably overreacting. It's most likely a scam."

"You sure?"

"Yeah."

"You seem scared."

"I'm fine. I'm a grown woman. If I get another call I'll file a report."

"Good. Look, I have to go. My flight's boarding. I'll talk to you when I get back."

After the call ended, Amelia stayed by the window for a few minutes, then climbed the stairs to take a shower, washing quickly, rinsing, and toweling off, all the time listening for the sound of her dog barking and thankful to have him for protection.

She considered calling her psychologist, Dr. Safeer Butt, who was still helping her work through the many mental issues stemming from her childhood. Tears welled in her eyes. The compulsive patterns of her own behavior reminded her of her mother. They shared the same obsessions with drink and sex, staying out late and partying all night, or staying in and drinking heavily at home.

Still feeling stressed after her shower, it took her a long time to calm down. After pulling on warm sweats and combing out her tangled, highlighted hair, she headed downstairs, not yet willing to call the police. Instead, she found a notepad and pen and wrote down the details of the phone call while she remembered them. A television had been on in the background. She recalled hearing the voice of the local weather forecaster.

Chapter 4

At 7.55 AM on Saturday morning, lead investigator John Doucette arrived at Pier 39, the suspected homicide crime scene, and added his name to the personnel log. The young patrol officer he encountered provided him with a few details.

"The victim is an adult male in his thirties. No wallet, no ID, no watch and no money. The only item found in his pockets is a silver cigarette lighter."

Doucette nodded. "Is there anything else?"

"Condition of the body is pretty good, only a little banged up, looks like he's been in a fight."

No call had come in from the Coast Guard, and no emergency call had come in from a suicidal man warning of his intention to jump.

Doucette had viewed the bodies of bridge jumpers in the past, and the condition of those bodies was gruesome. They could never be described as a little banged up. Bridge jumpers suffered horrific injuries including bones broken upon impact and internal organs crushed to nothing more than a pulpy mass.

As the bridge office had received no reports of suspicious persons or vehicles spotted near the bridge, and no one had reported sighting a jumper, Doucette felt certain they were not dealing with a suicide. In addition, no crowd had gathered to watch the final swan dive, though a small crowd appeared to be gathering now. With the dead man unable to tell him anything, Doucette's immediate interest lay in the person who'd found the body.

"Some guy out for an early morning run called it in on his cell phone." The young patrol cop spoke with a deep voice that seemed older than his years. "He's waiting for you over there."

Doucette glanced in the direction of a tall, athletically built man dressed in dark clothes, a dark hood, and dark sunglasses. He stood about twenty feet away and appeared to be watching them. Doucette spoke without removing his attention from the runner.

"You quizzed him yet?"

"Yeah."

"Catch him out in anything?"

"I don't think he lied."

"He could be the killer."

The young cop opened his notebook. "His name is Keith Sigmund; lives only a couple of blocks away. Says he runs regularly in the morning."

Doucette let his eyes scan the pier and then turned them toward the Golden Gate Bridge before returning his gaze to the runner. Murder could be arranged to look like suicide and suicide staged to give the impression of murder. The body had washed up on the San Francisco side of the Bay, not Marin. The perilous tide often pulled a corpse out into the Pacific. Doucette still had his eyes on the runner, wondering if someone had banked on that happening this time.

"Anyone touch the body?"

"No. The guy says he didn't go near it."

"Okay. Thanks for the info."

The dead man lay uncovered; another revealing indication. Shattered bodies of suicide jumpers were usually covered by a tarp. Doucette hated suicide, especially when it occurred from the bridge he drove over every day. He took several long strides to reach the body to carry out his own examination.

The victim lay on his back with his eyes and mouth open. His skin hadn't blistered and there were no organisms feeding off his face. His mouth and nostrils lacked the frothy mucus usually present in a drowning. His body showed no sign of bloating or decline. From experience, Doucette could tell he hadn't been in the water for long.

Pulling on a pair of rubber gloves, Doucette squatted on his heels and used his flashlight to look inside the mouth, noting a chipped front tooth and three teeth missing at the back, though not from a recent extraction or altercation. He studied the cuts on the forehead above the left eyebrow and the lacerations on the left cheek, the chin and the mouth. The injuries appeared relatively minor and could easily have resulted from either a fight or from the current smashing the body up against the rocks.

The victim might have been a boxer by the shape of his nose. He had a broad face, a shaved head, a short red beard, and a mighty thick neck. In Doucette's opinion, it would not have been easy to command authority over someone with this man's powerful build. Doucette was a big man himself at six feet tall and over two hundred pounds. The victim was taller and heavier, with Doucette estimating his weight to be probably north of two-fifty.

Doucette continued his examination, moving down the body. The victim wore business clothes consisting of black pants, a single-breasted black jacket, white shirt, and a blue tie in a loose knot around his neck. Silk, by the look of it. Even saturated with seawater, the tailored duds looked expensive.

A small tear in the jacket and a missing button caught

Doucette's trained eye. Definitely not dealing with a jumper, he thought. A jumper's clothing would be in shreds.

Doucette lifted back one flap of the jacket to reveal the suit label sewn inside; flashy, though not custom made. If the dead guy was rich, he was new to it and not from old money.

Nothing definite jumped out at Doucette. He could be dealing with a suicide, an accident, or a homicide. A robbery-homicide was his first guess, based on the injuries and the lack of jewelry, valuables or cash. It interested him that the dead man was missing his shoes and socks. Perhaps they came off in the water, or perhaps he died somewhere else and his body was dumped here. The unbroken blisters on his feet indicated he had not trekked far without his shoes.

With no identifiers on the body, he had a victim who could be single or married, a local or a foreigner, gay or straight or parked at any of the stations in between. He could be anyone. Doucette knew white males generally tended to kill other white males, and women who killed were more likely to use a firearm. If the victim was murdered, then he was probably looking for a white male.

Doucette stood, peeled off his gloves, and drew in a deep lungful of the cool, damp air. A popular tourist attraction, Pier 39 appealed to a miscellany of eccentric individuals including the homeless, drug addicts, misfits, and other unconventional oddballs. All of them contributed to the share of peculiarity. Travelers from all over the world came here to enjoy the sight of the fat sea lions lying on the foul-smelling docks or to take a cruise around the bay. Locals visited the pier to kill a day, or a weekend…maybe even a man.

The group gathering farther up on the pier was

growing. The killer might be among them. What a great day for tourism, Doucette thought, hoping that at least one of those tourists would prove good for a little help and have captured a useful shot on their camera or a phone.

Thankful to see no reporters present, Doucette turned his head toward the runner and made his way over.

Chapter 5

"Thanks for hanging around," Doucette said. "Can I get your name?"

"Keith Sigmund." The runner removed his sunglasses to reveal friendly brown eyes.

Doucette entered the name in his notebook. "I understand you found the body."

The man nodded. "They told me you'd want to talk to me. I can't tell you much. I didn't see anything."

"Then this probably won't take long. Mind telling me where you live?"

"Couple of miles east." The runner provided his address in The Presidio.

"Where were you heading when you saw the body?"

"Back toward the bridge and then home."

"Anyone running with you?"

"No. I went out by myself."

"You always run alone?"

"Usually with a group, but right now, I'm slow. Can't push the miles like I usually do." The runner moved his weight and winced. "Recovering from a groin injury."

"Right. I'll try not to keep you for long." Doucette noticed the man was barely breaking a sweat. "I'd like you to take me through what you saw."

"I was running close to the shoreline and I spotted a big object in the water. It looked like a dead whale or a sea lion. When I got closer, I could see it was a body floating face down."

"How long had you been running when you saw him?"

"About forty minutes. It was just starting to get light."

Doucette asked Keith Sigmund to detail his route, working out the timing in his head.

The runner provided the information, admitting this was not his usual route, stating he found The Embarcadero Waterfront too flat, too easy. "And there are way too many tourists." He explained to Doucette he preferred a hillier course, except when injured, and said he was training for the Marin Ultra Challenge, hoping to be fit enough to run the fifty-mile course in March.

"Fifty miles." Doucette raised an eyebrow. "Impressive."

"Takes a lot of work." Sigmund pushed his hands into his pockets. "Be my second time, if I make it."

He managed to share the achievement in a way that didn't sound like bragging.

"It's one hell of a hard race," Doucette said.

"You've run it before?"

Doucette smiled and shook his head. The race Sigmund planned to run was extreme and would present a tough challenge even for a serious runner in top form. Doucette had never been a serious runner, nor had he ever considered himself to be in top form. Too many sedentary days spent behind a desk had added the pounds and the inches to his waistline.

"Which club do you run with?"

"Local athletic group. They're called The Bay Stormers. Heard of them?"

"Yeah, I'm familiar with them."

Doucette had encountered the club in the past after a member was killed while running along one of the official club routes. This information he did not share with Keith

Sigmund. Instead, he asked the runner about the scar on his face.

Sigmund ran his index finger down his left cheek. "Motorcycle crash, a few years back."

"Still ride?" He had the rebellious, tough biker look about him.

"Never again."

"Some do, some don't." Doucette loved motorcycles. He missed riding them, having traded the bike for a car some time ago when his son Jack came into his life, deciding to hang up the leathers before his luck ran out.

He asked a couple more questions and then closed his notebook.

"I guess we're done here."

"Sorry I couldn't help much."

Doucette wished the runner good luck with the race and released him with the knowledge that he'd be required to come to the police station to provide a statement. He then took a moment to chat with a couple of the forensic technicians working the scene before returning to his car.

With no initial suspects to kick off the investigation, and no idea how the man died, he drove back to 850 Bryant Street, the police station where he currently worked, hoping someone had reported a man missing who matched the victim's description.

Chapter 6

Oliver Miller was a conman and a thief. Amelia Miller knew she had married a jerk, a man who gambled and cheated and tricked people out of their savings with his numerous petty schemes, yet he also had a good side and her desire to be with him remained steady.

She knew what people thought of her, and how she felt when she let them down, but her husband had never criticized nor blamed, perhaps because he was more flawed than her. He had accepted her deficiencies and stayed with her, until another woman entered his life and took him away.

Another vision of the new girlfriend made its way into her mind. Amelia dragged her fingers down her freshly tattooed arm, scratching around the irritated skin. This lovely young woman probably had no stretch marks, no cellulite, and she certainly had no wrinkles.

Filled with renewed anxiety, Amelia turned her thoughts back to the phone call and the man coming after her for payment, in no doubt about his intention to collect. A cold tightness settled in her chest. She had never felt this vulnerable, not since she was a child living under the care of a mother who loved her boyfriends more than her child.

Who the hell is Marcus Miller? Perhaps if she could figure that piece out, it would help her understand the rest.

Absorbed with the threat made against her, she crossed the room back and forth to the window, checking constantly for the return of the white car and noting the details of any man who appeared on the street outside her house. She considered her in-laws.

The people who had raised her husband were not his biological family. That was all he had ever told her about them, always careful with the information he gave out.

Oliver never talked about a brother, or a cousin, or any other relative named Marcus. She wondered why he would keep a family member hidden. Was it to protect Marcus, or to protect himself?

For some time, she stayed caught up on the notion that her husband had a brother that nobody in the family wanted to talk about. It intrigued her, and the last name convinced her. She pondered possible reasons for such a deep-rooted rift, for his family to reject one of their own.

Then her anger returned. What did any of this have to do with her? How far would this man calling and threatening her go for revenge? The fact she didn't know him, yet he knew her name and where she lived made it real and more frightening. It scared her to think that he might try to force his way into her home.

As she waited by the window, the house seemed too quiet. The strange stillness lifted the hair on her arms. Silence had its own sound, an understated and empty rhythm that pressed in on her, revealing the soft murmuring of fear, a hushed voice filling her ears and warning her of danger. It was impossible not to hear it.

She shivered and turned away from the window. With her dog at her side, she ventured through every room in the house, checking the locks on all the windows and shutting the doors, wondering how to keep herself safe from some unknown person who had targeted her and might want to hurt her.

A beer helped dull her nerves; at least enough for her

to settle down in the living room and curl her feet up on the couch. Minutes passed slowly, and the sun stayed hidden behind the clouds.

As her eyes closed, memories of her Irish homeland flashed behind them. Nights spent locked inside a basement, cowering in the dark, listening to the frantic rapping on the front door by one or another of her crazed mother's drunken boyfriends, always afraid they would find a way to get in to rape or kill her.

Her eyes opened. She took a deep breath and sat up, asked herself a question.

What made the caller believe Marcus Miller lived in her house?

She asked herself another one.

If the family had rejected him, how would Marcus know of the address?

A few more questions niggled.

If she went to the police, would they believe her? Would the message on her answer machine be enough to convince them of her innocence? If they didn't believe her, and this situation involved her husband, how would it affect her legal status in the country? America was her home now.

Perhaps it was time she looked for the money herself.

Searching for it gave her a sense of control. She checked all the hideaways she'd used in the past to conceal from Oliver the few valuables she owned to stop him pawning them to feed his gambling addiction. She tested the wooden floor in all the rooms for loose boards, felt along the walls for fake panels or secret compartments, then checked the staircase for any sections that looked like they might contain a hidden storage area.

The Doberman followed her, barking with excitement at this new game. Amelia stopped for a few minutes to scratch him behind the ears and then continued her search. She even unscrewed electrical wall plates and bolts in the air vents to look inside, but her effort turned up nothing.

Perhaps the clues lay in Oliver's routines and actions.

When he'd lived in this house, he'd often acted oddly, spending a lot of his time alone in the basement and keeping his desk down there, fully aware of how much she hated it. She had always refused to go down there because it brought back all the bad childhood memories. To her, the basement would always be a threat.

As she descended the narrow stairs to the lower level of the house, her stomach cramped and she almost changed her mind. She stared at the basement door for a long moment, psyching herself up, then opened it and entered the dark room.

Down here, the air felt cold and it carried a pungent musty smell. She groped for a light and jumped back as something sticky like a cobweb brushed across her face and her hair. She slapped at her face, wiping it away, then moved farther into the room.

This area had belonged exclusively to Oliver and even now, mostly empty, it still seemed infused with his presence. His old coffee mug still sat on his desk. She ran her fingers lightly over the top of the desk and left a trail in the dust.

She looked around. If there was any money hidden, it had to be in here, the one place he would expect she would never look.

There was nothing down here except for the desk under which she found a couple of boxes filled with papers, a few pieces of old furniture, and an empty suitcase.

Frustrated, she returned to the main level of the house and stood in the kitchen, staring out into the small rear yard, in need of inspiration.

Oliver loved working in the garden. When he was not in the basement, she would find him in the yard. What else would she find out there?

The idea seemed absurd, but it grew, and it continued to grow. Not willing to let go of it, she hunted around the house for the long-handled digging shovel, unlocked the back door, and then stopped.

The yard afforded no privacy from Laurel May, the nosy little woman who lived next door. The old woman would see her digging and ask questions.

Amelia decided she would have to wait until it grew dark.

Chapter 7

Some thirty minutes after Doucette returned to his desk, Keith Sigmund arrived at the Bryant Street police station to provide a statement, allowing Doucette no time to review his notes and information.

Doucette showed him to a tiny airless room used for interviews, and said he had a couple more questions he wanted to ask.

The runner sat up straight, his palms spread on his big thighs and his brown eyes fixed firmly on Doucette, waiting for him to start the discussion. This time, Doucette thought his eyes seemed a little less friendly.

"First, I want to thank you for coming in," he said. "We value your help on this."

"No problem."

Doucette started the interview with a couple of easy questions that Sigmund answered; however, sweat had already appeared on the man's forehead and Doucette noticed the way he clenched and unclenched his hands.

"You seem nervous," he said. "You're sweating."

"I've never done this before. What will happen to my statement?"

It was a reasonable question. "If a suspect is charged, it will be passed to the courts along with all the other evidence."

"Will I have to go to court?"

"Maybe." The sudden change in Sigmund's composure troubled Doucette. He remained silent for a moment, quietly observing and assessing, looking for signs. "Do you have a problem with that?"

"I've never appeared in a court."

"Is there anything that might prevent you from attending?"

"Would I have to give my name?"

"If necessary, your name could be withheld." Seated across the table, Doucette leaned forward on his elbows, intending to flush out anything that needed to be flushed. "Has someone threatened you, Mr. Sigmund?"

"No. Nothing like that."

Perhaps it was shock setting in. Stumbling upon a dead body would upset a lot of people.

"Is there a reason you feel you can't speak freely?" Doucette said.

"I can talk."

"I can see you have something on your mind. What's bothering you?"

Sigmund looked down at his hands. He caught his bottom lip between his teeth and chewed on it for a minute.

"I was thinking of the man's family. I'm not sure I could face them."

"Do you know them?"

"No."

"Then why is it an issue?"

The other man raised his head and stared Doucette in the face. "I don't want to see their devastation."

Doucette experienced a moment of confusion. At the pier, Sigmund showed no emotion. Now, he appeared to be quite distressed. Doucette wanted to know why.

"I think you'd better tell me what's going on here," he said. He waited some time for the other man to speak.

"I know what it's like to lose someone you love…in

this kind of way."

"What kind of way?"

"Suicide." Sigmund swept a strand of dark hair from his face. "I heard the guy took his own life."

"I see, and where did you hear that?"

"Is it true?"

"The cause of death is still under investigation."

"Suicide is a selfish act, don't you think?"

Doucette offered no insight into his own personal feelings on the subject. He clicked the end of his pen, sensing this went deeper. If Keith Sigmund was holding back information, then Doucette was intent on getting it.

"Mr. Sigmund, a lot of things can happen and a lot of cases never make it to trial. I'd like you to tell me again what you saw this morning, everything you remember."

"I already told you what I saw and everything I remember."

"I want you to go over it again."

Rolling his pen between his fingers, the only outward sign of his impatience, Doucette sat back and met Sigmund's gaze. By calling the police about the body, Sigmund had been willing to get involved, and now he seemed reluctant to talk. Perhaps he was afraid that what he said might be used against him.

The man repeated what he'd already told Doucette. His story didn't change. Determined to get to the truth, Doucette consulted his notebook and began again with a different type of question.

"How long have you lived at your current address?"

"Four years."

"So it's fair to say you know the area pretty well."

"Yeah, I guess."

"How long would it take to run from your house to

where you found the body?"

"I've already answered that question."

"I'm trying to get a clear understanding." Doucette smiled. "I noticed you don't wear a watch."

Sigmund let out a slow breath. "I left the house ten minutes before seven and I must have been running for about forty minutes when I called. You can check my cell phone if you want."

"Thank you. If it becomes necessary, I will do so. For the moment, I want to remind you that you are not here as a suspect."

"Then why do I feel like one?"

"I'm still sensing some reluctance and I need to understand it."

"Reluctance?"

"Look, I'm not trying to make trouble for you or trick you, and it's your decision whether you talk to me. A man has died, and I only want to get at the truth so we can solve the mystery of his death for his family."

"I wish I could help, but I've already told you I don't know anything. I only saw the body in the water. I didn't see what happened to him and I don't want to answer any more questions."

"You're free to exercise that right," Doucette said. "However, if you know something, this is your best opportunity to talk."

"I've told you all I can."

"Okay, but I can help you if you're in some kind of trouble."

"I'm not in any trouble."

"Okay." Doucette sat for a moment and then excused himself from the room.

"We're not getting the full story," he said to his

partner, Bruce Beaumont. "It's not in my imagination that this guy is keeping back information."

Beaumont agreed. "Want me to have a crack at him?"

"Not yet."

"Say the word and I'm in."

Doucette recognized the glint in Beaumont's ice-blue eyes. His more aggressive partner often succeeded in cutting through the bullshit and breaking a suspect down quickly. Doucette took longer and sometimes failed. Keith Sigmund was not a suspect, but he certainly knew more than he was willing to share. Doucette wanted to gain his confidence. He wanted this man to trust him.

He left Sigmund alone for ten minutes, and then returned with a cup of coffee in his hand to continue questioning the runner.

At Doucette's repeated request, the runner restated what he recalled. The story remained the same each time with nothing left out and no added detail. Though Doucette remained unsure, he handed the runner his card and told him he was free to go.

Sigmund rose from his chair, gritting his teeth. "What happens next?"

"We complete our investigation and hopefully we will make an arrest."

"How do you know a crime has been committed?"

"I don't." Doucette took a sip of his coffee and then set it on the table. "You asked me if I thought suicide was a selfish act."

Sigmund stood unmoving.

"It's not selfish," Doucette said. "It's an act of desperation. But for the survivors, it feels selfish. Your question tells me you're a survivor."

"I don't know what you mean."

"I think you do."

The runner stared at the wall. He seemed to lose himself for a couple of minutes.

"You could work with me to give this man's family some closure," Doucette said.

Keith Sigmund shook his head. "Closure does not come with knowing what happened, it does not come from catching the bad guys, and it does not come with time."

"You're right." Doucette tried to get a read on the man's thoughts. "Dealing with death is an awful finality."

"The pain never ends."

"Who did you lose, Mr. Sigmund?"

"My wife. She killed herself three years ago."

Now it made more sense. "I'm sorry for your loss." Even to Doucette, the words sounded inadequate.

Sigmund looked at him with his eyes half-closed. "She took sedatives and drowned in our pool. I came home and found her body in the water."

"It must have been terrible."

"She used to tell me that all human love ends in pain."

It was clear that this death evoked painful memories for the runner and that he was still suffering and adjusting to his own personal loss, yet something about it didn't feel quite right.

Doucette walked with Sigmund to the elevator and waited with him for it to arrive. As he waited, he sensed Sigmund sneaking a few glances at him and picked up on another change in his mood, but no words were spoken.

The elevator arrived. Keith Sigmund got in.

"Well, Mr. Sigmund. Thank you for your assistance."

The man stood stiff and silent, his face expressionless, yet the air felt charged with menace.

As the elevator doors closed, Doucette returned to his

desk, pondering the revelation and wondering what might have caused so much pain in Keith Sigmund's wife's life that she wanted to end it.

Chapter 8

Amelia Miller's scalp tingled at the same time her cell phone started ringing.

The display showed the caller as unknown, so she decided not to answer, heeding the bad feeling in her gut. After four rings, the phone went silent. The caller did not leave a message.

She held the phone in her hand, waiting for it to ring again. When it didn't, she set it down and poured a large glass of gin, gulped it down, added another inch of liquid to the glass and knocked it back, almost dropping the glass when the ringing started up again.

After four rings it shut off, exactly like before. It rang a third time, and a fourth. Same pattern. The caller cut it off every time after four rings with no message attached. Someone clearly wanted to talk to her and they did not want to leave her a message.

Grasping the caller's determination, she sat huddled on the stairs counting the missed calls until she could no longer remember. She got up and shoved the phone into a drawer, closed the door to the living room, and returned to sit on the stairs, still able to hear the damn thing ringing.

What would it take to get this man to leave her alone? What would happen to her if he didn't get his money? With the terrifying thought pounding through her brain, another loud noise made her start.

Someone was banging on the front door. Amelia held her breath. The dog barked and stayed right beside her. He didn't stop barking. She held onto him. Her chest hurt and it got harder to breathe.

Finally, when the dog stopped barking, she crept down the stairs to slip the chain on the front door, and then tiptoed into the living room to peer through the front window.

The white car had not returned. She saw no one prowling outside, but it did not mean there wasn't someone lurking somewhere nearby.

Would the assault come at night when she was lying in her bed, at her most vulnerable? What about tonight? Her dog could warn her, but could he protect her?

How much danger am I in?

She hesitated only for a minute, confused yet terrified by her thoughts, and then made a call to the local police to file a report.

Pushed to take a more aggressive tone than the one she intended by the attitude of the officer on the line, she snapped out an answer to a question she considered stupid.

"Of course I believe my personal safety is at risk. The guy made a threat against me."

"Please be specific."

"He didn't state explicitly what he would do to me, but I found his words abusive and intimidating."

"What were his demands?"

The question left her struggling for a response. Alerting the police to the missing money might raise awkward questions or cause the police to suspect her of some kind of involvement in a crime.

"Ma'am?"

"He said there was something left in my house that belongs to him and he wants it back. I don't know who this man is or why he is targeting me, but I live alone and I'm afraid he might try to break in."

"Has he tried to contact you again?"

"I think so, but he doesn't leave a message and I have to keep disconnecting the phone to stop it ringing through the night."

She decided not to say anything about the continuous calls to her cell phone or mention Marcus Miller, fearing the last name might suggest a link.

"Crank callers are often seeking attention. He may stop calling."

The officer sounded bored. "He used my first name," Amelia said. "It's not a crank call."

"Is there any reason he picked you?"

"Obviously. He believes I have something of his."

"It could be someone's idea of a practical joke."

A new edginess crept into her tone. "It wasn't a joke, and it wasn't a random crank call."

The officer sighed. "Have you contacted the phone company?"

Amelia fought to hold back angry tears that were threatening to spill. "The phone company won't help me because my estranged husband's name is still on the account."

"I suggest you give them a call."

She raised her voice to him. "A man threatened me. You're the police. You're supposed to help me."

"Let's just calm down," he said.

The situation was becoming tense. Amelia breathed in and forced herself to apologize. "I don't think you understand. I live alone and I'm afraid."

"It will all be okay."

His tone still revealed a lack of concern. "I just want you to take me seriously," she said. "I am afraid someone is going to hurt me."

"I'm sure your fear is unnecessary, but I'm going to fill out a report." He asked her a few questions about the call.

She took a deep breath and provided as much detail as she could.

"He said he'd been away."

"Away?"

"I assume he meant prison."

At this, the officer seemed to take a little more interest. He asked questions about what might be in her house, and then inquired about her estranged husband and what he did for a living, pushing her hard for the information.

She regretted calling. She kept her answers vague and tried not to panic. Realizing the mistake she'd already made, Amelia explained that her husband worked for himself and lived in Los Angeles, stating they'd had no contact for about four months, not since he left, and trying to convince the officer she did not have her husband's new address or any way in which to get in contact. It was the truth, but he seemed to doubt her.

"Is there anything else you remember about the call?"

"Not at this time. What should I do if he contacts me again?"

"I want you to document it. Place, date, time, and call back to report it. You could also ask your service provider to block the number."

"That's it?"

"If someone is harassing you, we can work with the phone company and arrange to place a device on your phone to track the calls and trace the numbers."

"Terrific."

She ended the call feeling dejected and considered calling Dr. Butt to relieve some of the anxiety and improve her psychological stability, the way his dialogue often did.

However, he wasn't always available when she needed him, which made her feel unimportant, and she feared that he might not be there for her today.

The police officer had done a decent job of making her feel worthless and that made her communicate much less effectively. A beer or a shot of gin could reach places of her psyche that Dr. Butt couldn't.

She sighed heavily. Why was everything such a nightmare?

Chapter 9

The surprise disclosure of Sigmund's wife's suicide stayed on Doucette's mind for a long time, temporarily distracting him from his investigation. Her suicide was not the issue. What bothered Doucette was the discovery of the body by the husband, a concern he raised with his partner.

"How many people come across a dead body in their lifetime?" he said. "This guy has discovered two."

"Yeah, I know." Beaumont shot him an irritated look. "Say what it is you want to say."

"Finding two dead bodies is horrendous bad luck."

"Maybe it's nothing more."

"Why is he the only one who called? Are you telling me no one else saw the body?"

Beaumont shrugged his massive shoulders. "People see what they want to see, and in a packed place they see less."

"Something's not right."

"If you feel something's not right about him, then why'd you let him go?"

"Don't have enough to charge him."

"So is he a suspect?"

"Two dead bodies is something I can't ignore."

"I get it," Beaumont said. "You got a hinky feeling about this, about him, but we've got real murder cases to solve."

"I have to go with my gut and my gut tells me it's not suicide and it's not an accident. Someone killed this man. Sole motive could be robbery."

"And you believe the guy who called it in did the deed?"

"I don't know yet. Perhaps he called because he wants to know what we know."

Keith Sigmund claimed he'd been running in the dark, yet he'd worn sunglasses and no reflective gear. Doucette decided he would try to find someone who knew Sigmund's route, and maybe a bit more about his past.

"Could be someone set him up to make the discovery," Beaumont said, interrupting Doucette's thoughts.

"Maybe. Except Sigmund changed his route this morning." It went down as another mark against him.

Beaumont leaned back in his seat and crossed his thick arms over his chest. "There's not much evidence of a struggle."

"Could be a business deal that went wrong."

"Don't smell like some shitty business deal that blew up."

Doucette agreed. It was not easy to beat the shit out of a big guy, and it didn't look much like anyone beat the shit out of the dead guy.

The victim was white. Most white people trusted the police. Perhaps the runner called for the right reason. Or maybe he believed someone saw him.

"Sigmund is a big, strong guy. He could take on a man weighing two-fifty."

"Yeah, maybe that's what happened," Beaumont said, "but I don't think so. For what it's worth, I also don't believe he got that scar in some biking accident. More like someone took a blade to his face."

"I thought the same thing. Too bad we can't prove it." The criminal database had revealed no record identifiable for Keith Sigmund. "You believe his story, then?"

"I'll admit it's unusual," Beaumont said, "but it's not enough to convince me that he's anything but one unlucky bastard."

"The dead dude wasn't on the pier fishing."

"Not fishing, maybe drinking."

"Might explain the missing shoes," Doucette said.

"Perhaps the guy lost it after a divorce. Statistics show more divorced men take their own lives than divorced women, and do you know why that is? It's because those crazy bitches are gold-digging whores; enough to push a man over the edge."

Doucette laughed. "You like those crazy, sleazy whores."

"I can't help myself. A guy like me loves a bitch."

"Sounds like a great investment for future happiness."

"I'm not thinking long-term."

"Relieved to hear it."

The playful exchange reminded Doucette of his ex-wife, who did everything she could to wreck their marriage. He sighed and popped the lid off his cup of coffee, saw it was empty and went to get a refill, grabbing an opportunity to call his girlfriend. Isabelle's voice always made him smile.

Isabelle didn't answer her phone. Doucette considered sending her a quick text to tell her he missed her, but changed his mind, shoving the phone back into his pocket. He loved her, but he had no desire to rush things.

He returned to his desk to find his partner standing with the phone clamped to his left ear. Beaumont placed his right hand near his crotch in a vulgar gesture, mouthing crude words and flashing a wild grin. The show of teeth reminded Doucette of a snarling dog.

"Hot date tonight," Beaumont said, ending the call.

"This one loves wearing handcuffs and sitting on my face."

Doucette pitied the poor, stupid woman. A wise woman would never agree to lose control to a guy like his partner. He turned his mind back to the case, hoping a public appeal would bring someone else forward.

Pier 39 got crowded as soon as it got light. Someone must have seen something. A well-dressed fat man with a shaved head and red beard, wandering the city without his shoes should stick in the memory. Someone must have noticed him. For a variety of reasons, people did not always call the police to report a crime. Perhaps there were other witnesses who simply did not consider it important.

With the body still awaiting identification, Doucette hoped the victim might have a family or loved one waiting for him at home, someone who would call to report him missing. So far, no one had.

"Maybe this will help us figure out who he is." Doucette picked up the evidence bag on his desk containing the silver cigarette lighter. He studied the design on the front. "What does the symbol of two crossed keys mean?"

"Might be a family crest or a coat of arms."

"What do you know about either of those?"

"Not much."

"Perhaps if you took a look at the damn thing."

Beaumont joined Doucette at his desk. "Let me see." Using a clean tissue, he removed the lighter from the little bag and turned the piece over in his hand. "Feels solid."

"More than a worthless piece of junk?"

"Might hold some value. Could be a collectible."

"Then why didn't the killer take it?"

"How the hell do I know? Maybe he missed it. Perhaps he doesn't smoke."

Doucette began tapping the keys at his computer.

"Looks old," Beaumont said. "Might be an antique. I know a little about antiques."

"Oh, yeah? Since when?"

"Since I came into some money a few months back. This is a good quality piece, sterling silver, and vintage. Got a few minor scratches, but they're barely noticeable. It's almost in mint condition."

Doucette raised an eyebrow. "I'm impressed you know about this stuff."

"Yeah, well I have my uses. Figured I'd starting investing in my future."

"Take my advice and sink your cash into property."

"Real estate's not my game."

Beaumont flicked open the lid of the lighter, commenting on the old decomposing flint inside. He tried unsuccessfully to light it, said he thought perhaps the flint wheel was too wet.

"Seeing as you know so damn much, what's the thing worth?" Doucette said.

"Probably quite a bit, but it's not the value I'm interested in right now. I might have seen this design before. I recognize the hallmarks. They're German."

Doucette watched with a mingled sense of amusement and irritation as his partner examined the lighter with the intensity of someone who knew what he was doing, his pug face all scrunched with concentration and his thick pink tongue pushing out from between his lips as he studied the crossed keys design on the front and the back.

"What can you get from the personalization?"

"Hmm." Beaumont read aloud the engraved initials. "E.V.P. Foreign tourist mugging?"

"Man, I sure hope not; however, it could be a clue to his identity."

"The initials could belong to the original owner, or a loved one, or the person who gifted it to him," Beaumont said. "The guy could be anyone from anywhere. You can buy this kind of thing off the Internet."

"Great."

"Give me a minute and I should be able to tell you what the keys mean." Beaumont returned to his own desk with the cigarette lighter and punched at the keys on his keyboard until an image appeared on the computer screen that matched the engraved design. "Here we go. Take a look at this. The keys look like the symbol of Saint Peter."

Doucette joined him and squinted at the screen. "Let me guess…you know all about Saint Peter."

"I will soon enough." Beaumont sourced another search engine, clicked open a new web page with more information, scrolled through the text and tapped away at his keys, eventually connecting the design to a papal coat of arms. He read the bits out loud about the connection to Regensburg Cathedral in Germany.

"You're saying we might have a dead patriotic Bavarian?" The victim was not dressed like a tourist.

"It's a start," Beaumont said.

"See what else you can find out."

Doucette returned to his desk wondering if the initials and the coat of arms were clues or of no significance at all. Had someone planted the lighter to mislead the investigation? With these questions in his head, he got to work on searching the database using the initials, hoping to connect them and identify the victim.

Chapter 10

The tension in her neck and shoulders grew worse, and her head felt like it might explode with the combination of booze and the warm sunlight shining through the blinds. Aware of her blood pressure rising, Amelia rubbed at her scalp and closed her eyes, trying to stay calm as her mind absorbed the reality of the situation.

The main facts seemed simple enough to understand. Either her estranged husband or someone with the same last name had crossed some bad people, got mixed up in some serious business, and vanished with a certain amount of money.

Prison terrified her husband and kept him from pushing things too far. Whatever crime he supposedly committed most likely amounted to one of his cons, but he was not violent. However, there was a lot she didn't know about him and his screwed-up family.

With the awful expectation of reprisal, there remained a strong sense of fear. He had run from his crime and in his absence, someone had turned to her to face the consequences.

The calls to her cell phone had ceased, yet the quiet environment seemed more ominous. As she got up to mix a drink, she glanced toward the front window, and froze. A man stood next to the tree right outside her house, and he seemed focused on her door.

Tall and thickset, he wore sunglasses and a dark baseball cap pulled down low as if to disguise his face. She could neither move nor take her eyes off him. Her heart raced and a rash of terrifying thoughts flitted through her brain. Why was he here? What did he want? What did he know about the chalk mark on the sidewalk? He seemed to be studying it.

She watched him until he turned and moved back toward a dark vehicle parked a little farther down the street, got into it and drove away.

After he left, she stepped away from the window and ran to the front door, desperate to completely erase the mark, unsure what it meant. As she came down the steps at the front of her house, a voice called out her name. She turned her head so fast it hurt her neck.

Laurel May stood in her front yard with her hands on her hips and shaking her head, a disapproving look on her face, clearly making her own observation and preparing to criticize.

Amelia ignored her, indifferent to the old woman's thoughts.

"I assume he was another of your gentleman callers," the old woman said.

"They're a lot of fun." She flung the careless comment over her shoulder. "You should try it. Perhaps you wouldn't be so lonely."

The old woman glanced down at the spade in her hand, color climbing into her cheeks. "There's no need to be so rude."

"And there's no need to be so nosy." Aware she'd probably gone too far, Amelia stopped, but refused to apologize. "I know you mean well, at least I'd like to think you do, but I don't appreciate your constant curiosity. It comes across as meddling."

"I understand." Laurel May's tight mouth relaxed. "It

must be quite difficult for you since your husband left and moved on with his life. I heard he's expecting a baby."

A sudden sharp pain stabbed her in the gut. Amelia stared at her neighbor. "Where did you hear that?"

"He told me himself."

"I don't believe you."

Bright red lipstick covered Laurel May's thin lips and some of her teeth. Her malevolent grin widened. "My mistake. I thought you knew."

"No, I didn't." Amelia kept her composure, though inside her heart was breaking. "When did he tell you?"

"Recently. I don't remember exactly."

"Because he didn't tell you. You're making it up."

"Oh, well now I wish I hadn't mentioned it. I didn't mean to upset you."

"Of course you did. You may be a tiny old woman, but you're packing a whole lot of mean inside that wrinkly old body."

"That's very unkind. There is no reason for a grown woman to be so offensive."

"You think I'm offensive? Well, you're downright disgusting," Amelia said, staring at her unblinking. "A hateful, evil old bitch without any friends."

Without another word, the old woman turned away and walked back inside her home, leaving Amelia to stare after her.

Was it true? A pang of pure hatred erupted in Amelia's heart. She breathed slowly, trying to get her emotions under control. It took her several long seconds to recover and remember the reason she'd come outside.

The white chalk spot on the street looked suspiciously like a message or a sign intended for someone else, as though her house had been marked. Amelia shuddered and rubbed away as much of it as she could with her foot, then headed back inside, slamming the front door in anger and locking it.

She tore a piece of paper from a notebook and jotted down a description of the man while she remembered it, conscious of another bad feeling sitting low in her stomach.

Chapter 11

Aggravated, Doucette drummed his fingers on the arms of his chair. The search for the initials engraved on the cigarette lighter had yielded no results, and no other witnesses had come forward.

"I don't believe it," he said, voicing his frustration to his partner. "All those damn tourists with cameras around their necks, and no one saw a thing. Not one single person."

Bruce Beaumont shrugged. "Fear keeps a lot of folk quiet."

"Yeah, well Taylor's not going to like it. He wants to speak to me to get an update and there's not a lot to go on. I need someone to hassle."

Cole Taylor was Doucette's superior. He wanted results quickly before another case went unsolved.

"We've identified a suspect who has no alibi. You can give him that."

"It's flimsy," Doucette said. "What's his motive?"

"Haven't got that far yet, but we'll figure out a connection."

Doucette agreed that their suspect—the runner, Keith Sigmund—was clearly a man who possessed the physical ability to commit the crime. He was also in the right place at the right time and he fit the profile they were building. The problem was an apparent lack of motive.

"I don't believe the groin injury," Doucette said, recalling the way Sigmund had walked to the elevator. "He forgot to limp."

Beaumont laughed. "We're going to need more than that."

"What are the possibilities of finding a dead body twice in a lifetime?"

"I'll admit it's unlikely."

"You don't think the statement he gave seemed a little too scripted? It was like he had rehearsed it."

"If you think he has something to hide, then bring him back in and make him sweat, see if he'll crack."

"I'm pretty sure he knows more than he's telling and for some reason he wants to keep it quiet." Doucette continued drumming his fingers. "We need more to break him."

"You're doing it again," Beaumont said.

"Doing what?"

"Tapping your fingers. It's annoying."

"Habit."

"A shitty one."

"Yeah, well, deal with it. I'm forced to tolerate enough of your bad habits."

"Like what?"

"Those snorting noises you make like you've got snot in the back of your throat. That's really annoying."

"I can spit it out if you like, but I've just kept it to snorting."

"It's horrible."

"There's an interesting lack of injury," Beaumont said. "The victim suffered only a few cuts and bruises which may have occurred in the water. It seems odd. He's a big guy to take down without a weapon."

"So, maybe some kind of conflict without a real intent to kill."

"Nah, I'm thinking more like an ambush, but that

would draw too much attention. The missing shoes point to suicide."

"Someone wants it to look like suicide," Doucette stopped drumming and stood. "I'm not convinced. Not when robbery appears to be a possible motive. I'm hungry. What time is it?"

Beaumont glanced down at his watch. "Eleven-thirty."

"Okay, let's go grab some lunch and we can continue to argue it out."

Some twenty minutes later, they were seated at a corner table inside one of his favorite inexpensive Vietnamese restaurants, still talking about their suspect. Doucette ordered a couple of dishes and a round of drinks. Food was coming out of the kitchen for other people waiting at the numerous tables and the whole place smelled great. His stomach grumbled.

Beaumont took a quick look around, caught the eye of a passing woman and grinned. She ignored him. Doucette's glance went to her, as if to apologize.

"Kind of a sweet little spot, huh?"

"Guess so," Beaumont said. "Too crowded for my taste. Means you gotta wait too long for the food."

"It's good food, and at a good price. Wait until you taste it. You can't beat it."

When the food arrived, Beaumont sniffed at it and grunted. "Portions are small."

"Better for your waistline." Doucette tucked into his chicken dish, talking about the case while he ate. "Robbery may not be the true motive."

"What is?"

"Don't know yet." Doucette talked around another bite. "I'm thinking about the nice designer duds. They'd have made him a target for muggers, for sure, but he had teeth missing, poor dental care. No one has called to report him missing. It doesn't quite jibe."

As he talked, Beaumont continued stuffing food into his mouth, eating like a ravenous wild dog and hardly pausing to breathe.

"I do believe someone caught this guy by surprise. Someone he knew, someone like Keith Sigmund, targeted him and stole his ID to delay the identification. I want to know why. I need to find the connection," Doucette said, knocking back a mouthful of soda.

"He's a member of a running club."

"I suspect he's lying about that."

"You're a runner. Shouldn't be too hard to find out."

"I'm thinking of joining them for a run."

"Good."

They consumed the rest of their meal without talking about the case. As Beaumont shoved down the last bite of his lunch and belched, the server put the check on the table.

Doucette stared at his partner. "How the hell can you eat like that?"

"Like what?"

"It's disgusting."

"It was good."

"Told you." Doucette got up to leave.

"Hey." Still seated, Beaumont stared after him. "How about some cash?"

"You're buying."

"Come on." Beaumont belched again. "Are you serious?"

"Sure."

"You picked the place. Why do I have to stump up?"

"Thought you recently came into some surprise money."

"Not much."

"Lunch shouldn't cost much, and I meant to ask you about the money. I wasn't aware you had any family who still gave a shit about you."

"Some old great-aunt died. I never met her."

"Really?" Doucette cocked a questioning eyebrow. "Yet she included you in her will."

"Not exactly. She left the money to my old man and he passed some of it to me."

"Time to cut ties, huh? Break out and live independently for a change."

"You can be a real ass at times." Beaumont reached for the check and pulled out his wallet.

They returned to the station to find the phone ringing on Doucette's desk. He snatched it up.

"Homicide, Doucette."

A woman spoke.

He held the phone tight in his hand and pressed hard against his ear, listening without interrupting, permitting her the angry outburst. He wished he had positive news to give her.

For two agonizing months, she had been waiting for a call from the police with news of an arrest in the case of her son's murder. As her son was addict, she had accused the police of not being interested in catching his killer, but she refused to accept that his killer might get away with it. Doucette also refused to believe it, telling her the police remained committed to solving the crime.

The youth, aged eighteen at the time of his murder, had been strangled. Small for his age, his body had been discovered in the basement of an unused building in The Castro less than a mile from his home. The crime did not appear to be sexually motivated and the body showed no signs of sexual abuse. No evidence existed to tell them if the teen had gone snooping in the basement out of curiosity, or if he'd been lured there.

Without a single suspect and no breakthrough in sight, the case remained unsolved, and it sickened Doucette. Murder always left him a little hollowed out inside.

He told the mother he would not stop looking for her son's killer. He wanted her to believe him, but he could tell that she didn't.

"What are you waiting for?" She started shouting and then she started crying.

Doucette repeated his promise to never stop looking. He felt as though he'd failed her and the weight of it sat heavily in his heart.

After the call ended, he sat with his elbows on his desk, fingers pushed deep into his hair, fighting an overwhelming desire to call his own son for no other reason than to hear the kid's voice.

His partner glanced over. "Bad news?"

"Bad all around."

Doucette reached for his glasses and put them on to reexamine the distinctive cigarette lighter, wondering why it was there. With no other items on the body, it looked like a plant.

Beaumont disagreed. "It's engraved, and there are no other clues. If the killer went to the trouble of removing all forms of this man's identity, he would have taken that, too. Seems he was trying to get rid of any evidence, so it's more likely he missed it."

"Then let's get the detail of this out fast," Doucette said. "Once we know the identity of the victim, we can start trying to figure out who killed him."

Chapter 12

Amelia realized she must have nodded off when the angry honk of a car horn woke her. The raised voices of men arguing reached her from the street. Amelia jumped up from the couch and immediately went to the window.

Two men stood outside her house, yelling at each other. One of the men she recognized as Adam Freeman, the owner of the dental clinic where she worked. A cold shiver ran through her body at the sight of him.

For several minutes she watched them, trying to figure out what was going on. Then one of the men climbed into a dark car with tinted windows and drove away, leaving Adam alone.

Amelia banged her fist against the window to get his attention. He acknowledged her with a wave and came up the path to her front door.

She opened it, but blocked his entrance.

"What the hell was that all about?"

"I have no idea. Do you know that guy?"

"No. Who was he?"

"I don't know, but he seemed to be paying a lot of attention to your place. I asked him what he was doing, but I couldn't get anything out of him."

"Did you ask him his name?"

"Yeah, he wouldn't say. It's okay if you know him. I'm not going to try and make you tell me."

"If I knew, I would say so."

"Hey?" Adam frowned. "You seem upset."

"That's because I am. What are you doing here?"

"I want to talk to you. Are you going to invite me in?"

"No."

"Amelia."

She shook her head. "I mean it. I don't want you in my house. You're supposed to be on a beach in Australia, reigniting the flame with your wife."

"Well, I'm not in Australia. I'm here, and I'd like to come in, unless it's inconvenient." He tried to peer around her.

"You could have called me," she said, stepping back to close the door.

"I called your cell phone repeatedly. You didn't answer."

"Why didn't you leave me a message?"

"I didn't want to leave a message. Look, is this a bad time?"

"Yeah."

"Is it?"

"Yes. It is." She stared into his round, expectant face. "It's Saturday. You can talk to me on Monday."

"I only want to talk."

"I don't want to listen, Adam. Go home to your wife."

"Amelia, please."

"I'll see you on Monday." She shut the door in his face.

Adam Freeman had been pursuing her for a while. People at work were beginning to notice, and Amelia had no interest in having sex with lying, cheating, married men. Adam was not handling the rejection well, and she put it down to arrogance. He thought he could have whatever he wanted, and he didn't like the fact that he couldn't.

She headed into the kitchen and poured herself a drink,

slumping down onto a barstool to reflect on the baby news divulged by Laurel May.

Oliver didn't like children. He'd said he never wanted them, and he would never agree to let her try. Amelia felt cheated yet again.

All four limbs ached and the energy drained from her body. The fresh tattoo on her arm stung like sunburn. She ran her thumb across it; the pain temporarily distracting, then she put her head in her hands and cried with the fucking unfairness.

She couldn't stop the tears. Laurel May's words had plagued her since she'd heard them, and the pain in her heart went deep.

The release left her head aching and her eyes sore. She cried some more, wrapped ice cubes in a cloth to hold to the puffy area, and then went to lie down.

Chapter 13

Sitting at his desk, Doucette went back over Keith Sigmund's statement, unable to shake the deep feeling in his gut that he might have let a killer go.

Using the route Sigmund said he took, Doucette calculated the distance from the runner's address in The Presidio to the location of the body and worked it out to be four miles. A young trained athlete running at a good steady pace could do it in a lot less time than the forty minutes Sigmund claimed it took him.

With a groin strain, Sigmund might be slower; however, as Doucette disbelieved the injury, it meant that Sigmund's timeframe freed up a short interval of unaccounted-for time, and Doucette's interest lay in those missing minutes. Where and for what was the time used?

The location of the body appeared to be a secondary crime scene. There was no physical evidence and Doucette believed the victim was probably already dead before his body hit the water. Adult homicidal drowning was uncommon and difficult to prove, but if the body sank or drifted out to sea, it solved a problem for the killer.

Keith Sigmund said he knew the area. Perhaps he knew it well enough to work out a route that almost fit the timing, Doucette thought, but not well enough to understand the tides.

He made a trip to the vending machine, returning to his desk with yet another cup of the department's shitty tasting coffee, and absorbed himself in the statement, searching for other consequential variations, muttering to himself.

"If you did it, I'm going to prove it."

For the next thirty minutes, he poured over the statement, and then tilted his head back and blew out a short breath.

At over six foot, Keith Sigmund looked solid and more muscular than the lean runners Doucette generally encountered. He recalled the race Sigmund said he planned to run and found the number for the running club.

The person who answered his call either could not provide him with even the smallest piece of information or did not want to get involved.

A big man like the victim would be hard to move. Sigmund was his primary suspect. Doucette now wondered if someone in the running club might be helping him.

Chapter 14

It could have been hours and it could have been minutes.

Wilkes Smith didn't know how long he'd been sitting in the coffee shop when the red-haired barista who'd served him came by his table and smiled.

"Here you go," she said. "Another latte, on the house."

"Thanks." He tried to hide his irritation. He didn't want her to remember him.

A horrible image of the fat man's dead body floating in the water flashed through his mind, tormenting him like a physical pain. With the sugar and caffeine pumping through his blood, the picture played over and over, no matter how many times he tried to blink it away.

"Bad day?" she said.

"What?"

The redhead sat down at his table. "You look like you're having a bad day."

"Do I?"

Her sociability worried him. In the minute she stayed seated, he did not attempt to fill the awkward silence.

"Never mind," she said. "I was only trying to be friendly."

Finally. She understood. He picked up his coffee and drank it, then moved away from the table feeling nothing but loathing for the girl. He'd merely wanted to rest for a while, not attract the attention of a woman or be subjected to her scrutiny. He realized he hadn't been too careful in letting her get a good look at him.

As he pushed the coffee shop door open, a mother entered with a young boy who looked to be about six or seven years old, the same age as Wilkes's own son. The two stared at each other. Wilkes forced a smile. The boy stuck out his tongue.

Outside on the street in the cold air, a deep ache hit him so hard that he wanted to cry out. His insides felt raw and bruised with the crushing private pain. Despair rushed through him. He wished he had more time. The inevitability of what was to come terrified him and he didn't know how to get through it. He'd read books and talked to friends in an attempt to understand the truth, yet it remained beyond his capability to accept it.

He wondered what the last moments would be like. Would they be peaceful or filled with pain? Was there anything he could have done to change the ending? Who could he blame? Someone had to be punished to justify his anger. Unable to share the extent of his grief, he'd kept it inside and allowed it to grow into a stronger more complicated emotion that he couldn't turn off.

At this point, he recognized the futility of hope. His heart and mind no longer believed in it and they would never do so again. His life had been shattered; he'd already lost parts of himself and saw no chance to claw his way back. His future remained out of his control, much like the unrestrained tears sliding down his cheeks.

He wished he could quit, disconnect, leave everything now, and stop caring, because caring made him weak and it led to too much hurt and pain. As he walked away from the café, he glanced back once. The young boy was by the window with his face pressed against the glass.

Wilkes moved along the street to his car, his feet

sinking into the soft, spongy ground as the sounds around him became muffled and the world started spinning.

He shook his head and took a breath. How could one person be dealt so much pain? How could one bad thing lead to something else so awful?

The woman he loved was waiting for him to come home. She needed him, but he was lost in his own heartache and finding it increasingly difficult to communicate with her, and he sensed himself losing some of his capacity for her grief.

A police vehicle passed him, traveling in the opposite direction. The sight of it sent the blood thundering through his veins. His stomach muscles tensed and he turned his head away, fighting a terrible sense of dread that they might be searching for him.

Upon reaching his car, he pulled off his wool hat and stuffed it into his pocket. He started the car and watched a girl of about sixteen sauntering across the street. He envied her youth and her freedom.

Out on the road, he forced himself to drive slowly, glancing in his mirror often, the tension building. He wanted to go to the police and confess, tell them this situation had escalated out of his control, turned deadly because of a bad decision, but he feared the police would not believe him.

Chapter 15

The air in the room had changed, grown colder. Dark shadows crept across the ceiling.

As her feet touched the cold tiles of her bathroom floor, Amelia swore. She shivered in her thin clothes, wondering how long she'd been asleep. It seemed like a long time since she'd shut the door on Adam and their short conversation.

It was almost dark and it would soon be time to dig. Amelia went downstairs and found her gloves and the shovel. The Doberman whined. She put out some food to shut him up.

After the recent rain, the ground would be easy to turn over. She pulled on a pair of old rubber boots and went outside into the back yard.

Glancing at the property next door, she saw no lights on or movement at the windows. Laurel May's house appeared to be in total darkness. Amelia knew the old woman went to bed early, rose early, slept lightly, and any noise disturbed her. She enjoyed spying on her neighbors the way other people enjoyed a soap opera.

A low wooden fence divided their yards. Her neighbor would be able to see over it. Amelia worked quickly and quietly, starting near the back door and working her way up and down the yard, using the moonlight to guide her. She watched the windows next door and continued to thrust the shovel into the ground for a couple of hours, lifting up clumps of earth and moving them aside. The work tired her, and she leaned against the little rotting shed to catch her breath.

Muscles burned in her shoulders and ached under the back of her skull. She took a couple of deep breaths and wiped the sweat from her face. Her damp pants and top clung to her skin and she started to shiver.

As she rested, a light went on in one of the upstairs rooms next door. Amelia picked up the shovel and headed inside, planning to come back out before dawn and fill in the holes. She had turned over so much earth that if Oliver had buried the money in the yard, she didn't feel confident that she would find it.

In the kitchen, she filled a cup with cold milk, swallowed a couple of pills, and ate a slice of toast, then refreshed herself with a quick shower and put on one of her husband's old t-shirts. Even now, she still liked to sleep in them.

It angered her that she still loved him after he'd left her for another woman. She missed him every day and felt his absence from the moment she woke up. Traumatic days and drunken nights filled the loneliness. His baby news made her heart squeeze painfully in her chest.

Laurel May was a mean and lonely old woman with a vicious tongue and Amelia decided she would try to steer clear of her. If anyone knew the real facts, it would be Penny Chapman, one of Oliver's oldest friends, and Penny would have told her. Amelia felt herself start to relax.

Chapter 16

Over the weekend, one of the main news stations and several independent Bay Area television stations aired the story about the unidentified body that had washed up on the shore.

By the time Doucette met with his supervisor on Monday morning to give him an update and go over tactics for solving the case, no one had called to file a missing persons report on the dead man.

On Monday afternoon, Doucette answered a phone call from Wade Richardson, the Chief Medical Examiner investigating the death.

"Tell me the man wasn't murdered for his shoes," Doucette said.

"Judging by the clothes, it could be considered a rational motive."

"I was kidding."

"Sometimes it's hard to tell. He was wearing a fifteen-hundred-dollar suit."

"I know."

"The shoes were probably expensive. No watch, no wallet. It suggests robbery."

"Why not walk away with the suit?"

"Perhaps it didn't fit the plan."

Doucette smiled. "I was joking. What else have we got?"

"Heart disease. The victim was an unhealthy male of around thirty-six, diabetic, type 1 from the blood-sugar levels, and at risk from complications of the condition. He could have lapsed into a coma and died."

No medical identity card or insulin pen had been discovered on or near the body. The items might not have existed or they might have been stolen.

"What's the probability that diabetic coma caused this man's death?"

"Difficult to determine."

"You had to ruin my mood."

Richardson let out a quick laugh. "You say it like it's the first time."

"Can we rule out suicide?"

"Not yet."

Doucette groaned. "Give me something to work with. I need answers."

"There is no evidence of previous attempts and there are also no fresh wounds on the hands." Richardson cleared his throat. "His fingers and nails show no sign of clawing or tearing to indicate any attempt to defend himself or free himself from the water."

"Can you tell me if he was dead before he went in?"

"I can tell you he died with no water in his lungs or his stomach. He would have been in trouble the minute he hit the water." Richardson explained that the man's diabetes would have increased the risk of hypothermia. "If conscious, he'd have gone quickly into shock and had a hard time keeping his head above the water. If he panicked or blacked out, a sudden seizure could have shut off the airway, which would account for the lack of water in his lungs. He may have asphyxiated under water."

"Anything else?"

"I did find a fair amount of sedatives in the bloodstream."

Doucette asked about the sedatives.

Richardson named several, including a commonly prescribed narcotic.

"Did the drugs play a part?"

"Most likely, but I can't yet confirm."

Doucette would have to wait a little longer for the toxicology report. With growing impatience, he inquired about needle marks to find out if the victim might have been an addict.

"In my opinion, no," Richardson said. "There are no marks in any of the typical places, but there is evidence of damage on the thighs and backside, probably from the insulin shots."

"Those injection sites could have been used for the sedative."

"Yes, if somebody wanted to go to the trouble to hide it."

"What can you tell me about the injuries?"

Wade Richardson took a long time to answer.

Doucette heard him chewing and then the sound of his lips smacking together. After viewing the gastric contents of a decedent, the Chief Medical Examiner often ate. He claimed the work left him hungry. Doucette found him quirky in a good way.

Richardson continued. "All soft tissue injuries are to the front of the body, mostly the face. There are no new broken bones, no internal bleeding, one chipped tooth in the front, several teeth missing in the back, his gums were not bleeding, but his face is swollen. This man had no significant marks and only a few innocuous scars on his body, but don't worry. I still have work to do."

"This man was murdered," Doucette said.

"Yes, it's quite possible that he was. Then again, the tear on the jacket does not match any wounds on the body so it might have been previously torn, and this man's death may have been accidental. It's unfortunate, John. I'm afraid the answers are not immediately obvious."

Doucette considered the medical examiner's information and the strong ocean current. Athletes had died in the freezing waters of the San Francisco Bay. Extreme cold-water temperatures could stop the heart of a healthy person. The current Bay water temperature was around fifty degrees Fahrenheit, and the dead man had a heart condition he may not have been aware of.

As Doucette knew no one had called 911 for help, he reasoned the victim had been on the pier alone. However, if he was alone and blacked out, it left an unanswered question about the missing shoes and socks.

No sane person walked barefoot around the city on a cold January night, and it left Doucette wondering if this man had recently been treated for a mental illness, possibly sedated to keep him under control, although the hospital hadn't called. No call had been received from the man's family or friends. No one was missing this guy or worrying about him.

"There is one more interesting detail I haven't yet mentioned," Richardson said. "Your victim had a compression bandage wrapped around his chest."

Richardson described the large dark bruises hidden beneath the bandage as non-fatal and symptomatic of a blow to the chest or possibly some kind of restraint.

"There are faint marks on his ankles and wrists."

Doucette got an extra beat in his heart. He thanked the Chief Medical Examiner and ended the call. What about alternative forms of restraint? He was thinking kink and bondage and knew at least two people he could ask for information.

Chapter 17

Doucette understood it took around eleven pounds of force to close off the carotid artery in the neck and fewer to close off the jugular vein. Convinced the crime scene had been staged, he put a question to his partner.

"What do you know about accidental asphyxiation?"

"It's usually an accident."

"How about suffocation for sexual arousal, also known as erotic asphyxiation?"

Beaumont continued reading without looking up. "Sounds fascinating, though not my typical routine."

"I thought you were into that sort of thing."

"You're fucking hilarious."

"What if the dead guy was a gasper?"

"What if he was?"

"There's a possibility he enjoyed being choked or strangled during sex. I think we need to explore it."

"Okay." Beaumont stopped reading. "You've aroused my curiosity."

"I just got some info from the ME." Doucette told his partner about the chest bruises and the compression bandage, and the marks on the victim's ankles and wrists. "Someone could have been kneeling on his chest during a sexual choking."

"Seriously? He was six-four and north of two-fifty. I don't think he was strangled by his girlfriend."

"There was a large amount of sedatives in the blood. It could have been used to control him. Maybe she didn't mean to kill him, or maybe she was angry with him. Hell, I don't know."

"A woman couldn't move the body by herself."

"If he belonged to a secret kink club she could have had help. It's worth considering."

"What about the runner?"

"I haven't forgotten." Doucette chewed the end of his pen. "Maybe he belongs to one of these types of clubs."

"I guess it's worth a look," Beaumont said. "I'm familiar with two or three groups with those kinds of members. The Exhibition, and The Experience strike me as the most likely. I'll see what I can dig up."

While Beaumont searched for the numbers, Doucette picked up the phone and tried to reach someone from his distant past, a woman with whom he shared a brief history, a woman by the name of Kitty Rose.

Ten years after Kitty Rose got married and moved away, she'd returned, unmarried, and the founder of a private business called Cat and Kitten.

Kitty Rose had first captured Doucette's attention a few years after they left the same high school when she moved into an apartment in the same building. He'd had no contact with her for a long time, but had not forgotten the few dates they shared nor the reason they broke up. It still made him feel embarrassed.

Kitty Rose answered her telephone on the second ring.

"Hi, Kitty-Kat," he said. "It's John."

She laughed. "You'll have to be more specific. I know a lot of men named John."

"That hurts a bit. It's me, John Doucette."

"I'm sorry. I don't remember."

"Yeah, well it's been a while."

"You'll have to refresh my memory."

He lowered his voice, not content to dig too far into the past. "You tied me up in my own bedroom."

She laughed again. "I do that to a lot of men. We never use real names."

"After high school, we dated for a few weeks. I flipped out."

"Let me think back. Nope, I don't recall."

"Come on, Kitty-Kat."

"It's been more than twenty years since I was in high school."

"It was my first bondage experience and they were complicated knots. I panicked."

"Was it your last?"

"What?" He felt his face flush. "Yeah, as it happens."

"You shouldn't be scared to try new things. Are you still mad at me?"

"So you do remember?"

"Of course I remember. How could I forget those beautiful moments we shared and your unwillingness to explore?"

"You still think about it?"

"I try not to, but I can't help it. You're the reason I started this business, to help shy people recognize their potential."

He cleared his throat. "How come you've never changed your number?"

"I was always hoping you'd get in touch with me again."

"I need your help," he said.

"Oh, well, I'm doing fine. Thanks for asking. How have you been?"

"I'm still scarred."

"I don't believe you."

"You tried to ruin me."

"You need to learn to have some fun, John," she said, breathing his name, her voice as soft and seductive as he remembered. "Are you now at least a little intrigued?"

"Are you trying to tempt me?"

"Sadly, no. You always were too much of a gentleman for me. I prefer to get mixed up with the more unsavory characters."

"You might like my partner. He can be truly nasty."

"Probably not. There is a certain art to being unsavory."

"Which he has not yet mastered."

"What can I do for you, John?"

The playful tone had gone from her voice. "I'm working on a case and I need your help." He gave her the details and a description of the victim, and told her his theory.

"You're suggesting he died after some violent sex game went wrong?"

"I'm wondering if he met someone at a certain type of party." Doucette explained that he didn't have the victim's name.

"It wouldn't matter," she said. "Most of the clients lie and don't use their real names. It's one of the reasons we don't keep that kind of information."

"What kind of information do you keep?"

"Preferences. Problems. My customers enjoy all kinds of kink and few of them are into plain old vanilla sex. There are occasional troubles, but we always manage to sort things out."

"Do you know of anyone who has ever pushed a partner too far?"

"I'd have to check."

"What about the use of sedatives?"

"That's one I haven't heard of."

"Is it possible?"

"Anything is possible. You have to understand that it's an alternative lifestyle and an escape. A lot of them are married. They're not here to seek out a caring relationship."

Doucette mentioned the issue of asphyxiation and asked about sadomasochism. "Subs can ask questions, am I right?"

"Of course."

"So they can find out in advance if they are going to be restrained in any way, or rendered unconscious?"

"Yes."

"And a sub can refuse an order if they don't want to do something?"

"We prefer to call it a command or a task, and yes, there is a safe word they can use any time they want to stop."

"Except if they are already unconscious."

"I'm not sure where you're going with this, John," she said. "Are you accusing me of something?"

He ignored the question. "Do you keep chat logs of conversations?"

"No."

"What about medical information?"

"It's private."

"The victim was diabetic. He had a weak heart and he may not have known about it."

"If a member or someone invited into my club died as a result of their participation, I would know. There have been no deaths. We screen our applicants and we check out everyone who visits before they are allowed in."

"Okay. If I get you a name, could you tell me if he ever

visited?"

Kitty Rose sighed. "I'll see what I can find out." She checked to see if she still had his number and told him she would call him back.

Chapter 18

Low on energy, Amelia Miller had dragged herself into work on Monday morning, still thinking about the last conversation with her boss. She sat behind the big reception desk in the dental office with a patient in front of her and no interest in what he said.

Digging in the back yard late at night and then going back out again at two o'clock in the morning to fill in some of the holes had left her fatigued and with strained muscles, plus the three consecutive restless nights had left her fighting to keep control of her temper.

The morning was turning out to be rough. A glitch with the computer system made scheduling impossible. Patients complained, tired of waiting to get to the back rooms. The air and temperature in the clogged reception area soon became stifling, thick with the smell of sweat, and the hectic atmosphere made her flustered.

She finished with the patient and another approached the desk. Amelia bit back her frustration. The phone on her desk rang three times. She interrupted the new patient to answer it and asked the caller to wait, putting them on hold. She'd skipped breakfast and now she was hungry and struggling to concentrate.

Thirty minutes later, during a rare letup in the flow, she stood up and announced she would be taking her break.

"I don't think so." The other receptionist, a young and brash woman Amelia neither liked nor trusted, turned to face her. "You don't get to take a break, Miller. You showed up almost fifty minutes late this morning and I'm not covering for you."

"I'm not asking you to, but I'm entitled to a break and I'm taking it now."

"Of course, you always do what you want and get away with it. We all know who the boss favors."

"What's that supposed to mean?"

"I'm sure you don't need me to explain." The other woman's red upper lip curled on one side, showing her contempt. "We can all see how he flirts and he only does it with you. We've all noticed the private meetings and the late sessions."

A hot angry flush burned Amelia's cheeks. "You have no idea what you're talking about."

"He saves the special treatment for you and we all know you're not that good at your job. I'd love to know how you do it. What are you trying to work your way up to? Wife?"

Amelia picked up her purse. "Maybe he would like you better if you were less of a bitch." She walked away.

Outside on the private patio area at the back of the building, she sat hunched on a small wooden bench, shivering despite the sun. The woman thrived on being a bitch and Amelia hated how she always let it get to her.

She sighed and lit a cigarette, inhaling the smoke and then releasing it into the air. As she watched it float away, she let it take her negative thoughts with it, and soon she started to loosen up.

Other staff members came outside to eat their lunch. Amelia got up and took a walk, not in the mood for conversation. The exercise and cool air cleared her head, until the abrupt ring of her cell phone shattered the calm and snapped her attention in another direction. She fumbled in her bag for the phone and checked the display. The number belonged to her boss.

She groaned and answered the call, knowing exactly what it would be about.

As expected, Adam asked her to come to his office, his tone stressing the importance of his request.

Reluctantly, she agreed and re-entered the building. Passing by the front desk, she heard a soft laugh.

"Get rid of her," she said to Adam, entering his office without knocking.

"Close the door," he said.

Amelia shut it and leaned against it, breathing in deeply, the blood pulsing in her neck. "I can guess the reason I'm here."

"I would like to know if what you've been accused of is true."

"It depends on what I've been accused of."

"Is it true that you called another member of my staff a bitch?"

"Yes, it's true."

Adam's tone remained solemn. "Your comment was overheard by one of my patients. I won't tolerate this kind of conduct."

"She pushed me to it. I'm not going to apologize. She is a bitch."

"Amelia, do you have a particular fondness for testing my boundaries?"

She held his gaze. "Are you sure you want to talk to me about inappropriate behavior?"

"I resent both the remark and your tone. You need to remember that I am your boss."

"Do you remember that when you're trying to get into my pants?"

Her comment enraged him, as she'd known it would. His nostrils flared. Amelia prepared herself, in the mood for a fight.

Surprisingly, he stayed quiet. He closed his eyes for a moment, then opened them and spread his hands on the desk.

"We'll deal with this later," he said. "Right now, I need to talk to you about another concern. It involves your husband."

Her belly did a little flip. "What about him?"

"Sit down."

"I'd rather not."

"Suit yourself. Adam unfolded the newspaper on his desk and pushed it across to her. "It's the late Saturday edition. Read it. Lower half of the front page."

She took the paper, read some of the words on the page, and thrust it back at him. "I don't understand. Why are you showing me this?"

"An unidentified body has washed up in the Bay and the description of the man matches your husband."

"There are lots of guys with a shaved head. It's not unusual."

"What about the red beard?"

"Also not unusual. Besides, Oliver was never overweight, just lumpy in a few places. The dead guy is a lot heavier. He could be anyone."

"When did you last hear from Oliver?"

"The day he moved out to go and live with that whore."

"Please don't use that word."

"Why not, if it fits?"

Adam sucked in his breath. "The police are treating the death as suspicious. Your husband made a lot of enemies."

Amelia diverted her gaze to the floor. "It's not him."

"How can you be sure?"

"He moved to LA."

"Your husband has friends here. Maybe he came back."

"I think you're being a little dramatic. The story is about someone else."

"Perhaps." A frown crossed Adam's face. "I hope I'm wrong."

"It's not him."

He folded the paper and put it aside. "Maybe you should call him."

"If it's him, I'm sure the police will get in touch with me."

"It might be better if you contacted them first."

She kept her voice level as the emotion built inside her. "Why should I? He's no longer my concern. Let his girlfriend make the call. I'm going to put it out of my mind."

Chapter 19

At the end of a long and tiring shift, Amelia left the dental clinic on Geary Boulevard and took an indirect route home, driving through Haight-Ashbury and the small Cole Valley neighborhood.

The hot sun beating down on her windshield raised the interior temperature and caused rivulets of sweat to run down her back and soak into her shirt. She sighed, cursing the heat and the broken air conditioning in her truck.

Unsure if her husband was dead or alive, she stopped at a gas station to buy water and beer, but mostly to peruse the local newspapers in the rack and search for a copy left over from Saturday. She didn't find one.

Back on the road, she drank greedily from a water bottle, continuing to glance in her rearview mirror, watching for the white car or anyone who might be following. Instead of a right turn at the next junction, she made a left. The vehicle behind her passed straight through.

When she finally reached home, she parked on the street and waited outside in the truck for a few minutes before letting herself into the house, wondering if she'd become a victim of her husband's crimes. How could she be married to such a jerk? She couldn't have known, having not seen it while they were dating, and given the choice knew she would do it all over again.

Could he truly be dead? The idea of it was awful. Seventy-two hours ago, he'd been alive and she'd been yelling in his face. The fight had been short, but explosive.

She pictured her husband's lifeless body floating in the water and tried to make sense of it. He couldn't swim. He would never go near the water.

A bar filled with people had witnessed the fight and many of them would have heard the threat she made. How long before one of them came forward?

Perhaps Adam is right. Maybe I should call the police.

Instead, she changed her clothes and took the dog for a quick walk, then returned home and cracked open the first beer.

She drank the next two beers in the bathtub, where she stayed until the water got cold. In the bar, she'd made her intention quite clear. She'd acted like a crazy person.

The same people who'd witnessed the argument in the bar also saw her husband leave, alive and well, so there was no reason for her to worry. Anyway, it wasn't him.

As she drank, the problem drifted away. She hurriedly toweled off and climbed into her pajamas. Knowing she wouldn't be able to sleep, she took a sedative, and then got into bed. The dog settled on the floor in her room and chewed on his paw. He wasn't that old. Poor thing must be bored, she thought. He needed playtime and more of her attention. She promised herself she would give it to him.

Soon, her eyelids drooped.

Chapter 20

Covered only by a light sheet, she tossed and turned until the loud noise woke her.

Amelia realized what it was. Apart from the dog barking, somebody was hammering on the front door. She opened her eyes and glanced at the small clock on the bedside table, shocked to see the time.

She'd only been asleep for two hours, and it took her a while to get going. She looked out of her window and saw a man at the foot of her driveway. He waved. A couple of seconds later, his fist was back hammering on the front door.

Sighing, she put on a robe and went downstairs to talk to him before the noise disturbed her neighbor.

She opened the door with the chain on. "Adam, this is hardly the time for a social visit."

"It's not even nine o'clock."

She wrapped the robe around her tightly. "What are you doing here?"

"I can't stop thinking about your husband. I can't get the notion out of my head, and I'm not leaving until you talk to me."

"Fine." She closed the door, slid off the chain, and opened it again. "You can't stay long. I don't need to give my neighbor a reason to gossip."

He stepped into the long hallway behind her. "Why does your house smell so bad?"

"It's dog poop. He has anxiety issues and sometimes

he shits on the floor."

"Damn. It stinks."

"If you find it offensive, Adam, you can leave."

"Don't you at least clean it up?"

"I haven't had time. Someone was banging on my front door. I suppose you want coffee."

"No, but can I switch on some lights?"

"I prefer it dark."

He sighed. "I can't talk to you if I can't see your face."

"That's the whole point."

Adam snapped on the light in the living room and stared at her. "You look awful."

"Thanks." She squinted against the brightness. "I'm not in the mood for company, so please make this quick."

"Have you tried to call your husband?"

"We're not in contact. I don't have his number."

He put one hand on her arm. "I want to help you."

She shook his hand off. "You want to sleep with me, Adam."

"I won't deny it, but you've made your feelings pretty clear. Anyway, it's not why I'm here."

Amelia took a seat on the couch, fingering the fabric beneath her thighs. Adam joined her on the couch. He smelled good. She noticed the wedding ring missing from his finger.

"Why did you come back early? I thought you and your wife were working things out."

He shrugged. "We tried. Australia was supposed to make a difference."

"Perhaps you should have gone to Europe."

"That's not funny."

"Sorry, but did you really think a vacation would change anything?"

"No, but I had to convince her I was willing to try. Anyway, we're getting a divorce."

"It's none of my business."

"We've been married for ten years and she doesn't want to make it work. She says she doesn't care anymore."

"Why are you telling me?"

"Because I want to make sure you understand that you're not the cause of her decision to leave me."

Amelia breathed in sharply. "Is that why you're here?"

"I know how you feel about cheating."

"It doesn't change anything." Amelia let out an exasperated sigh. "Adam, you're my boss and I don't want to have anything other than a business relationship with you. I never have and I never will."

"You're breaking my heart."

"No. I'm only bruising your ego."

"Perhaps that's true." He sat back and dragged his fingers through his hair, casting a quick glance at the coffee table. His smile vanished. "I see you're mixing alcohol with sleeping pills. Are you trying to kill yourself?"

"That is none of your business." She stood quickly. "You should go." She could tell the move surprised him.

His eyes widened, but he rose and made his way down the hall. "I'll see you tomorrow."

She opened the front door for him. "Goodnight, Adam. Tell your wife I said hello."

"I will not." He hesitated on the doorstep. "You need to listen to me, Amelia. Either call your husband or call the police."

She shut the front door and locked it, then made herself a cup of coffee and sat drinking it with her feet curled up on the couch, disturbed by the recurrent nagging suspicion that she knew would prevent her from sleeping.

In her mind, it was no coincidence that Oliver's sudden reappearance tied in with the threatening phone call, but she and Penny had been at the new bar for the first time. Oliver would not have known where to find them unless the information had been given to him, and Penny had decided on the venue. It meant Penny knew he had returned and had chosen not to tell her. Why? What did Penny know about the money?

For the first time, Amelia found herself questioning Penny's innocence and wondering about the true nature of their acquaintance. They'd come to know each other through Oliver, and had been friends for a number of years. Good friends, Amelia thought. She trusted this woman, but now found herself questioning the relationship, wondering if she could truly be a friend with her husband's ex.

Chapter 21

When Amelia arrived at work the next morning, she found Adam Freeman waiting for her. He asked her to come directly to his office, which aggravated the pain in her left temple.

"You're late," he said.

"Are you tracking my hours?"

"I stopped doing that a long time ago." He closed the door behind her. "I want to apologize for last night. I behaved inappropriately."

"How about an apology for all the other times you've behaved inappropriately?"

"Don't push it."

"Why do you want a relationship with me?" Amelia had been wondering about it for a long time. She wasn't pretty or petite, had small boobs, and nothing much to offer.

"I'm not sure. I like your personality."

"What is it about my personality that you like? I've been unpleasant to you."

"You have qualities I admire. I enjoy a woman who challenges me."

"Well, I'm unavailable."

"Perhaps that's what attracts me." He sat down at his desk. "Have you given any thought to what I said?"

"Not much."

"Have a seat." He pointed to one of the leather guest chairs. "You seem stressed."

"I hardly slept last night. I haven't for a few days.

That's why I need the sedatives." She sat and stroked her fingers across her forehead, massaging the pain. "I'm not ready to believe it."

"But you are considering the possibility?"

She nodded. "I guess I have to."

"What brought about the change?"

"I don't want to admit it, but you might be right." She told him about the threatening phone call. "He knew my name. I also think I'm being followed."

"What do you mean?"

"I keep seeing the same car, a white car with my initials as part of the plate. I see it everywhere I go and it's starting to freak me out."

"Well, this is madness."

"That's not all. I think my best friend is involved, either that or I'm losing my mind."

"What the hell is going on?" He stared at her. "You've got to call the police."

"I can't."

"Why not?"

"It gets worse." She bit her bottom lip. "I'm not sure how to say this." She hesitated for only a second before the truth spilled out of her. "I saw Oliver on Friday, the night before the body washed up. We had a fight and I made some threats."

"What kind of threats?"

"Serious ones. I didn't mean it."

"How serious?"

Amelia wrapped her arms around her body. "I said I would kill him."

Adam groaned. "I suppose you were overheard."

"By at least twenty people. It was his fault. He had his new girlfriend with him and I lost it when I saw her. I threatened to kill her, too."

"This could certainly complicate things."

She saw the concern creep into Adam's eyes. "He was alive when he left the bar, and she left at the same time. Well, if it's him, she would have called the police, wouldn't she?"

"Unless she couldn't."

"What are you saying?"

"Let's take a minute to think about this." Adam drew in a breath. "Other people saw him leave the bar, am I right?"

"I'm sure someone did. The place was full of people."

"You're sure they left together?"

"Yeah, quite sure. I saw them walk out."

"What time did you leave the bar?"

"I don't know, somewhere around ten-forty, maybe a little later. Why are you asking me this? I didn't do anything."

"You need to establish your alibi. If it's him, someone may be trying to set you up to look guilty."

"Why would anyone do that?"

Adam took a moment to respond. "I hate to say this, but your husband wasn't exactly an honorable person."

"There's only one body, so it might not be him."

"So far there's only one body."

Amelia wound a strand of hair around her finger. "Perhaps I should wait until the police make an identification. I don't want to become a part of their investigation if it's not him."

"How do you explain the phone call and the car you keep seeing?"

"I can't. Maybe I'm being paranoid."

"How do you explain Marcus Miller?"

She shook her head. "I can't explain that either."

"It's the same last name as your husband. It's probably not a coincidence."

"It's not an uncommon last name," she said.

"Your husband has a lot of enemies."

"I know, and I'm scared. I don't know what to do. If I call the police, I might be making it worse."

"I'd like to help," he said, "but I don't know how."

"It's my problem to sort out."

"Hey." He smiled. "I'm here if you need me. Try not to worry. You don't know what those people in the bar heard, and even if they did hear the threats, everyone experiences violent thoughts. It doesn't make them a killer."

Her face grew hot under his gaze. "Then why are you still reading the story? I noticed you've got the Saturday paper on your desk."

As he reached for it, there was a knock at the door. "Come in," Adam said.

Amelia stood and snatched the paper from his desk. "You're right," she said. "I need to call the police."

Adam viewed her story with skepticism, she could tell. If her husband was dead, then her life was going to change and she needed to be smart.

Chapter 22

Doucette's day started badly. He arrived at work early to find Cole Taylor waiting for him at his desk.

The frustrated Lieutenant launched into him, demanding a briefing on the new case.

With little evidence and not much progress made, Doucette explained he was waiting to hear from one of his contacts with some information.

Taylor frowned. "Are you guys going to be able to figure this one out?"

"I won't let this case go unsolved," Doucette said, sensing he should be doing more and still haunted by the murdered teenager investigation that remained unsolved.

"Different crime, same neighborhood," Taylor said. "It's not going to look good if you don't crack it."

The grilling made Doucette feel incompetent.

An hour after it ended, Isabelle called to cancel their date for tonight.

Now the phone was ringing again. Doucette snatched it up, stating his name tersely.

"Good morning, John." The low female voice spoke silkily into his ear. "Or is it not such a good morning?"

"Not for me, Kitty-Kat. You're early. What's up?"

"Might be early for some, but it's late for others." She laughed. "Anyway, I thought you would want to know what I've discovered, although I'm not confident it will help you."

"I'm looking for a name."

"Sorry. However, there is a client who disturbs me," she said. "He's hurt a few women, but he's still alive so he's not your guy."

Doucette grimaced. "You're right. It doesn't help."

"I couldn't find any information to suggest any of my members were involved with your victim."

"Never mind, thanks for checking."

"We hold all sorts of parties and events, John, and we allow guests to participate. He might have been someone's guest."

"How can I find out?"

"I keep a list. I'll see what I can do."

"Appreciate it."

"I think you might be allowing a few cuts and bruises to mislead you. Rough sex is standard. Some members like to be adventurous and it sometimes results in minor injuries. They're usually not serious and all activities are consensual."

"This guy suffered more than a few common injuries," Doucette said. "This is a murder investigation and we're exploring every angle."

"I don't like how you're trying to connect it to my business," she said, her soft voice turning hard. "You might think what we do is wrong, but these are good people."

"Of course they are. Some of the best in the world go to strip clubs."

"Be careful, John, or you could be looking out for your own reputation."

He apologized for the remark. "I didn't mean it, and I'm not usually such an ass. I realize I'm probably wasting my time and it frustrates me."

"Glad we're back to good cop; he's the one I prefer."

"If I got you a picture, would it help?"

"It might. Look, if you're going to ask around, please be tactful. Try not to freak them out."

Doucette thanked her and ended the call, glancing at his watch and forcing his thoughts back to his only suspect, the runner Keith Sigmund, the sense of doubt crawling deeper into his gut.

When he'd called the number Sigmund gave, he got a recorded message stating it had been disconnected. Doucette suspected the address Sigmund had provided in The Presidio would also turn out to be phony. He decided to take a drive there.

It took him twenty-five minutes to reach the address. He parked a few houses away and walked back to the building, an old duplex unit on Kobbe Avenue. Two trashcans, a motorcycle, and a black Dodge Charger sat parked on the gentle sloping driveway that led to a detached garage.

Doucette knocked on the door of the rear unit. No one answered. He knocked a second time, harder, and heard the sound of heels on a wooden floor. A shape appeared behind the glass, and a young female voice talked to him through the closed door.

"Who is it?"

"I'm with the San Francisco Police," he said. "I'd like to talk to you for a minute."

The door opened as far as the security chain would allow, and a teenager asked to see his ID. Doucette produced his badge.

"I'm looking for Keith Sigmund."

"I've never heard of him," the girl said, looking not at him or his badge, but at the phone in her hand. "You must have the wrong house."

"Is anyone else home?"

She shook her head. "My mom's at work."

"Where's your dad?"

"Don't have one."

"The Charger in the driveway belongs to your mom?"

"No." The girl made a face as if she thought he was stupid. "I just told you that she's at work."

"Right," he said. "Well, I need to talk to her. Can you give me her number?"

"Has she done something wrong?"

The teen looked shaken. After Doucette reassured her, she gave him the information he wanted. He retreated to his car and called the girl's mother at her place of work.

"What's it about?" the woman said.

"Your address has been connected to a murder investigation."

The girl's mother claimed Keith Sigmund was a name she'd heard, but not someone she knew, explaining he must have previously lived in her apartment as she still sometimes got his junk mail. She told Doucette the motorcycle in her driveway belonged to her boyfriend and then provided his name without being asked, adding that her boyfriend was trying to sell the bike. According to the mother, the other vehicle belonged to her neighbor, a single woman who rented the front unit.

"How do I get in touch with the landlord?"

She provided the number for the property management company, explaining the property belonged to an out-of-state investor.

Doucette thanked her, made a call to the number and left a message, then went back to the duplex and knocked on the door of the second apartment, pleased to find the tenant at home. However, after only a brief exchange, he left, realizing the futility in hanging around.

The second tenant told him she'd been raised in Southern California and moved to the Oakland neighborhood six weeks ago, and had never met the previous tenant in the other unit.

As there was nothing to be gained from talking to her, Doucette returned to his car and drove back to the station increasingly frustrated at the waste of his time.

Chapter 23

Staring at the computer screen hurt her eyes and her headache was developing into a migraine, so Amelia left work early with Adam's permission.

At home, she tossed a couple of pain pills into her mouth and struggled to get them down, then went upstairs to lie down on her bed.

Forty minutes of rest lessened the pain but did not get rid of it. As soon as she sat up, her brain revisited the matter of calling the police or not calling them, and the headache came back.

An attack of nausea gripped her at the sound of the telephone ringing somewhere else in the house. It kept ringing, following the same pattern as before. Breathing slowly, she closed her eyes, but the ring still penetrated her brain. The pain in her head intensified until she thought she would be sick.

When she felt well enough, she went downstairs and unplugged the phone.

The newspaper from Adam's office lay on the coffee table where she'd left it. Weak with the pain and still fighting the nausea, she located her cell phone in her bag and called to speak to the investigator on the case, pausing only for a moment to wrestle with her thoughts.

She waited for the call to be patched through.

When she heard the sound of his deep male voice, her heart beat a little faster. She ended the call without speaking.

Perhaps Adam is wrong. Though not quite convinced of it, she needed a bit more time to face up to the fact that her husband might be dead, that his past had caught up with him.

She lifted her hand and wiped her face, surprised to find tears on her cheek. Deep in her heart, she had always feared this might happen, that there might be somebody who would want to kill him. She had married a dishonest man, a rogue. Her best friend had tried to warn her, but Amelia had dismissed it, believing Penny was secretly bitter because she no longer had him for herself.

Her thoughts drifted back to the phone call. She recalled the menace in the man's words. Was he part of a local gang or a bigger criminal group? How long had he been watching her? Unless he got his money, something horrible was going to happen to her. He'd made that quite clear. Even with the dog in the house, she felt scared and vulnerable, sickened by the thoughts racing through her mind.

The dog let out a series of sharp staccato barks and scratched at the back door, a habit that drove her mad. She shouted at him to stop, then ran into the kitchen to see what might be getting him so keyed up.

His body was on alert. Amelia took a long hard look through the kitchen window. Nobody was in the back yard. She stayed by the kitchen window for a while, watching for signs of movement.

The dog's ears pricked forward and his claws skittered over the floor as he raced to the front door. This time, he barked louder.

There was no one at the front door, but the doubt would not leave her no matter how hard she tried to shake it off. She picked up her cell phone and called the police, this time without the hesitation.

Chapter 24

The canceled date with Isabelle bothered Doucette more than it would have if she had offered a reason or tried to reschedule, but she'd done neither and he felt a distance creeping in.

He knew his job made him hard to pin down, a difficult man to date. Perhaps she'd grown tired of getting less than she gave, of being treated as anything other than a priority. He couldn't blame her.

He sensed a pattern developing in their relationship and it was one he didn't like. They both had trust issues, and they shared the same stubbornness, or the same desire to make the other do the chasing. If she didn't call him for a few days, he didn't call her. He wanted to keep her close, but he could already sense her pulling away from him. A cool detachment was reflected in her voice and he could see it in her eyes. Losing her for a second time would be painful. They'd split up once before and got back together, but two breakups in less than five years might signal the end of the relationship and he didn't want to lose the only woman he'd loved since his wife had walked out, the woman he saw as part of his future.

Resigned to the fact he would be spending this evening alone—even his son had a date—he returned to his desk with a cup of coffee from the vending machine and grabbed the phone to answer another call that was patched through.

A female voice spoke.

"I need to talk to someone about the body that washed

up near the pier a couple of days ago," she said. "I may have some information."

"What kind of information?"

The voice dropped to a whisper. "I'm worried that he might be my husband."

"What makes you think he might be your husband?"

"He fits the description."

"Okay." Doucette grabbed a pen. "I'm the lead investigator on the case so I'm going to ask you for a few details."

He asked her for her name, contact details, and some facts about her husband, scribbling down the information she provided.

"He's my estranged husband," she said. "We separated four months ago when he traded me in for a younger model. His name is Oliver Miller."

"Does your husband have any identifying marks? Any scars, tattoos, birthmarks?"

After a momentary pause, she told him he didn't. "He does have some teeth missing," she said. "Oliver never went to the dentist unless it was an emergency."

Doucette invited her to come to the police station. "We have not yet been able to identify this man and we could use some answers."

She agreed to his request, adding that she needed some time to prepare.

Sensing her distress, Doucette thought she might need support and offered to send a car, which she declined.

While he waited for her to arrive, he reviewed the information he had on the case and the notes on his current suspect. This call could ignite his investigation.

Amelia Miller arrived an hour later, alone. Dressed casually, she wore light makeup, no jewelry, and cut an imposing figure at almost six feet in height with a large muscular frame. He smiled and held out his hand.

She gripped it with a hard shake. "I've never been invited to a police station before."

"Well, I appreciate you coming in to talk to me."

"I'm a little nervous."

"It's understandable." He guided her to the chair in the small room used for interviews and commented on her accent.

She did not smile or say anything in response.

"Irish, am I right?"

"I was born and raised in Belfast. Another life...different world." She opened the black bag on her shoulder. "I brought a recent photograph of my husband. I thought you might be able to use it to help with the identification."

He answered with a brief nod. "First, I have a few questions. When did you last see your husband?"

"I've had no contact with him since he moved out four months ago," she said. "He now lives in Los Angeles and I don't have his new phone number or address. He never wanted me to have the information."

Doucette noted the abrupt tone in which she delivered her answer. It suggested ongoing tension between the two.

"Does your husband have any enemies that you know of?"

She kept her brown eyes fixed on his face. "Of course he has enemies. Everyone has enemies."

"Can you tell me who they are?"

She shook her head, still maintaining his gaze.

"Who would want to hurt him?"

"I don't know."

"Mrs. Miller, is there any reason for you to feel that

you can't talk to me?"

"No." She broke eye contact and rubbed at her temples. "Man, I haven't been able to sleep for days. I could use a gin and tonic."

Doucette put down his pen and pushed back his chair. "I'm going to get myself a fresh cup of coffee. Can I get one for you?"

"Do you have anything stronger than coffee?"

"Not on the premises."

"Coffee with milk then, and three sugars please."

"I'll be right back."

Poor woman, he thought. He understood her anxiety and wanted to try and keep this as light as possible to help her with her nerves.

Before he returned, he spent a few minutes discussing her with his partner in the hall.

"She looks powerful," he said. "Capable of handling herself in a physical fight."

"Those were my initial thoughts." Beaumont rubbed his eyes. "Do you believe she could kill a man?"

"Can't make up my mind. Her husband left her for another woman. I'm not convinced she's over it."

"Revenge is a powerful motive."

"She came in voluntarily and she seems afraid, yet her actions are strange. I'm sensing there's something going on here, if I can get to the core of it."

Amelia Miller flinched when Doucette returned. He noted the reaction with interest.

"I'll warn you, it's not the best tasting coffee, but it's the best I can do," he said, placing one of the cups in his hand in front of her and dumping the three packets of sugar onto the table.

She thanked him, sweetened the drink and lifted the

cup to her lips, tasted the hot liquid, and then set the cup back down on the table.

"You're right. This is nasty."

"Sorry." Doucette noticed her hand trembling. He sipped his own coffee, deciding to take a different approach to get her to start talking without feeling so nervous. "Tell me how you and your husband met."

"By accident." A small smile crossed her lips. "It was on a blind date. He mistook me for someone else, and I went along with it because I had nothing else to do. We hit it off right away and we got married a year later."

"I met my ex-wife in high school," Doucette said. "We were married for ten years before she decided she liked someone else."

"That sucks."

"Yeah, and it hurts like a bitch, but hey, I'm still here."

"You think you've found the right one and then you discover things about the person you married and realize you never truly knew them at all."

"What things did you discover about your husband?"

"He was a trickster and a cheat." She chanced another sip of the horrible coffee. "Do you have any idea what it's like to wait years for that person only to have someone else come along and take them away?"

Oh, yes. The question reminded him of his ex-wife and a small piece of his heart went out to the woman in front of him. "I know this must be difficult," Doucette said.

"Yeah." She tried to smile. "Do you have any kids?"

"A son."

"You're lucky. I always assumed I'd have kids, but my husband didn't see them in his future. I couldn't force them on him, so I got a dog."

"Well, my son is a teenager now and sometimes I

wonder if I should have chosen a pet over becoming a parent."

"I'd be lost without mine."

Doucette turned to the photograph she'd brought with her. He noted the degree of similarity, although the man in her picture looked leaner with a sharp outline to his face and no beard; however, the eyes and nose were the same.

She leaned forward, her eyebrows drawn together. "Can you tell me if it's him?"

"There's definitely some resemblance." He placed another photograph facedown on a clipboard and put it on the table in front of her. Keeping his voice gentle, he instructed her to turn it over whenever she felt ready. "I want you to tell me if you believe the man in this picture is your husband."

Chapter 25

She sat twisting the strap of her bag and winding it around the palm of her hand, gazing at the clipboard, but not turning it over.

"Take as long as you need," Doucette said. "You must be prepared for the fact that it might be your husband."

"I feel sick."

"It's a natural reaction."

She kept her eyes down. "I'm afraid to look."

"Turn it over when you're ready. You're helping me by doing this."

Her hand trembled as she reached out and turned the photograph over.

He watched as her brain processed what she saw.

Though she did not cry, her reaction had the feel of true shock. She dipped her head lower and closed her eyes, then opened them and touched the face in the photograph with her fingers.

"Do you recognize him?"

She remained silent.

"Is he your husband?"

She pushed the blonde hair out of her face and nodded. "He's fatter. He always used to be in better shape. How did he die?"

"I'm afraid it's not yet clear. The cause of his death is still under investigation."

"So, you don't know if he was murdered?"

"We need the medical examiner to confirm it, but we

do believe a crime has occurred and we're treating the death as suspicious."

"I understand." She pushed the photograph away and sat back. "When did he die?"

"We believe sometime Friday night or Saturday morning. You said he lives in Los Angeles now?"

"Yes, that's right."

"Do you know what he would have been doing here?"

"I have no idea. We've had no contact."

"Is there anyone he might have come back to see?"

"He used to have friends here, so maybe he came back to see them."

"Can you give me any names?"

"They were his friends, not mine."

"I know this is hard for you," he said. "Any information you can give me will help."

"My husband had mostly undesirable connections. I tried to stay out of it."

She seemed to have recovered from her shock and he was starting to feel annoyed. Doucette leaned forward and put his elbows on the table.

"Do you know someone who has a reason to hurt him?"

"No."

"I'm sensing you do."

"Well, I don't."

She sat with her arms folded tightly across her body, deep lines forming in her forehead. He wondered if she'd been threatened.

"Are you afraid to talk to me?"

"Oliver was murdered," she said.

Her comment surprised him. "Are you involved in his death?"

"No."

"What makes you certain he was murdered?"

"He's afraid of the water. He almost drowned as a child and he never learned to swim. He would never go near the water."

It was an important piece of information and a buzz of anticipation ran through Doucette. He asked her what she knew about her husband's mental health.

"He didn't kill himself," she said. "This isn't a suicide."

"You seem pretty certain."

"I am."

"Is there anything you want to tell me?"

She glanced down at her hands. "Some guy is looking for him. That's all I know."

"What guy?"

"Someone he owes money."

"How do you know someone is looking for him if you've had no contact?"

"Because he called and threatened me, the man I mean, not my husband." She sucked in her breath. "He said if I called the police he would stab me in my bed. He knows my name, he knows I live alone, and he knows where I live."

"Then it's important that I find him." Doucette softened his tone. "Tell me about this man. What do you remember about him, about his voice?"

"Not much. He called the house, but I hung up after he threatened me."

"How would he have known your number?"

"It's still listed. I forgot to change it."

"How would he know your husband was back in the area?" Doucette noticed the slight shudder.

"I have no idea."

"You knew he was back."

"No, I didn't."

"He left you for another woman. You were angry with him."

"I would never hurt him. I still love him."

"Who does have reason to hurt him?"

"I've already told you, I don't know."

"I don't think you're telling me the truth. I believe you know why he came back and you know what he wanted."

"No." She shook her head.

"I can see that you're scared," he said, "but I can only help you if you tell me the truth."

"I don't know what else you want from me." She refused to meet his gaze. "I came here to identify him, and I've told you all that I can. I'd like to go now. I'm not feeling well."

Doucette sat back and studied her. He wanted to believe her, but the conversation and the change in her manner troubled him. Until he could get a better sense of her guilt or innocence, he intended to keep her at the station.

Chapter 26

As he continued to push Amelia Miller for information, she grew increasingly distressed. She began to falter, and she sounded exhausted. Sensing he might be able to break her, he added pressure, asking more questions about her husband.

"Where was he staying?"

She shook her head again. "I have no idea."

"He had no credit cards and no cash."

"Then I guess whoever killed him took his wallet."

"We found a silver cigarette lighter in your husband's pocket. In fact, it's the only thing we found." Doucette showed her a photograph of the lighter and asked her if she could identify it as belonging to her husband.

"Oliver didn't smoke." She glanced at it anyway. "I've never seen it before."

"The initials E.V.P. are engraved into it. What can you tell me about the initials?"

"Maybe it belongs to his girlfriend. Her first name is Eve. I don't know her last name, but I suppose it starts with P."

"Okay." Doucette accepted her explanation. "Tell me about the debt. Who did he owe?"

"I didn't say it was a debt. My guess is he stole the money. Since I married him, I've learned that Oliver is not a straightforward man, not exactly an upstanding citizen, maybe even a bit of a scoundrel."

"That's an interesting word." Doucette repeated it.

"What was he into?"

"If I knew, I would tell you." She slumped back in her seat and covered her face with her hands. "This is awful."

Doucette stopped for a moment and gave her a chance to calm down, and then continued pressing, keeping his tone firm.

She dragged her hands from her face and wrapped her arms around her body, hugging herself as she sat in the chair. She drew in a sharp breath and blew it out.

"The calls started a few days ago. I thought it might be a scam, but they haven't stopped."

"Tell me about the calls. What does he say?"

"The guy asked for Marcus Miller. I told him I don't know anyone called Marcus, but he didn't believe me, and that's when he threatened me."

"If you don't know anything about the money, why does this guy believe you do? Why would Marcus be using the address?"

"It's the same last name as my husband, so he must be connected in some way."

Doucette wanted to know what soured the relationship. Was there some dark secret or hidden past troubling the family? This case appeared to be getting more complicated.

"If I'm going to find whoever killed him, I need to know more about your husband and what he was doing here," he said. "Anything you can tell me might help."

"Oliver grew up in San Diego. He left home when he was young, and he never kept in contact with his family. He never talked about them. If he had a relationship with Marcus, he kept it a secret from me."

A long-lost or abandoned relative wasn't a new concept and reminded Doucette of an old murder case he'd worked involving robbery homicide. "Go on," he said, scratching at his forehead with his pen.

"We married a year after we met. I didn't know all that much about him, but I loved him. I thought it would be enough."

"What else do you remember about the caller?"

"He sounded young, but not very young, and he insisted Marcus lives at my address. It's not true."

She paused and asked for a second to compose herself.

It took her some time to think through what she wanted to say. Doucette wanted her to meet his gaze, to see what was in her eyes, but she kept staring at her hands.

"I wasn't totally honest with you before," she said.

"I suspected you might not have been. It's not too late."

"I saw Oliver a few days ago."

"Where?"

"In a bar in the city."

"There are a lot of bars in the city."

"It was a new bar, one I've never been to before. I wasn't expecting to see him. I didn't even know he'd returned to the area."

"Yet he knew where to find you. How would he know that, if you've had no contact?"

"It's a question I've been asking myself," she said. "We didn't arrange to meet, but I don't believe he was there by chance. Somebody must have told him."

"Who?"

"I don't have an answer."

"Okay. What happened when you saw him?"

"We exchanged angry words. He left after a couple of minutes. He had his new girlfriend with him, and that's when I kicked off. I think I scared him away. He was fine when he left."

"It was a mistake to withhold the information. Mistakes like that can hurt you. You should have mentioned it."

"Yes, I realize that." She blew out a breath. "Am I going to need an attorney?"

"You are not under arrest and free to leave at any time; however, if you've been threatened and you believe your husband is involved in some kind of crime, then I need you to tell me what you know."

"I panicked after I got the phone calls, and then I read the story in the paper. It's the only contact we've had since he left."

"I'm going to ask you this question again and I will know if you are not being honest," Doucette said, watching her closely for additional signs of deception. "What was your husband doing back in the city?"

"I promise, I am telling you the truth. I have no idea why he came back. I only know that he didn't return for me." She finally raised her eyes to meet his. "It wasn't a few days ago," she said. "I saw Oliver on Friday night, and I'm sorry I didn't tell you that before, but I was too scared."

The pulse throbbed in her neck. Doucette wondered what worried her the most; the fact she'd lied to him twice, or the conflict with her murdered husband.

She appeared genuinely upset, yet he still got the sense that she either knew more than she was willing to share or she was in some kind of trouble and she didn't want to tell him.

"You have motive and you had opportunity, and you keep lying to me," Doucette said, making no attempt to conceal his irritation. "Give me one good reason why I shouldn't arrest you."

"I had nothing to do with his death."

"So far, you haven't said anything to convince me."

She gripped the arm of her seat. "I'm not a violent person. I would never hurt anyone."

"That's not going to be enough."

"I was with my friend. We were having drinks, celebrating her birthday when Oliver walked into the bar. It must have been sometime around ten, but I can't be sure because I was pretty hammered. He left a few minutes later and I stayed in the bar. You can check if you want. There were plenty of witnesses."

"None of them have come forward."

"So?" She stared at him like a sulky child. "Perhaps it's because you intimidate people."

"I'm only doing my job. I'm not trying to intimidate or bully you in any way." Doucette smiled to let her know he was being kind. "Would you mind telling me what time you left?"

"About thirty or forty minutes after the fight with Oliver. It might have been an hour."

"Alone?"

"Yes. I made one stop on the way home to get a new tattoo and then I got a cab to my house."

She showed him the new ink on her arm and gave him details of the place where she got it done, plus she provided the name of the body artist.

He made a note of it. "I'll need to talk to your friend."

"Her name is Penny Chapman."

He wrote down the contact information she provided, and then asked her what she knew about the other woman in her husband's life, noting the bitterness in her response.

"That night was the first time I'd ever met her. Her name is Eve, she's blonde and about twenty-two."

And that's probably what upset you. Doucette

wondered again about the level of her involvement. "How do I get in contact with her?"

"I was wondering if she'd been in touch with you. I thought if this was about him, she would have reported him missing."

"We haven't heard from her."

"I don't understand. They left the bar together."

"Well, she appears to have vanished and we need to track her down."

Chapter 27

"What do you mean by vanished?"

"She may be hurt. We need to find her. As you may be one of the last people to have seen her, I'm hoping you can supply some information."

Amelia blinked. She said nothing.

"Can you think of anywhere she might have gone?"

"I don't know anything about her or her disappearance. I'm sorry, I can't offer you any help."

"I understand your anger," Doucette said. "Right now, I only want to find her and I'm hoping you can help me."

"You could ask my friend." Amelia managed to moderate her tone. "Penny and Oliver grew up together and they're still close. Maybe Penny would know where she might go."

"I'll talk to her."

"The calls were made locally," she said. "I know this because the first time he called he was watching television and I heard the weather forecast in the background. As the calls haven't stopped, I suspect he is still in the area. I also believe I'm being followed." She told him about the white car she kept seeing. "I've tried searching in the house for the money because I thought he might have left it hidden there, but I didn't find anything."

"I see."

"You don't believe me, do you?" Amelia gripped the corner of the table and looked directly into his eyes. "My husband has been murdered and I've been threatened. If Eve is missing, maybe someone took her."

"For what purpose?" There'd been no ransom demand.

"I don't know, but I do believe he is coming after me, and you need to find him."

"If you've been threatened, then I will do my best to help you, but until I know who killed your husband and why, then this might be a tough case to crack. You haven't given me a whole lot to work with."

"Is that it?"

"Not quite." Doucette stood up and excused himself to go and speak with his partner. He shut the door, but left it unlocked.

He found Bruce Beaumont sitting at his desk and handed over the piece of paper on which he'd written the name of the bar where Amelia Miller said she drank on the night in question, along with the details of the tattoo shop she said she'd used on her way home.

"Give these places a call and see if her alibi checks out," he said. "She's lied to me a couple of times and I need to know if she's still lying."

"Sure. You think she did it?"

"I don't believe I have all the details to understand the whole story, and I don't have the evidence to arrest her."

"So you're turning her loose?"

"I'm getting ready to."

"Mind if I talk to her?"

"Yeah, okay. Give me a few more minutes with her and then you can take a shot." He briefed his partner on the discussion with Amelia Miller, telling him he sensed this case involved a lot more than someone trying to retrieve some stolen money. "I believe money is involved, but there seems to be some weird family dynamic and I want to get to the truth about it. She seems a little vague on the information."

"Or she concocted the whole story."

When Doucette returned to Amelia Miller, he could see that she'd been crying. It made him uncomfortable.

"Here you go," he said, placing the beverage can in front of her. "The coffee here is so bad I brought you a soda."

She thanked him, but didn't touch it.

Doucette sat opposite. "I'm sorry about your husband and if I was a little harsh, I'd like to apologize for it."

She nodded.

He continued. "You said your husband is not a straightforward man. What exactly did you mean by that?"

She didn't hesitate. "He's a con man and I now suspect he is a thief."

"And you have absolutely no idea who he might have cheated?"

"No. None at all."

"Is it possible that your husband had a brother or a cousin that you didn't know about?"

"If you'd asked me this last week, I would have said no," she said. "Now, I believe it is entirely possible."

"One thing's confusing me," Doucette said, clicking the end of his pen. "Well, several things are puzzling, but we'll get to those later. For now, I'd like to know why your husband would leave his money in the old house?"

"Perhaps he thought it was safer. I'm certain it's the reason he came back. Marcus must be the answer," she said. "Whoever he is, he's hiding out and lying about his address. If you find out who he is, you might be able to figure out what the hell is going on."

"I'll be talking to everyone, and if I find any evidence, I may need to talk to you further."

"What will happen to my husband's body?"

"The death certificate will be filed and the body will be transported to a funeral home. If you like, I can put you in touch with someone who can help you decide what to do."

There was a knock at the door.

Doucette stood. "My partner has a couple of questions." He stepped out of the room, leaving Beaumont alone with her.

Back at his desk, he spent a couple of minutes thinking about her story. He believed a connection existed between the threatening phone call she'd received and the murder of her husband, and he knew he had to find the two people who might be connected to the murder. However, with the current whereabouts of Marcus Miller and Eve unknown, Doucette began to wonder if they might have disappeared together.

Chapter 28

After she left the police station, Amelia sat behind the wheel in her truck with her head bowed and her hands clenched on the back of her neck, wishing she could shut out the memories and turn off the emotions, but the pain refused to go away.

At the bar he'd looked different, much heavier than in the four months since she'd last seen him, but otherwise healthy. In the police photograph, he'd looked so pale and ghastly. Did death do these horrible, disgusting things to a person?

Oliver hadn't been faithful, yet the loss left a huge hole. Now, she supposed, she would finally get to meet his family. What horrible circumstances. She visualized their reaction, certain they would blame her.

What about Eve? What had happened to her to prevent her from coming forward?

For a moment, Amelia wished the worst possible fate upon the young woman, and then tried hard to regret it, acknowledging the cruelty of her desire. Maybe Eve just got scared and skipped out.

Amelia dried her tears on her sleeve and searched inside her bag for a painkiller to help ease the dull throbbing pain between her eyes.

Of the two cops, she trusted the older one. The younger, short and chunky one she didn't trust at all. He seemed callous and eager to arrest her.

Instead of going home, she drove to work. She parked

the truck in her usual spot at the front of the dental building and then moved it to a different one at the back, switched off the engine and looked around.

Satisfied that no one had followed her, she went inside the building and hurried to the restroom, hoping to slip inside it unseen.

Thankful to find the restroom empty, she inspected her puffy face and swollen eyes in the mirror, and then bent over the sink and splashed them with cold water.

As she reached for a paper towel to dry her face, she heard a voice she recognized and it was traveling in her direction. Amelia ducked into a stall and locked the door.

Two women entered the restroom. They spent the next few minutes on general chitchat before their conversation turned personal.

Amelia listened to what they said about her. One of them was the woman from the front desk. The other voice belonged to the hygienist, who was another gossiper on the team. As she listened to their acid remarks, she started to sweat. Her cheeks grew hot and the gnawing pain increased in her stomach. The comments reminded her of the way her mother used to demean her during the many drunken episodes that defined her childhood.

To stop the misery and end her pain, she pressed the handle to flush the toilet, unlocked the door, and stepped out of the stall.

Both women immediately stopped talking. Their stunned silence gave Amelia a sudden sense of power. The shocked expressions made her want to laugh.

She walked to the sink and washed her hands.

The awkward silence continued until the hygienist, clearly horrified at being overheard, made a feeble attempt at an apology.

"Save it," Amelia said.

The receptionist threw her head back and laughed.

The world was filled with spiteful bitches like these and a friendship with them was not important. Amelia left them in the restroom and returned to her position at the front desk. With no patients waiting, she began to file charts, until Adam Freeman appeared in front of her and took her back into his office.

He pulled a chair out, motioning for her to sit. His eyes flickered over her face.

"I can see you've been crying."

"I'm having some trouble with my contacts."

"You don't wear contacts."

"It's easier than admitting the truth."

"Which is what?"

"I've been to the police station to identify Oliver's body."

"What? Are you serious?"

"Deadly." Sick humor relieved some of the tension she felt.

"Amelia, this isn't funny."

"You're right. It's awful."

"I don't know what to say."

"Yeah, I'm struggling with it, too."

"I'm so sorry." He sat in the chair next to her, placing one of his big hands on top of hers. "Do the police know what happened?"

She pulled her hand away from his grasp. "Not yet, but they're treating his death as a homicide."

"I can't quite believe it. Do they have any idea why he was killed?"

"They don't have a clue."

"Did you tell them about the phone call?"

"Yep, and I told them about the fight."

"Do you think that was wise?"

"I threatened his life and now he's dead. Plenty of people heard it."

Adam let out a low whistle. "I don't know what to say."

"There is some good news," she said. "His girlfriend is missing."

"Missing?"

"Yes, Adam, as in absent, not there. No one knows where she is."

He frowned. "You're in shock and you're bound to be emotional. Perhaps you shouldn't be here."

"You're right. I'm not handling this well, but I don't want to go home."

"Then go stay with a friend. You need time to grieve."

"Whoever killed my husband knows where I live. What if he comes after me?"

Adam moved away from her and shoved his hands into his pockets. "I'd like to help, but we're about to have guests so I can't offer you a room."

"No, and I wouldn't be comfortable." Amelia sensed the change in his mood and thought she understood why. He wanted to distance himself to hide the truth about his infatuation with her in case he became a suspect.

"I'm sure everything is going to be okay," he said.

A moment of sickness washed over her. "I need to make a phone call. I have to find a way to contact his family."

"Of course."

She stood and made her way past him to the door. "Don't worry, Adam. I'll do my best to keep your name out of it."

Chapter 29

"Her alibi checks out," Beaumont said.

"Good."

"The tattooist said she tried to put the moves on him. His name's Finn Reed and he said it's not the first time. So she's not the brokenhearted widow."

"What else did you learn?"

"Husband drives a ten-year-old Mercedes-Benz; red with a personalized plate. He has some family living in San Diego. She couldn't give me an address or a phone number."

"Anything about a brother or someone they cut out of the family?"

"Nothing. Finn says she's a sex addict with serious jealousy issues."

"This Finn guy seems to know her pretty well," Doucette said.

"According to him, she gets around, has a lot of casual partners, and when she gets to drinking she does some crazy shit."

"How crazy?"

"Apparently, that's when she gets her kink on, and this past weekend she went on a bender. According to Finn, she's been doing it for a hell of a long time, screwing guys from all around the city, and for much longer than the four months she's been separated. Seems there are a lot of layers to this woman."

As Doucette listened to his partner talk, he learned

things about Amelia Miller that caused him to distrust her and question the love she had expressed for her dead husband. He remembered the compression bandage wrapped around the victim's chest and decided to make another call to Kitty Rose to see what she could dig up on this woman or her husband.

"You asked her about the claims made by this guy, what's his name?"

"Finn Reed. Sure, and she didn't like the question. She claims that she and the old man had a general understanding, that they were an open couple, swingers with rules."

"Interesting."

"She said it made the marriage stronger. Now, I've got nothing against an unconventional marriage, but it smelled a little bit too much like bullshit to me."

"Depends on the rules and whether someone broke them," Doucette said.

"One of her rules was no emotional attachment. If what Finn Reed says is true, then it would appear that her husband didn't give a damn who she slept with, and that don't sound much like an open relationship with rules."

"True. Is there anything else I should know?"

"Finn said he worked on her tattoo for an hour and then she passed out for a short time on his couch. When she woke up, he called for a cab to take her home."

Doucette still considered her a suspect. Just because her alibi checked out didn't mean she hadn't planned it, and he had witnessed her jealousy each time he mentioned her husband's new girlfriend. He decided he would have to go and have a chat with Finn Reed.

He clasped his hands behind his neck. "What do you think about the rest of her story?"

"You mean the brawl in the bar? The owner remembered her. She caused quite a scene and got especially angry when he asked her to leave."

"I was under the impression she left voluntarily."

"Nope. He kicked her out. Her and her friend."

"I actually meant the phone calls about the money," Doucette said. "Do you believe any of it?"

"I think she made it up. Her husband left her, replaced her with a younger woman, and she's afraid she's going to be charged with his murder."

"I'm not sure. I still believe there might be some truth in what she said."

"I'll admit, she's quite convincing, but she didn't fool me and she knows it."

"Why'd you let her go?"

"What'd you want me to say?"

"You fucked up. Tell me I'm not the only one."

Beaumont grinned. "I believe parts of her story, but I don't believe she killed him. If we want the full story, we've gotta track down the missing money."

"Have we established money as the motive?"

"She reported the phone calls and the threat made against her," Beaumont said, reading from his notes. "She filed the report on Saturday morning before the story hit the paper. That's what convinced me."

Doucette nodded. The murder piece had first been featured in the Saturday late edition. Unless she came up with the plan and set a trap arranging to have her husband killed, she wouldn't have known about the murder when she reported the phone calls.

"The girlfriend is still missing."

"I don't think she planned a double murder," Beaumont said.

Doucette thought about Amelia Miller's emotions. She'd displayed hate and jealousy, but not obsession. "I'm not sure what I believe." He sighed and rolled his neck to work out some of the kinks. "How does the girlfriend fit into this?"

"My guess is she got in the way."

"So we're left with the guy who found the body." Doucette leaned back in his chair. "The guy I let go is our only suspect."

"Yep. You really fucking screwed up."

"Come on," Doucette said. "Tell me what you think."

Beaumont put his feet up on his desk. "It must be a substantial amount of money if someone is willing to kill to get it back, enough for someone to be keeping an eye on her."

"That's her belief."

"But if he is following her, she could lead us to him."

"What about Marcus Miller in San Diego?"

"Ah, that's where I hit a problem. There's too many of them." Beaumont explained the name had produced numerous hits when he'd entered it into the database. "This one probably doesn't exist."

"I've got a new theory," Doucette said. "This whole story is not about Oliver, but about Eve. She hasn't been kidnapped or disappeared. She and Marcus are working together."

"Uh-huh, and how'd you put that together?"

"A man is dead and a woman is missing. Seems a little odd that no one has responded except the estranged wife, and she's right in the middle of it."

"Are you trying to make this more complicated?"

"Not intentionally."

Doucette turned to the page in his notebook where he'd

written the name and number for Penny Chapman, the friend Amelia Miller claimed she'd spent the evening in question with in the bar. As Penny had grown up with the victim, he hoped she might be able to tell him more about Marcus.

Chapter 30

Penny Chapman regretted answering her cell phone.

As soon as he identified himself, she wanted to cut the call, but it was too late. Her name had come up in a homicide investigation and the police officer on the other end of this call said he wanted to talk to her about the night in the bar.

She held her breath at the mention of Oliver Miller's name. As soon as heard it involved him, she knew it would be bad. She knew the kind of person he was. If he was dead, it explained why he hadn't been answering his phone.

"I'm sorry to give you such bad news," the officer said. "I understand you were a friend of his, and that you saw him on the night he died."

He couldn't be dead. The news refused to sink in. Her skin grew hot and she wanted to be sick. Why hadn't Amelia called to tell her? Did she even know?

"Miss Chapman?"

"Yes, I'm sorry."

"I'd like to ask you some questions. I understand you may have been with the victim on the night he died."

She struggled for an answer, the jolt of shock still passing through her. "How? When did it happen?"

"Perhaps you could just tell me when you last saw Oliver?"

"I saw him a few days ago."

"Could you be more specific?"

"Friday," she said. "I saw him last Friday."

"Where?"

"We were in a bar."

"Can you give me the name of the bar?"

She supplied it. "It's a new cocktail bar in the city."

"Yes, I've heard of it. Did you arrange to meet him there?"

"No. I was out with his wife, celebrating my birthday. Oliver turned up unexpectedly. He wasn't invited." This much was true.

"Okay, and when did you first become aware Oliver had returned to the area?"

"I only found out a couple of hours before I saw him," she said. Penny knew she had to be careful. She wanted to talk to Amelia before she answered any more questions.

"Does Oliver have any enemies?"

"A lot of people don't like him." She didn't know what else to say or how much she should reveal. Oliver had become the type of person who collected enemies.

"Miss Chapman, can you think of anyone with reason to hurt him?"

"No."

"No one at all?"

"Not enough to kill him."

"What about his wife? We know they were arguing."

"Are you suggesting she did this to him?"

"We can't rule out her involvement. Perhaps she hired someone to do it."

Penny couldn't believe it. "She isn't capable."

"Really? She seems quite capable."

"That's ridiculous." Her husband had left her, but murder? No. It was not possible.

"You're sure you can't name anyone else?"

"What about his girlfriend?" Penny said. There was no

point in lying to the police about the things they could easily confirm. "Have you talked to her? She was with him when he left the bar."

"We're still trying to locate her."

A moment of silence followed. Penny found it unnerving. She felt obligated to fill it with another comment, yet refrained, understanding it as a deliberate attempt by the police to unsettle her.

"It's clear to me that his death has come as quite a shock to you," Doucette said. "You're also friends with his wife so I'm surprised she hasn't told you about it. You haven't heard from her?"

"No, we haven't spoken since early Saturday morning. I'm in New York on business and I haven't been checking my phone."

"I see. When do you return?"

"I have a flight booked for tomorrow."

"Well, I'd like to meet with you when you return. Could you come to the station?"

"Of course." She wondered if she had a choice.

He asked her when it would be convenient.

Penny agreed to meet him at the station upon her return.

After the call ended, Penny changed her flight to catch the next one available with a seat open back to San Francisco, and then she checked out of her hotel.

She called Amelia on her landline and then on her cell phone and got no answer from either.

Chapter 31

Sitting in the departure lounge at John F Kennedy Airport waiting to board her flight, Penny tried to make sense of it all.

A restless uneasiness climbed over her. Nobody knew Oliver had planned to return. He said he had told no one and he'd made her promise not to mention it, not even to his wife. He wanted to see Penny in person, but he had refused to provide any information.

She remembered the conversation so well because it had filled her with panic. She knew by the tone of his voice that whatever he had to tell her, she would not want to hear.

When the police asked her about enemies, it had immediately brought Marcus to mind and she wondered why she hadn't come right out and told them about him. Perhaps because she couldn't admit it, that Marcus had managed to track them down.

Penny sat in the airport in a daze, ignoring everyone around her. She knew Marcus had to be behind Oliver's murder, but Marcus was supposed to be in prison. Was he out? It seemed to her to be the only possible explanation, the only reason Oliver would come back, and now he'd been killed trying to protect her.

Her temples throbbed and the knot in her stomach got worse. She wanted to call Oliver's mother, Barbara Miller, yet refrained, not ready to hear the agony in her voice, plus she could not give her any answers. Besides, she knew the police would contact Oliver's parents. That was part of their job.

Passengers lined up to board the plane. Penny stared at them. The thought of going home scared her to death. Without Oliver, she felt lost, and the news of his murder was threatening to overwhelm her.

As one of the last passengers to get on the plane, she found her seat at the back by the window, and was dismayed when a big bald man with a vicious face heaved himself into the next seat. The sight of him made her nervous. She wanted to switch to sit next to the aisle, but on a crowded flight every seat was filled and she was stuck.

Wedged between his beefy body and the window, she felt trapped and desperate to escape. She breathed deeply and made sure she had a sick bag in the seat pocket in front of her.

"I don't like flying," she said to a flight attendant coming through the aircraft.

The man next to her leaned over. "Landings are the most dangerous."

She shoved her bag under the seat in front of her and put on headphones to listen to some music while she waited for the aircraft to leave the ground. Terrible thoughts ran through her mind. Marcus had threatened to find her, and in her heart she always knew he would. No one could protect her. Oliver tried. Not even the police could keep Marcus out of her life.

The big man was sweating. She could smell it. She cocked a glance at him, at the grimace on his face, and noted the clenched fists. Perhaps he hated flying, too. The thought distracted her from her own fears.

Due to the delayed arrival and the cleaning crew completing their task, the plane took off behind schedule, some forty minutes late. As it rose into the air, Penny sat back, comforting herself with the thought that approximately seven hours from now, she would be rid of the man in the next seat.

When the drinks cart reached her, she ordered a juice. The man next to her drank hard liquor for the whole flight.

As the plane got closer to its destination, her breath tightened and her heart pounded. She wished she had someone meeting her at the airport, someone waiting for her at home.

The moment the plane landed, she reached for her bag, anxious to get off. It seemed to take a long time for it to reach the gate, but finally the seatbelt sign went out and passengers filled the aisles. Then there was another long wait before the lines began to move.

Penny wanted off, but the big man was blocking her way. His massive legs barely fit into the small gap, forcing her to wait while he struggled to get out of his seat. She moved into the aisle behind him, staring at the thickness of his back.

Inside the airport terminal, she forgot about him as soon as she lost sight of him. She recovered her suitcase and stopped in the gift shop to buy a newspaper, then walked outside to join another line for a cab.

She didn't have to wait long.

The driver started the ignition and asked for her destination. She gave it, but as he pulled away from the curbside she turned her head and saw the fat man from the plane climbing into the taxicab behind hers.

Penny located her cell phone in her bag and made a quick call. Then she asked the driver to change the destination, instructing him to take her to a hotel instead, afraid to go home in case Marcus had someone following her.

She caught the cab driver's eye in the rearview mirror. "Can you turn right at the next light and let me know if the car behind follows?"

He complied. "Are you okay, Miss?"

"Yeah. Slow down. I don't want us to get separated."

After the driver made the right turn and checked his mirror again, he turned his head. "He crossed through the intersection. Want me to follow?"

"No." She smiled. "It doesn't matter."

When he dropped her off at the hotel, she pushed the cab fare into his hand, grabbed her bag and ran inside the hotel to check in.

"One room key," she said to the desk clerk. "I have a jealous ex-boyfriend who might try to find me and I don't want to see him. Please, would you be able to let me know if anyone comes in here asking for me?"

"Of course, Miss Chapman. I'll make a note."

Her room on the fourth floor overlooked the pool. Penny stared down at the blue water shimmering under the outdoor lights. The room itself was small and fairly basic, with a single bed, a TV, and a coffee maker in the bathroom.

After checking the door lock and security latch, Penny checked her phone for messages, hoping to see one from Amelia. Disappointed and confused not to have received a call, she went into the bathroom and turned on the hot water to fill the tub, and got undressed.

Oliver was more than a friend. She did not want to live the rest of her life without him. She closed her eyes and let the tears flow without restraint. Few people experienced the real side to Oliver Miller, the buried part of his character that Penny knew. He was decent, a good man.

Her body ached with sorrow and emptiness. The warm

soak did nothing to soothe it. She toweled off as her emotions welled again, and then curled up on the bed, wondering if her heart and her head would ever heal. Finally, fatigue overtook her. As she drifted off to sleep, her last thoughts were of Amelia.

Chapter 32

Amelia Miller craved a warm male body, someone to hold her, to help her forget and to make her feel good.

Lovers filled an emptiness stemming from her childhood, a hollow restlessness and a sense of something that was permanently missing. Other men provided a short-term connection, a thin cover over the void, temporarily making her feel wanted.

These men would never love her, never satisfy her nor take away the loneliness, but it felt good to be in the arms of another person for a while.

Instead of a lover, she took a shower, then got into bed early, alone in a basic budget motel room. She slid down under the covers, knowing she would not sleep much tonight. Her mind stayed on the man out on the streets, tracking her movements and making terrifying plans.

Her cell phone rang almost immediately. Before she answered it, she got out of bed and checked through the window to see if anyone was outside on the street. Habit.

Then she answered the call, wishing she had someone with her in the motel room.

"I'm not a patient man, Amelia."

His voice set off a nervous fluttering in her stomach. She remained silent. Perhaps by refusing to respond, she would deny him what he wanted: power and control.

"I've given you a couple of days to consider what I said, and I can't wait much longer. I meant what I said. I want my money."

He was trying to remain calm, but she could sense his growing frustration.

"You may think you can control me," he said, "but you don't know what I'm capable of."

As he tried to provoke her, she listened to the noise in the background and the sound of a woman's voice. The call ended abruptly when the woman called out a name.

The woman had called him G. It must be a nickname, or an initial, and it was her first clue to his identity.

Amelia set the phone on the bedside table and used the motel pen and paper to log the detail. She thought the woman sounded of a similar age, early to mid thirties, which meant G was a husband, a boyfriend, or possibly a brother.

She wondered how he might be connected to Marcus. For a while, her mind stayed on the police investigator's suggestion that her husband had a brother. She wished she knew more about the complex man she'd married, a man with secrets and a family she'd never met. The cops would make the notification, but she felt it would be better if they received the news of Oliver's death from someone they knew.

If a brother existed, Penny had to know. Why would she conceal it? Amelia wanted the answer, but she couldn't face talking to her and for that reason had not answered any of Penny's calls. She considered the secret as bad as a lie.

Chapter 33

"It's nine o'clock," Bruce Beaumont said, getting up from his desk and stretching, then grabbing his jacket. "I'm guessing you don't have plans for tonight."

Doucette looked up from his case file. "I'm working late. Those are my plans."

"Come on. Let's grab a bite."

"You go ahead. I don't need to eat."

"Yes, you do, and I'm starving. I can't work on an empty stomach and you already skipped lunch." Beaumont hunted around the mess on his desk for his keys.

"Fine. I guess I could use a break." Doucette threw down his pen and stretched his neck and shoulders. His eyes hurt and he needed to pee. "First, I need to make a phone call."

"Don't go bailing on me now." Beaumont located his keys and threw them into the air, catching them in his palm. "I'll drive. Tell the little hottie I said hi."

Doucette sighed. On his way to the bathroom he called Isabelle's home number, but she didn't answer. He tried her cell phone and got no answer there. Then he sent a text. When he didn't get one in return, he tried not to let it bother him.

In the car, he sat thinking about the case and the missing woman, wondering if she was involved or an unintended target, suspecting that if it were the latter they might already be too late to find her alive. His mood darkened. At least Penny Chapman would be able to provide some new information in the morning.

"Mind if I pick the place?" Beaumont said, interrupting Doucette's thoughts.

"You know the drill."

"Yeah, yeah, I pick, you pay."

"That's not how it works."

"Suits me. The place I have in mind is cheap with big portions. You'll love it."

"I doubt it."

Beaumont stopped along the route for gas. As he got out of the car, Doucette made one final effort to reach Isabelle with no result. Was she busy or avoiding him?

As his partner pushed open the door to the little Italian place on Geary Boulevard, the incredible garlic smells inside made Doucette salivate. His stomach let out a loud growl.

"Don't need to eat, huh?" Beaumont laughed.

A young greeter welcomed them and showed them to a table near the door. Doucette looked around and spotted a man he recognized sitting at a table across the room.

"Give me a second," he said to his partner, and made his way over.

"Mark." He slapped the man on the back. "How've you been doing?"

Mark Thoeny was a friend and the owner of another eatery in the city. Doucette hadn't seen him for a little while, not since an incident that had occurred three months ago when Doucette had been getting lunch in Mark's Grill Bar late one afternoon and two gunmen had burst in, robbing the register and assaulting two of the male employees. Doucette had managed to stop it from turning deadly, and he wanted to catch up.

"John." Mark's shiny face broke into a grin. "It's good

to see you and even better under these circumstances."

"You're damn right. How are the guys?"

"Doing well and glad to be alive, thanks to you."

"They're alive mostly thanks to you, but...hey, don't try wrestling with a guy pointing a gun at you again."

"Sounds like a solid piece of advice."

Doucette glanced at the faces of the two other men seated with Mark at his table. "Sorry to interrupt. Enjoy your meal," he said.

As he was about to turn and head back to his own table, Mark made a comment about the recent story in the news, the one concerning the body that had washed up on the shore.

"We were just talking about it," he said. "My friend here thinks he might have seen him."

"Oh, yeah? When was this?" Doucette pulled up a seat next to the friend Mark indicated, a guy named Gerry.

"Sometime last week, Thursday I believe," Gerry said, unfolding a newspaper. "I've been out of town for a few days and I didn't know anything about it until I got home this evening and saw this story."

"Where did you see him?"

Gerry named a hotel restaurant outside of the city.

Doucette took a quick look at the photograph in the paper and saw that it was indeed connected to his murder case. Anticipation tugged up the hairs on the back of his neck.

"I was there having dinner with my wife and some family from out-of-state," Gerry said. "This guy came in with a woman, a small, pretty blonde who looked way too young for him."

"You're certain it was this man?"

"Well, not a hundred percent, but I believe it was him.

There's something familiar about his face and I remember the couple."

"Because of the age gap?" Mark said.

"No, because he complained about the food. He was a real ass. Sounded to me like he just didn't want to pay for it."

"What else do you remember?" Doucette said.

"Not much. Apart from the age difference, they seemed like any ordinary couple."

"Do you recall if there was any trouble, or anyone who appeared to be paying them any particular attention?"

"No, I don't think so."

"Okay." Doucette thanked Gerry for the information and produced one of his cards. "If you remember anything else that could help our investigation, I'd like you to call me."

"You got it."

Doucette shook hands with Mark Thoeny and returned to his own table to give his order of chicken and rice to the waiter, and then sat massaging his temples, still trying to piece it all together.

Beaumont studied him. "What's up?"

"Got a bit of a headache coming on." Doucette expelled a long breath and ran his hands through his hair. "I'm tired. It's been a long day."

"She hasn't called you back, has she?"

"Who?"

"The little hottie."

"Her name is Isabelle."

"I know. If you want my advice, stop calling. Make her want you."

"Thanks, but I don't want your advice. I can figure out my own shit."

"Fine. So, what was that all about with your buddy over there?"

"One of the guys at the table believes he saw the victim last week, dining with a woman at a place in Oakland."

"You're not convinced."

"He thinks he saw him, but he can't say for sure."

"It's worth checking out."

The meal arrived. Doucette ate fast, wanting to get it out of the way. The portions were huge and the food delicious. Unable to eat everything on his plate, he asked for his leftovers to be boxed so he could take them away.

Beaumont tossed some money onto the table without complaint and picked up his jacket.

After Beaumont drove them back to the station, Doucette got out of the car and left him with instructions to check out a couple of things in the morning, and then climbed into his own vehicle and headed out, intending to go home. Instead, he drove to Isabelle's Sea Cliff address.

Her car was not in the driveway where he expected it to be. He sighed with frustration and disappointment. Things hadn't been right between them for a while and he blamed himself because it was easier than blaming her.

Neither of them seemed willing to talk about the distance creeping in, but he was sure they both felt it. Perhaps it was his fault and his reluctance to commit. His past failed marriage still clouded his views, and he sensed it driving Isabelle away.

Her first marriage had ended in divorce and she'd made it clear that she wanted to find another husband before she lost the chance to have children, which presented Doucette with a potential problem and another issue to consider. Jack was now a teenager and the baby stage had been tough. Doucette wasn't sure he wanted to have any more children.

For a few months, they'd been having the same conversation without making progress. He cleared his mind of the subject and drove away from her home.

As he turned down his street and parked in front of his own average two-bedroom abode, he received a call on his cell phone from Amelia Miller. He switched off the engine and sat in his truck listening as she told him she'd received another threatening phone call from the same man.

"I heard a name mentioned," she said. "A woman called him G. I don't know if it's a first name or an initial, but that's what I heard come out of her mouth."

"Okay, good. It's a start."

"Can you trace the calls?"

"It can take time," Doucette said.

"What do I do if he contacts me again?"

"Try not to panic. Keep a diary of the calls. Write down everything he says and call me."

Doucette got out of his vehicle and stood on the sidewalk, considering the name Amelia said she heard. Mark Thoeny's friend's name was Gerry, and he claimed to have seen the victim shortly before he died. Probably nothing, he thought, but decided he needed to know more about this friend. It never hurt to have the right information.

With no real inclination to move from his truck or go inside, Doucette stared at the windows of his apartment, the only one he could see with no lights on inside. His only son was growing up and spending more time away. The place seemed empty, more of a shell than a home, and he took his time entering.

He switched on the light and hung his jacket next to the empty hook on the wall, then made his way to the kitchen, put his leftovers on the counter and grabbed a couple of beers from the refrigerator before settling into a chair in front of the television in the living room.

After a few minutes, with the Miller case consuming him, he switched the television off and returned the beers to the fridge, then pulled on sweats and running shoes and headed out.

Chapter 34

His route took him in a southwest direction, through a series of right and left turns and part of Haight-Ashbury, his pace strong and hard for three miles, until he reached Kezar Stadium in the southeast corner of Golden Gate Park.

Stopping under the arch on the west side of the stadium to catch his breath, Doucette watched bright lights bobbing in the distance. Loud voices reached him, carried along by the wind. He jogged on the spot to keep warm, waiting for the small group of runners.

As he moved out from under the arch, the three adult males glanced across. Doucette spoke first.

"Are you guys from the Bay Stormers Running Club?"

The lead runner stopped. "Who wants to know?"

Doucette sensed the man judging him. His instincts told him he'd found the right club.

"I'm investigating a homicide and I'm looking to speak to someone from your club."

"We're a private group," the runner said. "Who passed you the info?"

"Keith Sigmund. He said you guys meet Tuesdays and Thursdays. Today is Tuesday." Doucette had remembered the schedule from working on an old case involving a dead runner.

A second runner with close-cut hair, presumably to disguise the fact it was thinning, moved up behind the lead guy. "Sigmund. You mean Freud." He turned and yelled to the third runner approaching. "Hey, Freud. Got someone here who wants to talk to you."

A bigger man jogged up beside his two smaller buddies. His height and build matched the suspect. As Doucette searched his face for the scar, he realized he had never met this man before.

"I'm Keith Sigmund," the third runner said. "What do you want to talk to me about?"

"A homicide."

"Don't say anything." One of Sigmund's running buddy's interjected with the piece of advice.

"You want to talk to me about a murder?" Sigmund used one of his huge hands to wipe his sweaty hair out of his face. "Why do you want to talk to me?"

"Your name came up in my investigation."

"My name?"

"That's what I said."

"Well, I don't know how. I don't know anything about a murder."

"I have some questions and I'd appreciate an opportunity to talk to you."

"What the hell about? I just told you, I don't know anything about a murder."

"Then you have nothing to fear and you won't mind giving me your full cooperation."

Sigmund demanded to see some ID. Doucette provided it.

"Look, I'm not trying to obstruct your investigation," Sigmund said, "but I don't know why my name came up. I'm going to guess it's not by coincidence, but I'm not the guy you're looking for."

"That so? I have a witness who connected you to the case and he gave me the name of your running club."

"Now, hold on a minute." Sigmund cast a quick glance

at his friends. "What witness? Who is this fucker?"

Doucette noted the rage in his eyes. "You got some identification?"

"This has to be a fucking joke." Continuing to protest his innocence, Sigmund produced a driver's license from his belt. "I'm not your guy. Someone is trying to set me up."

Doucette narrowed his eyes against the bright light coming from the headlamp Sigmund wore. He asked him to turn it off. The man complied.

"Why would someone try to frame you for murder?"

"I can come up with a few reasons."

"So you admit you have a problem?"

Sigmund gave the others an upward flick of the chin, signaling his desire for them to go on without him. He zipped up his jacket and stood with his feet apart, breathing hard. At least he appeared willing to talk.

"I've pissed off a lot of people. At some point, one of them was going to hit back."

"You speak as if you treat people like shit, and you seem to be an angry man."

"Yeah, you're damn right I'm angry, but I've done nothing wrong. I'm a social worker in The Tenderloin. It's a hard line of work in a hellish neighborhood. I'm sure you can understand what it's like."

"Must be tough."

"I deal with a lot of shit. It's not always easy to keep everything under control. Clients get rough. Sometimes I have to get rough back. It's a hostile environment."

"I get it. It's a power thing. You use violence as a restraint."

"Sometimes, it's necessary. Kind of like your job, huh?"

Doucette did not react to the deliberate provocation. "You involved in any recent conflicts?"

One corner of the man's mouth lifted in an attempt at a smile. "Am I a suspect?"

"It depends on what you tell me."

"I deal with some pretty dangerous situations and sometimes I have to take a hard line. You have to understand something. I work with sadistic types, all kinds of paranoid people. Some refuse to take their medication. Most don't want our help. They want money for drugs."

"Then perhaps this whole case is not actually about the victim, but about you," Doucette said.

Sigmund frowned. "If someone wants to hurt me, isn't killing another human being to do it a little extreme?"

"There's usually a reasonable explanation."

"Psychotic breaks happen. Some of our clients believe everything we do is a personal attack and they hit back, but they do it directly."

"Yeah? Well, this seems personal."

"Someone is using my identity. I'm not involved."

"You know anyone called G or Mr. G?"

"Nope, never heard of him."

"Pity. This is going to be a lot more complicated than I thought."

"Look, I'm sure there's been a mistake," Sigmund said.

"Oh, there's definitely been a mistake."

The man's demeanor had changed and sudden warmth crept into his manner. He stared at Doucette with an expression of frankness, as if the eye contact would be enough to convince him the words coming out of Sigmund's mouth were the truth, and he spoke politely.

"It's clear to me that someone wanted you to find me, and I would like to help you resolve this."

"Good." The transformation made Doucette uncomfortable. "I'm willing to listen to what you have to say."

"There are quite a few people who have grudges against me. One of them is trying to make me look guilty."

"One of them?"

"One, maybe more. You'll have to decide this for yourself, but I am telling you the truth. I don't know what's happened, but I haven't killed anyone. I'm not a murderer."

"Noted." Doucette paused for a moment. "I've got to account for everyone's whereabouts, so do you mind telling where you were from about ten on Friday night until around eight o'clock on Saturday morning?"

For a second, Keith Sigmund became flustered.

Chapter 35

"I was seeing someone."

"Who?"

"An ex-girlfriend. We went out of town for a drink. I picked her up at nine o'clock on Friday night and I got home at seven the next morning."

"Can anyone verify it?"

"My wife."

"Your wife?" Doucette remembered the conversation with the runner at the pier about his wife's suicide. "So, she's alive?"

"What? Of course she's alive."

"Good." Doucette hoped it would stay that way. "Please continue."

Sigmund's tone dipped lower. "I told her I was working."

"Well, you seem remorseful."

"She was waiting up for me when I got in. I also have a receipt at home for the motel."

"I'll need to see it. I noticed your driver's license shows an old address," Doucette said. "When did you move?"

"It's been a couple of years. I never got around to changing it."

"The guy I'm looking for knows your old address. Seems like he doesn't know you've moved, so he could be someone you haven't seen in a while."

"Hell, I don't know."

"Would help if you could come up with a name. He's around thirty years of age, dark hair, six-four, big scar running down the left side of his face. Sound like anyone you know?"

"I can't remember much about the past couple of years. I drink a lot. It's how I get through the madness."

"This guy has a serious problem with you," Doucette said. "Something must have happened to him that triggered his desire for revenge, and he hasn't forgotten you. Whatever happened must have been significant. What can you remember?"

"Fuck man, beats me." Sigmund removed his headlamp and raked his fingers through his hair. "I'm working with a young guy whose father cut him when he was a kid, but he's a short dude and I don't have any problems with him."

"It's not easy to frame someone for murder, and there's usually a motive. This guy believes there's a good chance you'll be found guilty, so I'm not convinced that I'm getting all the facts here," Doucette said. "I need to know if there's anything you haven't told me."

"There's nothing else to tell."

Doucette remembered a small detail he thought might jog something loose. The silent pun amused him. "This guy mentioned the Marin Ultra Challenge. You ever run it?"

"Once. You think he's a past member?"

"Unlikely; too easy to track him, but he's familiar with the club and the events."

"I don't understand," Sigmund said. "Why hasn't he come after me directly?"

"Consider yourself lucky. Someone else pissed him off more. Maybe you'll recognize the name of the victim. Oliver Miller."

"Miller?"

"How do you know him?"

"We used to be friends."

"Used to be?"

"We lost contact a long time ago."

"Do you know if he was involved in anything?"

Sigmund shook his head. "I haven't seen him in years, but now I understand why the dude you're looking for picked me. There's bad history between Miller and me, real bad, and whoever got to him knows the story, but a lot of people know the story."

"What's the story?"

"I don't know if I should be talking to you without a lawyer," Sigmund said, an ugly flush spreading across his face.

"I'm not arresting you." Doucette shivered in his sweat-soaked shirt. "Look, it's been a long night and I'm sure you'd like to go home. I know I would, so the sooner we can straighten this out the better for everyone."

"If I talk to you, I want to make one thing clear. I understand that what I'm going to tell you gives me motive, but I didn't kill him. I wish I had, but his death has nothing to do with me."

"Understood."

Keith Sigmund took a long, hard look at the ground. "Miller used to date my sister. They only went out for a while. The night before she died they had a fight and he locked her out of his apartment, made her sleep all night in the car."

"What happened to her?"

"She'd had too much to drink and she couldn't drive. In the morning, when she couldn't get inside the apartment, she tried to make it over to my place, but she was still intoxicated and she crashed her car into a stone wall."

"I'm sorry."

"She'd called me to come and get her, but I was busy, too caught up in my own shit to answer my phone and by the time I got her message, it was too late. She was dead."

"You can't blame yourself."

"I don't." Sigmund sucked the air in hard through his nose. "She was young and she must have been cold and hungry because she would never drive if she had been drinking. She made a terrible mistake. He may not have killed her directly, but Miller caused my sister's death. If he hadn't locked her out, she would never have been on the road that morning."

"When did this happen?"

"It's been seven years. I wanted to kill him, but I wouldn't have waited seven years. I haven't seen him since the day of her funeral."

"He attended?"

"Oh, yeah, even after he was asked to stay away. The man had no respect for my family, no appreciation for our wishes, and absolutely no regard for boundaries," Sigmund said. "I struggled to keep my distance and it's only because of my family that I didn't go after him myself. We've already lost enough."

"What do you know about his family?" Doucette said, noting a rising level of aggression in the other man's voice. Sigmund seemed to be struggling with some kind of split personality, one minute cold and then warmer. "Does Oliver Miller have a brother?" Doucette had not yet been able to reach any member of the dead man's family.

"I don't know and I don't care. I don't even want to hear that man's name."

"I'm trying to connect someone called Marcus Miller

to this case."

"I've never heard of him." Sigmund tilted his head to the left and then to the right as if to work out his anger. "What about the asshole who committed the murder, the one using my name and trying to make it look like I did it? Why aren't you out looking for him?"

"We're tying to trace him, but without any information, it's difficult. In the meantime, you have motive, like you said, so I'll be checking up on your alibi, and I may have some more questions." Doucette returned the ID.

"I'll answer your questions, but you better find him because I'm not involved and I want my name out of it." Keith Sigmund provided his phone number and his current address. "You can contact me any time."

"Appreciate it. You'd have no idea why Miller was returning to the city?"

"Returning?"

"He moved away, returned sometime last week."

"I wasn't aware."

"Seems he didn't make regular trips," Doucette said, "so we're still trying to figure out why and thought perhaps he might be meeting someone."

"Not me."

"Okay. Well, thanks for your time."

Doucette watched Keith Sigmund as he headed out of the park, glancing back once.

Chapter 36

When he returned home from his run, Doucette grabbed a quick shower, and then ate the rest of the chicken and rice meal he'd left out on the kitchen counter. While he ate, he checked his cell phone for messages and found a text from his son Jack, but nothing from his partner or Isabelle.

A full stomach and an hour in front of the TV led to lethargy and his eyes began to close. He rested them for a bit and then headed to bed, passing his son's room on the way and pausing outside the door, even though he knew the kid was not in the room. He missed having a wife and a family waiting for him when he came in late from work. With the house to himself, at least he didn't have to be quiet.

Disgruntled, he sat at the computer desk in his bedroom and worked on the case for a while, searching various archives, accessing and retrieving information and assessing its value, until his eyes grew heavy again and he shut down the computer in favor of the comfort of his bed.

He slept on and off for a few hours, waking with severe abdominal pain and a violent urge for the bathroom. He stayed in there for a long time, sweating and then shivering, ejecting fluids and other nastiness from both ends.

Finally, he washed his face, rinsed his mouth, and swallowed two antacids to reduce the pain, then crawled back into bed, weak, exhausted, and wondering if it was food poisoning or a virus that was making him feel so awful.

After another trip to the bathroom at five o'clock in the

morning, his stomach began to settle. Doucette took a warm shower to soothe his aching muscles, drank a glass of water, and decided he might as well work.

The phone rang once before Kitty Rose answered. She sounded tense and slightly angry. He apologized for the early morning call.

"I'm glad it's you and not your partner," she said. "He certainly knows how to be an asshole."

"What's up?"

"We hit a bit of a rough spot tonight. I can handle it, but he's causing me some serious problems."

Doucette asked about it and she gave him the details.

"Yep, he can be an asshole. I'll talk to him."

"I appreciate it."

"I need your help," he said.

"I don't know what I can do for you. After last night and your partner, it's kind of soured my feelings."

"Do I have to beg?"

She laughed. "No, that'll only make me horny."

"It's about my new murder case."

"I really wish it wasn't."

In spite of his weak and shaky condition, Doucette laughed. "When is this flirting going to stop?"

"Why does it have to stop?"

"Because I'm old and boring and in love with someone else. You don't want a man like me, Kitty-Kat."

"Maybe, maybe not, but you can't deny that the chase is addictive."

"I'm glad you get a kick out of it," he said.

"I do, especially when you're the one calling for my services."

"You mean your resources," he said, correcting her. A little flirting felt good. Privately, Doucette enjoyed it, although he would never admit it. "The victim in this case is Oliver Miller. His widow is a sex addict and I believe she or the victim could be linked to your club."

Kitty Rose sighed. "Why do I get such a strong sense you're trying to ruin my business?"

"I'm not out to mess with your business. All I'm trying to do is solve a murder and it's the clues that are leading me here."

"Only the clues?"

"Yep. This guy or his wife might have been leading a double life."

"Most of my clients are leading a double life. Perhaps you should come in here and bust everyone."

"It's tempting. I might have to consider it if I don't get any evidence."

"Boy, I'm glad we're friends," she said, "because you can be a total shit when you want to."

"All part of the charm."

Doucette had no intention of going after her club. He saw no benefit in losing Kitty Rose as an informant.

"If you promise me your partner won't cause me any more trouble, I'll check it out."

"You got it, and thanks."

"Happy to do it." Her tone said otherwise.

Doucette had a few more questions he wanted to ask, but ended the call, unable to concentrate as the pain in his stomach and the nausea had returned, made worse with the smell of the take-out food lingering in the apartment.

Clutching his stomach, he raced for the bathroom and immediately threw up, then went into the living room to lie down, returning to the bathroom a few minutes later for another loose bowel movement and to vomit again.

Chapter 37

Woken by a bad dream that made her cry out in her sleep, Penny Chapman got out of bed and took a shower to wash the sticky sweat from her body. Standing under the warm water, she kept her eyes open to distract her mind from the disturbing images.

She stepped out of the shower, dried, and wept into the rough towel. One thought occupied her mind. Marcus Miller had carried out his threat. He'd tracked Oliver down and paid someone to kill him, he'd threatened Amelia, and now he'd found her. Why else would Oliver have come back?

As she wept, she thought she understood why Amelia had failed to call her or answer any of her calls. Her friend must be grieving, too.

Using the writing paper and pen in her hotel room, Penny wrote down the details of the man from the plane to tell the police, then made a note to tell them about another man she feared Marcus might have murdered.

Next, she used the hotel phone and called the number of a friend, a young lawyer with a large firm in town. His answer machine clicked on. Penny left him a message.

Feeling broken, she made a cup of coffee in her room and turned on the television, hoping for some news of the murder. Oliver had wanted to tell her something important, something he could not be persuaded to tell her over the phone. Now she would never know.

She turned the television off and sat on her bed, staring at a crack in the wall. "Damn you, Marcus."

Whatever his reason, Oliver had made a mistake in coming back. Marcus seemed to have eyes hidden everywhere. He knew everything and always seemed to have someone willing to do his work. Every instinct told her he was involved. Locking him up would never be enough.

The desperate fear filling her mind was escalating into panic, dropping her deeper into the massive dark hole in which she'd lived for years, forcing her to use the same breathing technique she'd been taught ten years ago to calm herself.

Amelia needed help.

Penny realized the mistake she'd made. Amelia had already been threatened, but she remained ignorant of the danger she was in. Penny called her number and again got no answer. She tried several times. Each attempt brought no response.

My best friend is dead.

She made herself think it, say it out loud, and accept it to remind herself of what was real. It hurt like hell, but it strengthened her grip on reality.

Someone had to comfort his mother.

In the midst of her own pain, Penny remembered all that his mother had done to help her. Barbara Miller was a widow. Even though they'd had no contact for years, Penny loved her. If Barbara didn't already know, then Penny wanted the terrible news to be delivered to Oliver's mother with the kindness of someone who loved her, not by an indifferent police officer.

First, she made sure she had the number. Then she finished her cup of coffee. Sick at the task that lay ahead of her, she stared at the phone on the bed. How could she explain it? What words should she use? She took a deep breath and went into the bathroom.

"Barbara, I'm so sorry to tell you. Oliver died. Barbara, your son is dead. Oliver has been murdered."

Standing in front of the mirror, she practiced saying what she knew she had to say until she thought she could get it right.

Tears streamed down her face. When she felt strong enough, she went back to her phone. Her heart raced. With shaking fingers and a breaking heart, she made the call, forgetting that his mother might have no one with her to help her absorb the unimaginable news.

She could only tell Barbara what she knew, that the son she loved had died. That was all. The rest would have to come from the police.

Chapter 38

The Jaguar drew too much attention.

This morning, Wilkes Smith sat behind the wheel of his own aging black car drinking a lukewarm cup of coffee and fiddling with the radio. The loss of his money was not the biggest problem he faced.

Until a few months ago, he'd never heard of the man who'd been murdered. The killing brought him no satisfaction. His complicity in the crime still left him bewildered and he realized that he'd been manipulated and tricked, but none of that mattered now.

His girlfriend would be worried. Three days had gone by with no contact. The separation added to both his suffering and hers. He'd left her to cope with an indescribable situation while he went after the man who'd deprived them of any peace in the final few months.

His thoughts shifted quickly to his seven-year-old son at home and he struggled to catch his breath. With the end coming soon he thought his heart might stop, and he could barely stand the agony of waiting. He did not know how to prepare himself to say goodbye, and he felt like he was losing his mind. Right now, he needed to regain focus, to get what he came for and get home to his family.

Across the street from him, the green and white house sat empty. He'd been watching it for long enough to establish that the owner wasn't at home. He needed to get inside and search the place, find the money that belonged to him or take what he could lay his hands on, and get out of there before anyone returned. Instead, he sat fidgeting and fretting, his adrenaline flowing.

A man was approaching on the opposite side of the street. He appeared to be watching the cars carefully, and then looking around as if he might be contemplating breaking into one of them. Wilkes watched him. It was starting to freak him out. The man was fat, with long, dark hair, and he didn't look like a cop. Perhaps that was intentional.

Another vehicle drove past and slowed. Wilkes suspected trouble. The fat man stepped out in front of it. Then he went around to the passenger side and got in. Wilkes watched the car until it disappeared. Satisfied, he sank lower in the seat and continued to observe the early morning movements of the residents, in particular those of the occupant of the yellow house next door to the green and white one. The lights in the yellow house were on in the downstairs front room and he'd noticed the security camera the old lady had installed.

A car filled with people pulled up in front of the yellow house. Wilkes saw a familiar shape appear at the window. The old lady waved at the dark-haired woman getting out of the car. The younger woman waved back, then walked around to the rear door and opened it for two small children to climb out. Together, the three of them walked up the path of the yellow house and disappeared inside it. A few minutes later, the young woman returned to the car without the children.

Predicting that the elderly neighbor would be occupied with the kids, Wilkes took advantage of the opportunity to get inside the green and white house. He zipped up his jacket with the crowbar tucked inside it, and pulled the wool hat over his head.

As he jogged across the road, stopping once beneath the palm tree at the foot of the driveway before continuing his approach, he heard a loud barking. He'd forgotten all about the damn dog, and it was a big dog, one he did not want to deal with. He stopped again and listened.

The animal sounded alert and aggressive, as if it knew he was there and it viewed him as a threat. The barking continued. What if the neighbor came outside to investigate the noise? What if she or someone else had been tasked with taking care of the dog while the owner was at work? Wilkes decided he couldn't risk it and he wasn't up to the job of killing a dog.

Frustrated, he returned to his car and drove away, knowing he would have to return. He had to get inside that house.

Chapter 39

Amelia Miller heard the muffled ring of her cell phone. She poked her head out from under the pillows, planning to let it go to voicemail, but decided she'd better answer it when she saw Penny's number on the display.

"I've been calling you and getting no answer," Penny said. "Where are you?"

"In bed."

"Are you drinking?"

"I won't answer that question," Amelia said. It angered and offended her, and it made her feel judged.

"You don't really need to. I'm sure you've heard the news."

"I assume you mean about Oliver? Yes, I know."

"You should have called me."

"I meant to."

"Is that all you have to say?"

"What exactly is it you want me to say, Penny?"

"He was my friend, my best friend."

"This isn't about you." Amelia wondered how her friend could be so selfish, so insensitive.

"I'm sorry," Penny said. "I know you love him. You must be devastated."

"He was my husband."

"You can't imagine what it's like to lose a friend like Oliver, someone who's been there for you at the worst time of your life."

"And you can't imagine what it's like to go to the

police station to identify the dead body of your husband."

"You're right," Penny said. "Forgive me."

"I'm a suspect."

"It's too awful."

"I'm still trying to process it, so you'll have to forgive me that I didn't immediately think of calling you."

"I'm truly sorry."

The sympathy Amelia heard in the apology removed some of her tension. "Thank you." It was all she could summon up the energy to say.

"You didn't have to call his mother and hear her reaction when I told her that her son had died," Penny said in a soft voice.

"I thought the police would have told her."

"No. I did it, and hearing her sobbing was awful."

"I'm sorry." Amelia sat up in the bed, her whole body trembling as she listened to the long awkward silence and the sound of her friend crying. She fought to hold back her own tears. "This must be equally as terrible for you."

"It is," Penny said. "I still can't believe it's happened."

"Neither can I." Amelia pushed her original anger aside. Temporarily. "I wanted to call you, but I didn't know if you knew and I didn't want to tell you over the phone. Are you still in New York?"

"I got back last night. The police called. As soon as I heard, I changed my flight. You gave them my details?"

"As part of their investigation."

"They want to talk to me today."

"I'll go with you."

"It's probably better if you don't."

Amelia frowned at the comment but didn't ask.

"I wanted to speak with you first, so I could figure out what to say based on what you've already told them,"

Penny said.

"I'm not sure I understand what you mean." Wrapping herself in the soft duvet, Amelia leaned against the pillows.

"You know exactly what I mean. I'm talking about the fight in the bar."

"Oh. Well, don't worry. I told the police all about it."

"Did you mention the threats?"

"Yeah, I told them everything, including the phone calls."

"I meant the personal threats you made against your husband," Penny said.

"The police know about those. They also know about the demand for money. I suggested that Oliver stole it."

"Why?"

"Because I believe it's what happened, and it probably got him killed."

"You don't know what got him killed."

"Come on, Penny." Amelia sighed. "I know you want to be loyal and so do I, but we both know what Oliver was like. He must have conned someone or robbed someone because nothing else makes sense."

"You don't know if it's the truth and you shouldn't have accused him."

"Well, what does it matter? He's dead."

"I can't do this now," Penny said.

"Do what?" Amelia felt her anger growing. "Look, I appreciate your devotion to my husband, and I'm glad you mentioned the truth because I've been wondering about it myself, and I thought perhaps it's time you told me the truth."

"What are you talking about?"

"My husband's family."

"What about them?"

"The guy who called the house asked to speak to Marcus Miller, then the police tossed out the idea that my husband might have a brother and I haven't been able to get the idea out of my head. I don't know much about his family, but you do."

"What do you want to know, Amelia?"

"Did Oliver have a brother?"

"Yes. His name is Marcus."

Amelia ran a hand over her face, sickened by the answer. "Why didn't you tell me?"

"I couldn't."

"Why?"

"It's difficult to explain."

She sensed the change in Penny's tone. "What happened to him?"

"The family disowned him."

"Why?"

"I haven't got time to do this over the phone," Penny said. "Why don't you come over later and we'll talk about it."

"Does his brother have anything to do with the reason Oliver moved?"

"Marcus has everything to do with why he moved."

"Is his brother the reason he never let me meet his parents?"

"Yes."

"Is he dangerous?"

"Yes."

"I can't believe you kept it from me." Amelia felt a deep level of anger and resentment. "I trusted you."

"I know, and I'm sorry. I regret that we didn't tell you. It was a mistake."

"I'll see you later, and I want to know everything."

Amelia ended the call and curled up on the bed. What the hell were they all hiding? Was his family as toxic as hers?

The room was quiet and cool. Tears rolled from the corners of her eyes and fell into her hair. She wanted to sleep and never wake up. Then she remembered the dog she'd left at home.

All four limbs felt like lead weights attached to her torso, and it took enormous effort to drag her body up off the bed and get dressed.

By the time she left the motel room, the morning traffic had become a little quieter. Amelia preferred the longer route home, the one that took her past the bars where she often drank, places filled with drunken laughter and the chaos of other people with troubled lives.

The whining, barking greeting she got from her dog at home filled her with warmth. She let him out into the backyard and put some food in a bowl.

With no intention of showing up for work today, she called her boss, then reached for a bottle of red wine and uncapped it, poured herself a glass and swallowed a large mouthful.

"If it's going to be a stressful day," she said, "I might as well start it off right."

Chapter 40

Doucette eased himself off the sofa, showered and shaved, put on a fresh shirt, and then headed in to work. Still with stabbing pains in his stomach, he arrived at his desk much later than he intended.

His partner greeted him with a scowl. "You don't look so good."

"Started last night, must be something I ate."

"You gonna be okay?"

"Yeah, I think the worst of it has passed."

Instead of his usual coffee routine, Doucette uncapped a bottle of water and drank some while he checked his voicemail for new messages. He returned a call to the fraught mother of the strangled teen, still desperate for answers, and assured her he would continue to do everything he could to find her son's killer.

He left messages for Mark Thoeny concerning his friend Gerry, and then turned to the case file on his desk and reviewed his notes on the Miller murder.

Beaumont informed him of his lack of progress on the matter of where the victim might have stayed.

"There are a lot of places in Oakland. I'm still working on it."

"Keep at it and speed it up."

Doucette grimaced. His inflamed stomach had started to bother him again. He tried to settle it with more water and an antacid.

His partner looked across at him. "We ate the same

thing and I feel perfectly fine."

"I'm not used to dining at these hole-in-the-wall places."

"Plenty of good places serve dodgy food. Sometimes you gotta take the risk."

Doucette closed his eyes and breathed out. "I'm not trying to pin it on the place. I probably left the food sitting out for too long." He took another sip of water and updated his partner on his meeting with the real Keith Sigmund and his conversation with Penny Chapman.

"It's a compelling motive," Beaumont said. "I'd have killed the man myself if I had a little sister and he'd treated her like that."

"Sigmund has a fairly solid alibi. I still have to check it out, but I don't think he did it."

"Pissed off the wrong person, then."

"Freely admits it. He's pissed off a lot of people, but he couldn't come up with the name of a single person who might be trying to incriminate him."

"Can't? Or won't?"

"Nah, he was mad," Doucette said. "He's not protecting anyone."

"Which means we don't know who found the body."

"I also talked to Kitty Rose this morning. She said you went after some of her clients last night, and you went in hot."

The phone on Doucette's desk rang, cutting him short. He grabbed it and growled his name.

Penny Chapman told him she was on her way in to see him, approximately five minutes from reaching her destination.

When she arrived, he did not keep her waiting.

He strode across the lobby to greet her, noting the hard

yet pretty features and rigid look of the small, neatly dressed woman.

"My name is John Doucette and I'm the lead investigator on this case. I appreciate your willingness to come in and talk with me today."

"I wasn't aware I had a choice."

She removed her sunglasses and lifted her gaze to meet his; her narrowed eyes communicated her displeasure.

"You came here willingly," Doucette said, reminding her she was not under arrest and free to leave at any time.

So she would talk freely and tell him what she knew, he wanted her to relax and feel comfortable. Thinking that one of the small interview rooms might not be the best setting, he suggested they take a walk outside first.

"If you don't mind, I'd rather stay inside," she said.

"That's fine." He directed her to the elevator.

"Do you have any suspects?"

"We have several."

"Is Amelia a suspect?"

"She's helping us with our investigation."

Doucette seated her at his desk, offered her water or coffee, which she declined, and caught his partner regarding her with interest.

"I understand you were close to Oliver Miller and you must be hurting. If this happened to someone I love, I would want answers, and I want you to know I'm going to do everything I can to get them for you."

"Thank you. I'm pleased to hear it, but isn't that your job?"

Her brusque tone and manner revealed antagonism toward the police and Doucette was determined not to make this worse for her. He wanted to gain her trust.

"I can see how much you loved him, and I appreciate

you coming in here. I'm willing to listen to anything you have to say."

"I'm not surprised this has happened," she said. "Look, I came here because I know who did it. You should be looking at Marcus Miller. He is responsible for Oliver's death."

"Do you have any proof?"

"Right here." She pointed to the barely visible scar above her right eye that had not escaped the attention of Doucette's trained eye. "Marcus attacked me, almost eleven years ago. I was a student at UCSD and it happened one afternoon on my way home from school. He raped me and he left me for dead. That's what started this."

No tears came, but her eyes filled with anger as she told him the details. Doucette did not interrupt her. When she finished, he thanked her for telling him.

"Oliver and I used to date a long time ago. A year after the rape, we left San Diego and came here. I thought the distance would make me feel safer, but it didn't."

"I'm sorry for what you've been through." He pressed her gently. "Why didn't you mention his name when I asked you if Oliver had any enemies?"

"I should have told you." She ran the back of her hand across her mouth. "Marcus is Oliver's older brother and he has been in prison for eight years. He has about a year left on his sentence before he gets out. He must have hired someone to do this."

"Why would Marcus murder his own brother?"

"Because it was Oliver who turned him in." She took a deep breath. "I was a coward and too afraid of him to report it. I was young and terrified of what he might do, but Oliver stood up to his brother and wouldn't back down. He wasn't going to let Marcus get away with it. Marcus has been a bastard since he was born."

Based on what she was telling him, Doucette sensed robbery might not be the motivation for Oliver Miller's murder. He immediately saw a link between the demand for money and the murder, and if Marcus had hired someone to take out his brother, then this killer-for-hire could be an ex-con and he was probably the person making the phone calls to Amelia Miller, looking for his payment. However, this scenario didn't fit with a non-violent murder.

"It's not the first time he's done this," she said. "Marcus paid to have someone killed in San Diego."

"You have evidence to support this?"

"After Marcus went to prison, we knew he would find a way to retaliate, so Oliver paid someone to watch his brother's friends while Marcus was inside. One night, there was a robbery at this guy's house and the guy was murdered." She sighed. "Look, I don't know for sure if Marcus is guilty or innocent, but I'd say he was probably involved."

Doucette wrote down the details Penny gave him about the man Oliver Miller had hired in San Diego along with the date of the robbery homicide, intending to look into the other investigation and see if any data collected could be applied to his own case.

"Marcus is intelligent and evil and he has a way of controlling people to get what he wants," she said. "People are afraid to go against him."

Her theory that Marcus had arranged to have his brother killed seemed reasonable, though he considered it improbable. Logically, not all of the pieces fit together. The caller had asked for Marcus. Tying Marcus's name to the hit would risk exposing the man he'd hired. If Marcus was behind it, someone else was using his name.

"Marcus is a dangerous man," Penny said, as if reading his thoughts. "He has contacts, thugs who are prepared to do whatever he wants for the right kind of money. He may not have killed his brother, but he is behind it."

Doucette asked her for the contact details for the family in San Diego, which she provided immediately.

"They won't be able to tell you anything. Not long after we moved, Oliver cut off all contact with his family. He did it to protect his mother and to save me. He never even told his wife that he had a brother."

"Do you know if they're still living in San Diego?"

She nodded. "They're still at the same address, and they kept the same number. I called his mother before I came here."

"Okay." Doucette leaned back in his chair. "Can you think of anything else that might help?"

"I'm not sure." She told him about the man on the plane.

"We'll check it out." He made a note. "What do you know about Eve?"

"Oliver's girlfriend? Not much."

"What do you know about their relationship? Did they fight a lot?"

"No, I don't think so. Why?"

"If they left the bar together, I'm wondering how they got separated."

"I don't know."

"How did she seem to you that night in the bar?"

"Normal. Happy. They seemed happy together."

"So you knew her?"

"I've met her before, but it's not like we're friends. She's quite a lot younger, so we don't have much in common."

Doucette paused as the pain worsened in the lower portion of his stomach. Unsure from which end of his body the rest of the contaminated food was going to be ejected, he made a quick exit and headed for the bathroom.

Chapter 41

The questions about Eve reminded Penny of something important.

Four months ago, Oliver had taken his girlfriend to Las Vegas on what was supposed to have been a guys' trip, and Penny had gone along to provide her with some female company. The group included some of Oliver's friends, people Penny barely knew, and they were all drinking heavily, partying hard, and hitting all the clubs. For a lot of the time Oliver was drunk and Eve was embarrassed. Penny remembered the last conversation she'd had with her.

Eve had confronted him during the week about one specific incident when he'd grabbed her by the hair and bent her over, forcing her head into his crotch and completely disrespecting her in front of his friends. It was out of character and it shocked Penny, but she'd put it down to him being around the guys. She'd told Eve that Oliver meant no harm, but that he sometimes made stupid decisions. Eve had confided to her that day that she wanted to leave him. Penny assumed they'd left the problem in Las Vegas, because they'd stayed together.

Even before the crotch incident, Oliver had started behaving strangely. He was a gambler, and they were only two days into the trip when he ran out of money and asked his girlfriend if he could borrow some. She withdrew some savings from her account and loaned it to him. He kept on gambling until he lost it, and then they argued. Finally, it was Penny who told him he had to stop, but he was unable to walk away.

After that, he didn't talk to her for a few days. Then he took off and was not answering his phone. He didn't come back for some time, and when she next saw him he was spending a lot of cash, thousands of dollars. He told her he'd collected a debt.

Penny knew it wasn't the first time he'd stolen, but it might have been the first time he'd lied to her. Nobody else seemed to realize it.

As the week progressed, Oliver spent more time with the guys and less with Eve. Right after the trip, he walked out of the house with whatever he could carry and never returned to his wife. Penny had also had no contact with him, until a few days ago.

She communicated all of this to Doucette when he returned, rubbing a hand across his ribcage.

"Something horrible happened," she said. "I've always suspected it was the reason he left the city. It reminded me of what he was like when we left San Diego, like he was trying to avoid someone."

She gave Doucette the dates of the trip so he could check for reports of any burglaries around the time.

"When we spoke over the phone, you said that Oliver turned up in the bar unexpectedly," Doucette said. "Do you have any idea why he came back?"

"No, I never got the chance to find out."

He asked her to go over the facts of the evening again, from the moment Oliver entered the bar until he left, reminding her that she was not a suspect.

Penny repeated what she'd already told him, this time adding the detail about the fierce argument between Oliver and Amelia before Oliver and his girlfriend left the bar.

"Amelia would never have carried out her threat to kill

him," she said. "She was drunk. Oliver was never in any danger from his wife."

"She threatened to kill him?"

Penny saw something she didn't like flit across the investigator's face. "Amelia said she told you all this."

"She must have forgotten to mention it. Has she ever threatened him before?"

"Not in my presence. She's never been physically violent. She doesn't even own a gun."

"A threat to kill someone is a little bit more than an argument; however, we do know that Oliver and his girl left the bar alive. I've spoken to some of the bar staff who confirmed it. We know he was in the area for at least two or three days before he died and we're trying to figure out where he stayed. I'm hoping you can help us with that?"

Penny shook her head. "He didn't make regular trips back here. He wanted to see me, but I never told anyone he was here, not even his wife. He left before we had a chance to talk." She stared at her hands as she spoke. "Oliver would never have come back if everything was okay."

"Then whatever he wanted to discuss with you must have been of extreme importance. Surely you have some idea what it might have been."

"I don't. I can't think of anything, but something must have been wrong."

Doucette rubbed his finger against his chin, pondering what could have been so important that the victim had chosen to make the long drive from Los Angeles, dragging his girlfriend along, instead of just communicating the problem in a phone call. The fact he had not confirmed the meeting place in advance definitely indicated an attempt to avoid someone and could be viewed as a sign of uneasiness. It added to the mystery.

"We got a tip that he might have been in Oakland," Doucette said. "Does he have any friends or business there?"

"Possibly, though none that I know."

"You said he only got in touch with you shortly before you saw him and you never told anyone he was in the city."

"That's correct."

"Then how would his killer know exactly where he would be and when they could get to him?"

She sighed. "Seems Marcus can find out anything."

Her response left Doucette feeling troubled. It was not an acceptable explanation. "Is there anything at all you want to add?" he said.

"You haven't told me how he died. Was he shot, stabbed, or is it too gruesome to discuss?"

"We're still investigating the cause of death."

"That's what I don't understand." Concentration lines appeared on her forehead. "Marcus hated his brother. He would have made him suffer."

Chapter 42

After Penny left, Doucette read through his notes and spent some time analyzing the information, separating facts from assumption and breaking it all down to decide what might be important.

Instead of moving his case forward and closer to a resolution, this new information set him back, making it more difficult to nail down one solid suspect. Now he had several possible suspects and a lot of unanswered questions. The victim's life may have included a network of scumbags and criminals and any one of them could have killed him.

Both women seemed convinced they were being followed, though based on their stories it couldn't be by the same man. From what he'd learned, Marcus Miller was a convicted rapist still serving time. For now, Doucette moved his name to the bottom of his list of suspects, and then he made a call to the victim's family.

An older woman answered.

As soon as Doucette identified himself, Barbara Miller wanted to know how her son died. Her voice sounded strained, as if she'd been crying, and she spoke with a significant stutter that made it hard for him to understand her. He wished he could tell her how or why, not that it would ease her anguish in any way to be told the details of how her son had been murdered.

"I'm afraid we don't yet know," he said, and offered his condolences. It was all he had to give her and it seemed hollow and insincere, but he used the opportunity to talk about her rapist son, Marcus and at least get a measure of whether she thought he could be in any way to blame.

"Yes, I do believe it's possible that he was involved," she said, handling the inquiry far better than he'd anticipated.

The conversation led to Doucette gaining more essential information, including the fact that not only had Marcus Miller been released from prison early, he seemed to have disappeared. No one knew of his current location.

As the contact she'd tried to maintain with her murdered son had ended a long time ago, she could not confirm if Oliver had known of his bother's release prior to his murder.

"He stopped returning my calls and changed his phone number," she said. "I know he loved me and he did it to protect me."

She then asked about Penny Chapman. "Her life will be in danger until Marcus is found," she said. "I'm afraid he won't stop until he punishes her for sending him to prison. He should have been put away for life."

Doucette gave her his personal cell phone number so she could call him more easily if she got any news or wanted to keep informed.

Next, he put a call in to the prison, spoke to several different individuals, and finally got the information he wanted, which was confirmation of the date of Marcus's release. The timing couldn't be a coincidence, he thought, yet an ex-con connecting his name with a demand for money from the family of a murder victim seemed unlikely, even for a stupid ex-con.

He turned to his partner. "Marcus may be in San Francisco. I want you to find the parole officer and see if he can give us some info."

Doucette updated his case file with the information and called Penny Chapman's cell phone number to inform her of the bad news. He'd believed Barbara when she said Penny might be in danger.

"You've got to be kidding." She sounded incredulous and furious. He couldn't blame her. "When did he get out?"

"Last July."

"How the hell could that happen?"

He knew she must feel betrayed. "I will do my absolute best to find him."

"Before he finds me?"

"We're searching for him and we're going to find him."

"I had broken bones and a collapsed lung and I damn nearly died. I was in the hospital for more than a week. How could he disappear? Isn't he supposed to be monitored?"

"I'm going to give you my personal cell phone number and you can call me at any time if you feel threatened," he said.

"I already have your number. If he killed Oliver, he probably knows where I live. Can't you do anything to protect me?"

"I'm going to talk to my superior and see what can be arranged."

"That bastard never showed even a little bit of regret." She swore. "He should never have been let out."

In his heart, Doucette agreed. He would never understand what some men could do. "Try not to panic," he said. "I'm not suggesting he was in the bar, but do you remember if anyone followed Oliver out or left the bar around the same time?"

"The place was packed, so it's possible. Can't you check with the bar? It's a new place. They must have some of those cameras set up."

Unfortunately, the cocktail bar's surveillance system had failed to capture anything that might have been useful. Doucette was not yet convinced that Marcus had killed his brother, but if he did do it then someone was probably helping him. Doucette still considered the runner who'd found the body and was assuming a fake identity as his most important suspect.

"I want you to call me if you can think of anyone who might know where he is, or anyone who might be willing to help him," he said.

"Marcus was into pornography and prostitutes. Before he went to prison, he would go to brothels, so if anyone knows where he is then it's probably a woman."

"Thank you, Penny. I'll be in touch."

Chapter 43

The anticipation of Oliver's death and the shocking suddenness of it appeared such a confusing contradiction.

For years, Penny had sensed someone in the shadows, someone following her tracks and monitoring her movements, looking for the right opportunity. The news of Marcus's release left her struggling to comprehend the legal system or understand the meaning of justice.

It had taken years, but her life had become stable again. Now he was free to come after her to fulfill the promise he'd made a decade ago, and this time she didn't have Oliver to protect her.

She remembered the calls Amelia had told her about. Someone connected to the case was looking for Marcus. Why would the hired killer use Marcus's real name? It made no sense to her, but if they had a connection to Amelia, then Amelia's life was in danger. Penny had to warn her. Not willing to lose another friend, she pulled out her cell phone and made a call.

Amelia's voice sounded slurred. Penny knew at once that her friend had been drinking. Amelia's choices made her angry, but this time she said nothing about it.

"We need to talk," she said. "I'm on my way over to you now."

"Now isn't the best time."

"Don't push me away, Amelia. I would never do that to you."

"I trusted you, but you've been keeping secrets."

"I know, but I need to talk to you right now, and you shouldn't be alone."

"Fine." A short paused ensued. "What time is it?"

Penny checked her watch. "Ten."

"I'll make us some coffee."

As she drove, Penny tried to recall the faces in the bar. One of them might have been Marcus. She shuddered. Years had passed. His appearance would have changed.

She'd allowed the fear of his release to paralyze her for years and the sudden surge of emotions breaking to the surface was making her head hurt so much it became impossible to concentrate on driving. She stopped at the nearest coffee shop and ordered a breakfast she couldn't eat.

When she closed her eyes she saw Marcus grabbing her, and when she opened them she still saw him. A chill flowed over her skin like ice water. Her hands shook and her heart raced every time her thoughts returned to Marcus. He could be anywhere, even here, watching her as she struggled not to fall apart.

Penny paid for her uneaten meal and returned to her car. Having recovered enough to drive, she found a packet of cigarettes in her bag and lit one, took a few quick puffs and threw the rest of it away before she started out on the remainder of her journey.

The damn dog barked as soon as she knocked on her friend's door. The stupid dumb animal barked at everything.

A few seconds later, Amelia opened the front door dressed in a robe. Penny gazed into the eyes of her friend and saw a similar pain reflected there. She stepped up and embraced her, then released her to enter the house. The stench hit her instantly.

Amelia said nothing as she closed the front door and followed Penny into the kitchen.

Penny also made no comment about the filth and the chaotic state of the place. Instead, she sat quietly on a bar stool in the kitchen and watched her friend rinse out two mugs, sensing a deep tension in the air.

Amelia spoke first.

"How are you doing?"

"The same as you, I expect," Penny said.

"No, it's worse for me because you only lost him once and I've lost him twice, and now I know he's never coming back."

Penny traced a finger down the surface of the table where the wood had split. "You think you have it worse, that you've suffered more than me?"

"I've lost my husband. You've lost a friend. You have other friends."

"You've known him for a few years and I've known him since childhood. He was my best friend."

"I thought I was your friend, yet you lied to me."

"I didn't lie."

"Okay, then you kept something important from me; it amounts to about the same thing. You should have told me my husband had a brother."

"Turns out that you lied to me, too," Penny said. "You said you'd told the police that you threatened Oliver, but I've just talked to them and they didn't know anything about it."

"I thought I did. If I forgot to mention it, it was an oversight."

"A fucking big one."

"Well, it's not my fault. I've never done anything like this before."

Amelia brought the mugs to the table. Penny saw the exhaustion etched into her friend's face. "Oliver asked me not to tell you about Marcus," she said.

"Oliver is dead now, so you don't have to keep any more of his secrets."

"You know, it's interesting to hear you accusing me of keeping secrets. What about the secrets you're keeping from me?"

"What are you talking about?"

"You've been cheating on your husband."

"I don't know where you got that idea." Amelia opened the door of the refrigerator and searched inside it. "I don't have any milk, so you'll have to drink it black."

"Yeah, I don't mind." For a moment, Penny wished she were alone. Her friend's hostility and the awful smell in her home made this so much harder. She drew in a shallow breath and let it out slowly. "You don't have to pretend," she said. "I know you've been having sex with men for money. I've known it for a while."

Amelia said nothing. She sat down in a chair and pulled the robe tighter around her body.

"Why do you do it?"

"It's a compulsion."

"So you don't deny it?"

"What would be the point?"

Penny spooned sugar into her coffee, keeping her eyes down and wishing she knew what to say to fill the silence.

"I'm not a whore," Amelia said.

"Of course not." Penny sipped her coffee. "What would you call it?"

"Therapy."

"You might have to explain that to me."

"Sex is how I deal with stress. Without it, I can't cope."

"You could take anxiety medication."

"Yeah, that would be better. Look, I know it's wrong, but I've been this way since I was about sixteen and I can't change it."

"Did Oliver know?"

"He accepted it. Anyway, Oliver had other women."

"Is that why you do it? To get back at him?"

"No, and I don't want to discuss it with you, so if this is why you came over you can save us both some time and leave."

"It's not why I'm here."

"Then it's your turn to talk," Amelia said. "Tell me the big mystery about Oliver's brother. I want to know why I was never told about him."

Penny kept her eyes fixed on the dark liquid in her cup. Too many thoughts were flying through her mind.

"Why was he kept a secret?"

"He's a convicted rapist."

"You didn't think I had a right to know this?"

"The family cut him out of their lives a long time ago."

"I'm supposed to be a part of the family."

"I had to respect their wishes."

"To hell with respect, Penny." Amelia placed the coffee cup in her hands on the kitchen table. "Where is he now?"

"That's what I want to talk to you about."

Chapter 44

"Your husband chose not to tell you about Marcus because he didn't want you to judge him by what his brother did."

"Stop calling him my husband," Amelia said. "He had a name. Oliver. Call him Oliver."

"This is a mistake." Penny stood. "Perhaps I should go."

"No. Stay. I want to hear what it is you came here to say."

With no one waiting for her at home, Penny agreed. "As long as there is no fighting," she said. Amelia appeared more hurt and vulnerable than Penny had ever seen her. "We both love him and we need to support each other."

"I miss him. I never got to say goodbye."

"It's hard to believe we'll never see him again. Oliver was my first love."

"I know. You never told me why you broke up."

"We broke up because of his brother." Penny gave her friend a sad little smile. "I was twenty when Marcus raped me."

Amelia rubbed at her temples. "I'm so sorry."

"Oliver blamed himself because he knew his brother had raped a girl before. He thought it was his fault because he hadn't told me."

Amelia stopped rubbing and looked at her friend. "How could he think it was his fault?"

"The day the attack happened, Oliver was supposed to

pick me up from school, but Marcus tricked him and showed up instead. If I'd known Marcus had raped a girl, I would never have gotten into his car."

"Oh, Penny. I don't know what to say."

"After it all happened, Oliver started to lose control. The attack changed him. The lovely old Oliver was gone and you married what was left. Now you know the truth about his family."

Amelia picked up her mug and rotated it in her hands, finding a small amount of private relief in the knowledge that someone else's family was more screwed up than her own. "You said you want to talk to me about Marcus. Do you know where he is?"

"All I know is that he's out of prison. He only got nine years and they let him out early."

"When?"

"About six months ago. Nobody knows where he is. I think Oliver might have come back to warn me."

"I don't. Why would he wait so long to tell you something so important? If he knew his brother was out of prison, he would have told you immediately over the phone or come back sooner," Amelia said.

"Maybe he didn't know." Penny bowed her head. "It's so confusing and I'm terrified that if Marcus killed his brother he's going to hurt me again."

Amelia reached across the table and squeezed Penny's hand. "I'm glad Oliver was there for you back then, and now that's he's gone, I'm here for you."

"That's the problem. I'm worried that Marcus might be the man following you," Penny said.

"Why would he come after me?"

"I can think of a couple of good reasons. You're my friend. You married the brother he despised."

"There's also this issue of the money with Marcus's name attached to it."

"What are we going to do?"

"Well, we're not going to sit around." Amelia opened a kitchen drawer and pulled out a new notepad. She tore off a page, scribbled on it, and pushed it across the table to Penny. "Here's a clue."

Penny stared at what her friend had written. "It's an initial. What does it mean?"

"The guy demanding money is still in contact. He called yesterday and I heard a woman's voice. She referred to him as G, so this might not have anything to do with Marcus."

"G?"

"I know it's not much, but it's all I heard."

"That could be from a first name or a last name. It's not enough to go on."

"He knows my name, my address, and my phone number. He even knows my cell. This guy seems to know all about me and I don't have many friends, so he has to be someone who knew Oliver."

"It's still not enough."

"I know, but we've got to try. How many people do you know with that initial who could be connected to both Oliver and a situation involving stolen money?"

Penny glanced at the strained expression on her friend's face. She sat silently, fist pressed against her lips, thinking hard for a moment. Then she gave a soft laugh.

"Actually, there is someone."

Chapter 45

"Have you ever heard of Greg Grace?"

"I don't think so," Amelia said. "Who is he?"

"A friend of Oliver's, or he was at one time," Penny said, looking her friend in the eyes. "I can't believe I didn't think of it before. I'm an idiot."

"Think of what?" Amelia stared back.

"Do you remember the group vacation last September, the all-guys week in Las Vegas?"

"Of course I remember it."

"What did Oliver tell you?"

"He never talked about it and I never got the chance to ask."

"Of course. I'd forgotten."

"What do you know about that trip?"

Penny said nothing. She shifted her gaze.

Amelia eyed her friend. "You were there, weren't you? I knew it. Why did you never tell me?"

"It's not important right now."

"Perhaps not to you."

"G could mean Greg Grace," Penny said. "Greg was part of Oliver's group and they were involved in some strange business." She told Amelia the same thing she'd told the police.

"Hang on a second," Amelia said. "Oliver was many things, but never a bank robber. The risks would be too great for one thing. He was a good conman, but not that good. He'd never get away with robbing a bank."

"Well, okay, maybe not a bank, but perhaps a restaurant or some other place. He had to have robbed someone to get all that cash."

"How much cash?"

"It must have been a lot because he was spending it like crazy and he had to split it with his partner."

"What partner?" Amelia's eyes widened. "Do you mean Eve?"

"No, Greg. I'm sure Greg was with him because they both disappeared that day."

"I don't know." Amelia bit on her thumbnail. "I'm not so sure about this."

"Well I'm not sure about any of it either, but it's possible. I know he didn't win it. I checked the news reports for weeks and there were a number of burglaries reported in the area around the time."

"You told the police this?"

"I did, and they're looking into it."

"He left me right after he got back. Never said a word. Just packed a bag and walked out." Amelia turned her head away. "He must have hated life with me. It must have been unbearable."

"You're not the reason he left," Penny said. "I'm sure he was running away, but not from you. He loved you. He should have been a better husband."

"He left me for that child, for Eve."

"He didn't love Eve. I saw how he treated her. They were fighting a lot in Las Vegas."

"She was there? What was she doing there? I thought it was supposed to be all guys."

"That's what he wanted you to think."

Amelia frowned. "Another thing you kept from me."

"I'm sorry, but being torn between you and Oliver

wasn't easy. I always tried to do my best."

"At least you're finally willing to admit that Oliver is a thief."

Penny got up and took her coffee to the sink. "It was around the same time that Oliver stopped returning my calls." She stared at the pile of dirty dishes. "I think he was afraid to talk to me in case he let anything slip. He knew Greg would have a problem with me if I found out."

"Where do we go from here?"

"Well, we have a choice." Penny rejoined her friend. "We can leave it to the police, or we can try to find our own evidence."

"You said it was a lot of money. How much are we actually talking about?"

"Thousands of dollars."

"Where does Marcus fit into this? The caller asked for Marcus."

"I don't have it all figured out." Penny put her hand on top of Amelia's, noting the black lines of dirt under her friend's fingernails. "I'm not even sure anymore that this has anything to do with Marcus. Someone is using his name, and it has to be someone who knows Oliver. Maybe someone from San Diego."

"Or someone who learned about Marcus from Oliver."

"Whoever it is knows that using Marcus's name would terrify me. Marcus is also easy to frame."

"If it's not Marcus following me, then who is?"

"You said someone is watching your house. Greg Grace lives locally."

Amelia closed her eyes and put her head in her hands. "I don't understand any of this."

"I know. It's complicated and it probably won't be any easier to understand tomorrow." Penny patted Amelia's shoulder. "Oliver risked a lot to come back here. I'm not going to let it be for nothing."

"What are you suggesting?"

"I'm going to find out everything I can about Greg Grace."

"I'll help." Amelia got up from her seat. "Give me a few minutes."

"Where are you going?"

"Oliver left some of his boxes in the basement. Perhaps there's something in them that might help."

Chapter 46

While Amelia was down in the basement, Penny took an opportunity to wander through the house and saw things that dismayed her, signs that her friend wasn't coping. There were the unwashed dishes, dog mess on the kitchen floor, piles of dirty laundry, and muddles in every room. The kitchen cupboards contained no food. She found bottles of booze hidden behind some old rags that were clearly not being used for cleaning.

In need of a snifter, she grabbed a bottle and uncapped it.

"Don't bother to put it away."

The voice startled her so much she almost dropped the bottle on the floor. "I'm sorry," she said, her face burning. "I needed a drink." She set the bottle on the table, her pulse racing.

"You were checking up on me."

"I didn't mean to. Look, you don't need to hide it from me."

"I don't," Amelia said, dumping two boxes on the kitchen floor. "I hide it from myself." She held the bottle to her lips, tipped some of the liquid down her throat, and recapped the bottle.

Penny cast her eyes to the boxes. "Do you think you'll find anything?"

"No idea, but at least I'm doing something. Going through these will keep me occupied."

"This must be overwhelming," Penny said. "I can see

that you're struggling. I'd like to help."

"Everyone is struggling, Penny. Life is hard."

"They're not facing what you're going through."

"For some people, it's worse. I'll survive it."

"Why don't you stay with me for a while?"

"So you can monitor my drinking?" Amelia smiled and shook her head. "Thanks, Penny, but no."

"I'd enjoy the company."

"You only have one bedroom."

"We'll make it work. We'd be safer if we stay together."

"I don't agree, and I'd like you to stop worrying about me. It might not look like it to you, but I can take care of myself. This mess in here…this is how I live. Now, let's get to work."

Watching Amelia as she opened the first box, Penny realized a few unpleasant truths about herself, such as how quick she'd been to condemn her friend's negative behaviors. It was clear that Amelia had problems, yet she was afraid to share them because Penny was judgmental and unsupportive, often rude.

What she'd believed about Amelia wasn't true. The excessive drinking and the sex were because of her depression instead of a way to manage it. Amelia already hated herself. She didn't need anyone else to make her feel worthless.

Penny hid her thoughts by helping Amelia sort through the contents of the boxes. Amelia deserved a better friend. Recognizing this brought Penny a little closer to understanding.

"Greg has a younger brother," she said, sharing what she knew. "They're not close. In Vegas, I could sense some distance between them."

"Two unrelated pairs of brothers from two similar backgrounds. It's disturbing."

"Steven Grace has been in trouble before. He has a dark side. I didn't like him at all." Penny remembered the incident in Las Vegas. "There was a fight between Steven and Oliver that involved Eve."

Amelia looked up from her sorting. "This could be important."

"It was over quickly, but it got violent."

"Is it true that she's pregnant?"

"I don't know. Where did you hear that?"

"The old bitch next door. She said Oliver told her. She spoke to him recently."

"That means somebody knew he was back," Penny said. "We have to talk to her. Maybe she knows something that could help us."

"Let the police talk to her," Amelia said. "I'd love an opportunity to hit her back."

Chapter 47

"I've been going over it for an hour and it's still screwy," Doucette said, wishing he could figure out the pieces that would help him with his case. "I don't have anything to show that Marcus Miller is involved, and I'm pretty certain he didn't hire someone to kill his brother. It's not consistent."

"I talked to a couple of the Las Vegas detectives and a number of robberies fit the timeframe," Beaumont said, swallowing a mouthful of soda. "Most of them are unsolved."

"Marcus was reporting to his parole officer until last month, so he wasn't in Vegas last September; however, I still think Vegas is the connection." Doucette picked up his keys from the desk. "I'm heading out."

He intended to follow up on the lead Amelia Miller had mentioned. Although she'd only been able to provide him with an initial, he considered it worth the short drive to the Oakland hotel where Mark Thoeny's friend Gerry had dined with his wife, in the hope that the incident Gerry had witnessed would lead to information on the location of the missing woman. Perhaps some of the hotel staff remembered the dissatisfied customer from his complaint about the food.

With all lanes crowded on the bridge into Oakland, Doucette eased his aging vehicle along the road, often slowing to almost a crawl, which allowed him the time to reflect on a few of the facts, including whether the victim had been notified of his brother's early release from prison. It seemed the most likely reason for his return, yet Doucette remained unconvinced.

Unacquainted with the new manager of the small hotel, Doucette introduced himself to the slightly scruffy young man and showed him a crime scene photograph of the victim's face.

"He was murdered last week. I'm trying to trace his movements in the days leading up to the murder, and we have a witness who placed him here the night before he died. I'm hoping you can tell me if he was a guest here."

"Last week?" The manager stared hard at the picture as if remembering a far more distant event. "Yeah, I saw him with a pretty hot little number here in the restaurant."

"You're sure?"

"Yeah. They ate a meal, but they didn't have a room. Not even for the hour."

"You remember all your guests?"

"Only the pretty ones and she was sweet, way too good for a bald and middle-aged fat dude like him."

"More in your age range, but out of your league, huh?"

A hot ugly flush burned on the man's cheeks. "Like I said, they didn't have a room."

"We need to talk with her," Doucette said, disliking this cocky piece of shit. "We're trying to locate her. Is there anything you can tell me about them or their behavior that night?"

The manager shrugged, clearly annoyed. "Nothing comes to mind."

"Take another look at the photograph."

He didn't bother. "I told you, I don't recall anything unusual."

"Then you won't mind if I check your guest records for

the past week."

"Got a warrant?"

"I can come back with one, and maybe I'll dig deeper, see what else I can find."

"Hey, I'm only trying to make a joke," the manager said, losing the cocky bravado. "I'm not against the police." He provided a list of guest registrations for the past week. "Here, help yourself. You won't find anything."

Doucette searched through the list, failing to find the victim's name or any other person with a first or last name beginning with the initial G. It pissed him off. He asked to see the dining area, determined not to leave this place with nothing to show for his time.

"I heard a complaint was made," he said. "The victim was upset."

"Yeah, about the meal. He didn't like it and when I came into the restaurant to deal with it he carried on being rude. I think he'd forgotten he was eating free food."

"Free food?"

"I took his meal off the bill."

"What else do you remember about the evening?"

"He seemed anxious or agitated. She also seemed unhappy and a little tense. I thought maybe they'd had a fight."

"Interesting." Contrary to everyone else he'd asked who'd thought the couple seemed happy. Doucette's eyes scanned the small room. "You have a video surveillance system here, right?"

"Usually we do, but the camera got damaged. We had a couple of drunks in here who got a little out of hand, so unfortunately there's no footage."

"That right?" Disappointed, Doucette turned to leave.

"We keep a full record of all vehicles parked on the

property," the manager said, now noticeably more helpful. "Name, address, make, model, and license plate. It will show you the time he arrived and the time he left. I'll get you the data on your way out."

He showed Doucette back to the front reception area and located the paper records with the information the hotel had collected from their customers. Doucette found the name of the victim and his guest plus the details of the vehicle. It was a break, though not enough.

Oliver Miller had been driving a red Mercedes Benz with a personalized plate. Doucette considered it odd for someone trying to stay hidden. The address Oliver had given was his old residence. The name of the woman with him was Eve Powell.

Satisfied that he could now put the victim and his girlfriend in Oakland the night before the murder, Doucette thanked the manager for the extra bit of information and returned to his vehicle. Hoping to find clues that would lead to the whereabouts of the missing woman, he called his partner and asked him to dig up any records on Eve Powell.

"I'll check on it right away. Hey, thought you'd want to know Sigmund's wife called and verified his alibi."

"Well, then, I guess that means he's innocent," Doucette said with irritation.

"He's still a suspect?"

"He may have proved he was somewhere else on the night of the murder, but he had motive and he was in Oakland around the time his old enemy returned."

"He may be in the clear," Beaumont said.

"If he is then someone is trying pretty hard to make it look like he committed the crime. Someone familiar with his history and his movements."

It didn't fit with the use of Sigmund's old address, but

Doucette figured that was intended to dupe everyone and to conceal the real killer's identity. However, until he knew why Sigmund was being set up, he was not willing to rule him out.

With the hotel Sigmund said he had used only a block away, Doucette decided to go there next and check out the alibi. Maybe he'd get lucky and get another break.

Chapter 48

Marcus wanted to meet him.

Without the money, Wilkes Smith knew this next encounter would not go well. Marcus was a vile man, a manipulative murderer bent on securing his own revenge. Wilkes only wanted his money. He'd never intended to execute the man who stole it and the killing filled him with remorse.

He'd been tricked and lured, and now he was trapped. The signs were there from the beginning and he'd refused to take notice of them. Driven to distraction by the double grief that had been inflicted upon his family, he'd allowed it to carry all his rage until the belief in his own cause became a dangerous obsession. He'd dismissed all logic, surrendered to impulse, and he'd learned nothing along the way.

Desperate men were easy to control, and Marcus refused to be deterred, dragging Wilkes much too far into the game now to withdraw. Sitting in his stolen car with his life pitched into an even deeper hell, he didn't know what to do. He scrubbed a hand over his face, thinking of his family and of the young woman being held hostage. Shutting his eyes, he tried to block it out, but that only worsened his thoughts.

In his other hand, he held the dead man's wallet with his driver's license still inside it, minus the cash and credit cards that Marcus took. The property address on the license matched the house half a block away that Wilkes had tried to break into, the home of the man they'd killed. Getting inside the dead man's home without being noticed would be difficult. The old woman living in the house next to it never slept. Always at her window and watching the street, she made him nervous.

Wilkes stuffed the wallet in his pocket. He understood his position and the consequence of bucking the plan. The young woman's life depended on him, on the successful completion of this job and on Marcus getting his share of the money, but Wilkes didn't trust the man who'd directed him here. He doubted that Marcus was even his real name.

His decision meant sacrificing the hostage. She should never have been there, and Marcus would kill her anyway. The man was insane.

Worried about the police, who might be touring the city and looking for him, Wilkes started the engine and drove his car through the San Francisco streets, navigating the steep roads and turns, planning to get on the freeway before they caught him.

He followed the same van for a mile, staring at the back of it as if hypnotized. He still had a family and the thought of going home to them gave him back his strength. His child might have a few weeks or a few months, but he'd not yet lost the passion for life and Wilkes wanted to see him again, before it was too late.

A sharp pang of pain ran through him at the thought of his family. They were counting on him to bring back the sixteen thousand dollars that had been stolen from them several months ago in the middle of a hot Las Vegas afternoon.

The money was supposed to pay for medical expenses. The loss of it had been devastating for his family and he couldn't return without it. His lover trusted him to fix this and he could not let her down or face the heaviness of her disappointment. Everything else became insignificant. Without knowing how the fuck he was going to accomplish it, he realized he no longer had a choice.

Feeling the anxiety rising inside him, he drove to the nearest quiet spot where he could get out of the car for a few minutes and sort out his head. He accepted that the choice he'd made had led him to this and he admitted that perhaps he'd made the wrong one. Murder had changed him, thrust him into a dark world, and it would follow him forever. Nothing would ever be normal. Revenge had become an obsession and he'd pursued it regardless of the price. Perhaps he and Marcus were no different.

He realized what he had to do, and now that he'd made up his mind he had no time to waste. Returning to the Dolores Heights neighborhood, he hoped to see the blue truck gone from its usual spot outside the dead man's house. Desperately tired and scared, his spirits sank lower at the sight of it. His head began to throb and his fingers closed around the crowbar in his lap, knowing he could neither wait for her to leave nor come back.

As he parked and opened the car door to get out, a generously proportioned woman with straight blonde hair and dark roots came out of the little wooden house across the street. Wilkes pulled the door shut and stayed in the vehicle, watching her through the cracked windshield.

She came down the front steps with the big black dog beside her and glanced once across the road, though not at him. She was a sizeable woman, taller than him, with harsh features and an uneasy manner. As she set off down the street, heading away from him, her stride was long and her pace hurried, as if she might be troubled. Her husband had caused him so much pain and agitation, and he wished he could be of equal distress to her.

The considerable height and build of this woman made her seem less vulnerable and a part of him appreciated it. He regarded her as a threat and that put them on a par.

Holding the short crowbar beneath his jacket, he pulled the hoodie up over his head and exited the vehicle, sprinting across the road, wary of the neighbor and ready to take his chance with her should she get in his way.

Wilkes skipped the front door and slipped up the left side of the house. He unlatched the side gate to enter the property through the back, figuring it his best chance of breaking in unseen.

The damp ground absorbed the sound of his feet. A low dividing fence afforded the nosy neighbor a decent view of the small rear yard and the few thin trees provided minimal cover. He stopped when he saw all the holes in the backyard with mounds of soil waiting to fill them, and then proceeded to the house.

He'd hoped for a sliding glass door with an old roller that could be lifted easily to force the frame off its track. A back door made of solid wood, like the one he was confronted with, presented him with a bigger challenge. He tried it and found it locked.

Two windows without bars gave him his way in and he used the crowbar to break one of them, careful not to cut his skin on any of the sharp pieces of jagged glass.

The house reeked. The horrible stench of dog shit filled his nose and throat and made him gag. Months of searching and a relentless determination had finally led him to this moment and brought him to this stinking, repulsive place. He glanced around, detesting this house, hating the man who'd once lived in it for what he'd done, and feeling no sympathy for the woman left behind.

After checking for a fast way out if interrupted, Wilkes headed straight for the master bedroom and began rifling through cupboards and drawers, turning the room inside out, frenzied in his search for whatever cash or valuables he could grab in the few minutes he could afford to spend here.

Dark suits, jackets, and dress shirts hung from a rail in the cramped closet space. Wilkes found the steel fire safe behind them, locked and bolted to the floor. Without the tools, the time, or the skills to break into it, he let out a loud string of curses. The sense of frustration almost crushed him.

He searched the room, finding nothing worth taking except a small wad of cash hidden in a pot on a bookcase, then headed back downstairs, his heart pounding.

During the short time he spent searching the rest of the house, he found nothing of value, no jewelry, not even a watch. As he turned to leave, a framed photograph on the wall caught his gaze.

Wilkes stared unblinking at the smiling pink face of the bride and the neutral expression of the groom. Even on his wedding day, the groom looked like a man with no emotions, his cool stare almost evil, and the sight of him filled Wilkes with rage. He responded by ripping the frame from the wall and hurling it to the ground as hard as possible, satisfied as the glass exploded, and then grinding his muddy boot heel into the picture. Small jagged pieces of glass from the frame sprayed out across the tiled floor. He hoped the woman got it embedded in her skin.

On a hook behind the photograph, she'd hung a key. Wilkes lifted it from the hook and clutched it in his hand. He tried it in the back door, expecting it would fit, and when it did he took it with him, imagining her return and knowing full well the anguish she would go through at finding her home had been ransacked.

As he ran down the side of the house with the crowbar in his hand, he tossed the empty wallet with her dead husband's ID inside it onto the driveway, mocking the widow the way he believed her husband had mocked him.

Upon reaching his vehicle, he had recovered and caught his breath, his pulse no longer racing. He climbed in, started the ignition, and drove away before anyone saw him.

Chapter 49

As Wilkes drove, he listened to the radio and tried to sing along to one of his favorite songs, but nothing worked to distract him from his thoughts. He knew that behind and in front of him there lay no roads of escape, no way out.

Hot and airless inside his vehicle, he opened the window and breathed in the polluted morning air. His hands were shaking and the memories jammed his mind. The pain increased in his chest, making it hard to breathe.

His son's life would be cut short and Wilkes knew he might not be able to return home for the end of it. Nothing could change it. The boy was too young to understand, and Wilkes believed himself too weak to handle it. When the time came, his lover would have to face it without him. He couldn't be sure if that hadn't always been his intention.

He thought about killing himself, of driving to the bridge and jumping off, but he didn't want to feel the impact, and if he had a gun he would have lacked the guts to shoot himself in the head on the way down.

The temperature marked fifty-seven degrees on the thermometer in his car. It seemed hotter. He turned his head to one side and then the other, trying to dislodge the strange buzz in his ears, but it only grew louder. A smoky haze hovered in the air, thick and insidious, pressing in on him and turning the sky brown. Wilkes drove past two parked cars and almost hit the third.

On Castro Street, he found a space to park and pulled into it, determined to save what remained of his family, prepared to sacrifice himself and suffer his lover's punishment to keep her out of prison. First, he wanted to taste another cup of coffee and to savor one last moment of freedom.

The air outside smelled of dog shit and pot. It reminded him of that stinking house and the bastard people who lived in it; things he didn't want to think about.

Inside the coffee shop, there was live music playing, art on the walls, and lots of happy people. Wilkes closed his eyes and breathed in, soaking up the sounds and trying to let his body absorb the vibe. This world seemed artificial, dreamlike, and so far from reality that his mind felt disconnected.

He stood in line waiting his turn. As the people moved forward, he moved with them until he reached the counter, slowly shuffling a few baby steps each time like he was already a shackled prisoner. He managed a smile at the counter, knowing that for the moment he was safe.

Taking his coffee to an isolated table, he sat down and pulled his phone from his pocket, holding it in his palm for a long moment, not sure if he could make the call and commit himself to letting her go.

The strong caffeine aided the blood flow to his brain and gave him a temporary shot of energy, clearing his head. He punched in the number.

His beloved answered before he even heard it ring. Her voice sounded distant, miles from this horrible moment, and he wished so hard he were home.

"I've been waiting for your call," she said. "I'm worried."

"I'm sorry." His voice cracked. "I miss you."

"I miss you, too. Is everything okay?"

"Yeah." He cleared his throat until it became easier to

speak. "Everything is fine." It was the repeat of an earlier conversation. They never seemed to have anything else to say to each other.

"That's not very reassuring."

"I don't want you to worry."

"I can't help it when I don't know what's happening. What you're doing is dangerous and there's nothing I can do to help you."

He sighed, saddened by the monotony of it all. Over the past four months, her weight had been dropping and her hair thinning. He'd put it down to anxiety and hoped it wasn't an indication of anything more serious. "I need you to stay strong," he said.

"Do you have any chance of getting the money?"

"I don't know."

"It doesn't matter. I need you to come home, and you shouldn't be out there alone."

"I can't come home," he said. "Not tonight."

"When?"

"It's complicated." Wilkes watched the people around him, his heart aching in his chest at the hellish thought of never seeing her again. He didn't want to lie, and yet he couldn't tell her the truth. "I don't have the money and I won't have another opportunity."

She started crying.

"Listen to me." Her sobs almost made him change his mind. "I know you're afraid, but it's going to be all right." He squeezed his eyes shut and thought of the boy. Babies needed their mothers. "I love you. I will always love you, but I can't give you what you need. I want you to forget about me and move forward with your life."

He cut the call and switched off his phone before she could respond. There was nothing left to say. He'd taken a big risk and it had not gone as planned. He'd helped kill a man and he could not run away from it. To protect her, he had to clean up his mess.

Wilkes Smith finished his coffee and left the coffee shop, a lost and empty husk of a man, truly broken and with nothing left to fight for.

Chapter 50

The Oakland motel lobby stank of old cigarette smoke that was probably trapped in the carpets and the drapes. The place looked like it had been decorated in the seventies and it was grubbier than a truck stop, with old water stains showing through the paint on the ceiling.

Doucette approached the front desk. The agent took no notice of him, immersed in an argument over the phone in a foreign language. Doucette waited patiently for the agent to finish his call, and then stated his business.

Though courteous and helpful, the agent treated him coolly, accommodating his request and checking the guest registry. He verified Keith Sigmund had stayed at the motel on the date in question and paid by credit card.

Satisfied, Doucette left. He returned to his car and drove in the general direction of the Bay Bridge, stopping once to get a quick cup of coffee and use the restroom. As he exited the coffee shop, his cell phone rang. The number on the display belonged to Penny Chapman.

Surprised to be hearing from her again so soon, Doucette answered the call leaning against his car, watching a man dressed all in black jogging down the opposite side of the street.

"Everything okay, Penny?"

"I'm fine," she said. "I'm calling you because I believe I know who might have murdered my friend."

Terrific. Exactly what I need is another suspect, Doucette thought, trying not to be too skeptical. She'd first suspected Marcus and it seemed now she'd come up with a new name. "Go ahead, tell me," he said, expecting this might be another wild guess. "Who do you think it is?"

"His name is Greg Grace and he has a brother called Steven Grace who might also have been involved."

"Uh-huh, and what was the relationship between Greg Grace and the victim?"

"They were friends, but not close."

Doucette's attention remained on the jogger. "What reason would he have for killing his friend?"

"I'm not sure, but it's got to be worth talking to him. He lives locally and he recently lost his job. He was also in Las Vegas with Oliver and Eve. I forgot to mention his name when we spoke before."

"Why do you suspect him?"

"Both of the brothers have big gambling debts and Steven has a rap sheet. There was a bit of trouble between them all during that week."

"I see. What kind of trouble are we talking about?"

As Penny told him what she remembered about the violent encounter that had taken place between Steven and Oliver, and about the romantic infatuation she believed Greg Grace had for Eve, Doucette made up his mind to pursue it. It was enough to raise his suspicion.

"I appreciate the call and the information," he said.

"Did you check if there were any robberies reported around the same time?"

"We did, and we're still checking."

"I feel like the Grace brothers are watching me," she said. "They may have helped Oliver steal the money, and they know I was there."

"How well do you know them?"

"I'd heard about them, but never met them before the

Vegas week. I didn't like Steven at all. I got a bad feeling about him from the moment I met him."

"I must ask you not to contact them, or be careful what you say if they contact you, but it would be best not talk to them."

"So you'll look into them?"

"I'll let you know what I find out," he said, ending the call.

With the jogger now out of his sight, he climbed into his car and started the drive across the bridge, arriving at his desk at the Bryant Street station to find another situation developing.

His partner repeated the information he'd just received from someone claiming to have had some involvement in the murder. The man had refused to reveal his name, but he'd provided specific details about the crime and imparted additional information including the location of the victim's vehicle.

Beaumont said the caller had offered the name of Marcus Miller as the accomplice he'd accused of the actual killing, and would be willing to divulge more information when he called back, but only if he could speak to Doucette.

Doucette whistled. "Let's hope he resurfaces, but I'm not going to base this case on it."

A killer with a conscience was not entirely unusual; guys who couldn't live with what they'd done and turned against more cold-blooded partners. Marcus was still a big piece of the puzzle he had to solve and now his name had been thrust back into the mix of suspects.

"Find out anything on Eve Powell?" he said, hoping for, though not anticipating, good news.

"Nothing." Beaumont shook his head. "Absolutely no idea what's happened to her."

"I can offer a suggestion." Doucette updated his partner on the progress he'd made in Oakland, and then preceded to tell him about the other two new suspects. "I'm particularly interested in talking to Steven Grace."

Chapter 51

According to the mobile detector Steven Grace used to warn him of the presence of cops, there were none currently operating in the immediate area.

Half a mile down the road from the designated meeting place, he slowed the car and took a good look around. No one paid him any attention. He continued his approach toward the sports bar, watchful and ready to abandon the meetup at the first sign of trouble.

Leaving his vehicle in a side street, he jogged the rest of the way and entered the parking area on foot to avoid being issued a ticket and thereby leaving a trace.

His attention went directly to the vehicle in the parking space nearest the street. It was white, with one male occupant sitting in the front seat. He grinned, pleased to see that the asshole he planned to meet could follow a simple instruction.

As he approached the vehicle, another guy who appeared from nowhere ran over and jumped into the waiting car before the driver sped off, leaving Steven staring after them, an unpleasant emotion stirring within him.

Then Steven heard the siren and saw a patrol car in the distance. He watched it pick up speed and follow the white car.

"Fuck." He laughed softly to himself. "That was close."

He checked his watch. Waiting around put him at risk.

Five minutes passed before he checked his watch again. Then another five, and another five, until it hit him that the fucker wasn't coming.

His face grew hot and his head started to hurt. In prison, he'd learned how to make hard and dangerous men do what he wanted, and he'd thrived because of his ability to control others. Now this weak and pathetic character had gone against him and his brother and screwed up their well-thought-out plan.

Smith lacked serious skills in the killing business. No guns or knives had been used, yet the idiot had reacted so badly that some of the people on the pier became aware of them near the body, forcing them to call the cops.

The ex-con returned to his car hell-bent on getting his hands on the money that belonged to him and his brother, and then on finishing this business with Wilkes Smith. As the raw rage flowed through him, he balled his hand into a fist and struck the steering wheel repeatedly, his blood pressure boiling.

Unable to calm himself, he drove crazily, screeching his tires to stop at a set of traffic lights and laughing hysterically at the look of terror on the face of a jaywalker.

For a moment, he allowed his thoughts to rest upon the woman in his basement. He cared nothing for her life, though he cared passionately about getting even with those who deceived him. Oliver Miller thought he could run and hide, but he got caught and he paid for his mistake, and now another punk who'd underestimated him would also be made to pay.

The woman might already be dead, and she would have died with her boyfriend if the decision had been left to him. It no longer benefitted him to keep her alive and it irked him to see his brother so weak because of some stupid crazy obsession with a woman.

Behind him, a driver blasted his horn. The light had changed again, and Steven pressed his foot hard on the pedal.

The search for Wilkes Smith engrossed him, and he drove for a while until he ran low on fuel and had to pull off the road to fill up at a gas station. As he pumped the gasoline into his car, his phone rang. The number on the display belonged to Wilkes Smith.

Steven hesitated. Sensing it might be a trap he disregarded the call, pushing the phone back into his pocket where it sat against his thigh. It rang again and he ignored it. If Smith had been caught he would crack and confess. Steven regretted his brother's decision to use him. It presented too much risk.

He lit a cigarette and noticed a truck driver observing him in a way that made him uncomfortable. He pinched off the tip and put it behind his ear, not wanting to be remembered. The cell phone in his pocket kept ringing. The truck driver continued to stare at him.

He finished pumping fuel into his car and then hopped back behind the wheel and drove away, glancing in his rearview mirror once to see a couple of patrol vehicles pull off the road and head in. He experienced a few seconds of fear and then a frisson of excitement at the realization that they were not there for him.

The cops would be looking at Keith Sigmund for this. In Vegas, Oliver Miller had let the drink take over before he realized he'd talked too much about himself. Steven despised successful people like Keith Sigmund. It seemed reasonable that Sigmund should do penance for the murder.

The feeling of euphoria did not last long. The cops had surprised him, and cops had a way of reappearing.

Unsure of the situation with Wilkes Smith, Steven considered calling his brother and sending him to the basement apartment to make sure Smith understood the consequences of his actions.

After a little time to cool off, he reconsidered. Like his brother, he'd been chasing this opportunity for months and he needed the money. Instead of calling his brother, he drove to a quiet side street and called Wilkes Smith.

Smith answered the call as if he'd been waiting for it. "I've been trying to reach you," he said. "You didn't answer your phone."

Steven forced himself to stay calm. "Did you forget the time?"

"I didn't forget."

"Then where the hell are you?"

"It's not important."

"What the fuck does that mean?"

"It means I did what you asked me to do. I went over the whole place and I didn't find anything."

Steven got out of the car and paced around. "You're lying to me."

"I'm not. There is no money in the house."

"Well, you'd better get it. Remember what I said. Screw me over and I'll come after your whole family."

"Think carefully before you threaten me."

"You think you have options? Listen to me, asshole. You're not going to fucking cross me. Think about the woman. You know what will happen to her. Do you want to live with that on your conscience?"

"She's dead anyway."

An incredulous laugh got stuck in Steven's throat. He pressed the phone hard against his ear. "Well, what the hell are you going to do now?"

"What I should have done four months ago."

"You'll go to prison for a long time."

"Well, I can't do anything about that."

"You're making a mistake. You have no idea what they'll do to you in prison."

"Freedom is a luxury neither of us deserve."

Wilkes cut the call.

Steven tried to call him back and got no answer. Conscious of the fact he was swaying on his feet, he opened the car door and climbed in, raging and ready to burst. His thoughts turned to violence. No one violated his trust and got away unscathed. Someone had to pay. Someone always had to be punished.

He pulled out behind a passing car and stamped his foot on the accelerator pedal, his mind working through his problem. The situation was out of his control and this stirred the brute within him. He drove for five miles before he called his brother.

Chapter 52

Amelia Miller made four deliberate left turns, then cut the walk short and headed home, desperate to reach the house even though she felt quite sure she had not been followed. She tried to walk past her neighbor without noticing, but Laurel May called out her name.

Sensing a familiar thrill of dislike, Amelia pointed to her watch. "Sorry, I can't stop." She knew she was being rude.

"While you were out, a man got inside your home. I thought you should know."

The alarming words stopped her. Amelia stared down into a pair of cool blue eyes. "What man?"

"He entered through the back and he returned to the car with a crowbar."

"Are you sure?"

"Quite sure. I've already called the police." Laurel May stood in her front yard clutching a garden spade in her hand. "He wasn't your husband, but he dropped this."

Her neighbor handed her a battered and stained wallet. Amelia recognized it instantly and opened it to see her husband's credit cards were missing, but his ID remained inside. The hairs stood up on her skin. Her husband's killer must have taken it. He knew where she lived and he was letting her know that he could get inside her house whenever he wanted.

"What's going on here?" Laurel said. "Is this man someone you know?"

"No." Amelia held her husband's wallet tightly between her fingers. "Something terrible has happened."

"My goodness. Are you all right?"

The question was asked with real concern, the only time Amelia had ever heard sympathy from her neighbor, and it made her want to cry. She crushed the emotion.

"No. I am not all right. Someone needs to help me."

The old woman pressed her hand to her chest. "You're scaring me."

"A man has been following me," Amelia said, twisting her wrist and winding the dog leash around her palm, pulling the Doberman close. "He's been here before and he's going to hurt me."

"Who's going to hurt you, dear? What on earth are you talking about?"

Amelia gazed at her house, afraid to approach it. "What did he look like?"

"Well, I didn't get a good look at him. He was wearing a dark jacket with a hood pulled over his head."

"What about his face?"

"I can't remember."

"It's easy to remember a face."

"I'm sorry?"

"It doesn't matter. When did you become aware of him?"

"I heard the glass break, and then I saw a man run across the road to his car."

Amelia's heart thundered in her chest. "I don't know what's happening, but my husband is dead, and I believe this man had something to do with it."

"What do you mean, your husband is dead?"

"Dead as in not breathing." Amelia couldn't stop herself from running her tongue, even though she knew her next words would distress her old neighbor. "He was murdered."

Laurel May gasped. "Was he selling drugs?"

Amelia stared at her. "You know something," she said, not sure whether to laugh or cry at the absurdity of the situation. "That's probably what happened."

"Is that why all the men come to your house?"

"You have no idea." Amelia shot her a hateful glance. "It's better if you stay out of it."

She began walking up the path to her front door, holding her breath and preparing to go inside, giving her dog a quick rub to help build her nerve. She would have preferred to wait out on the street for the police to arrive but had no intention of continuing a conversation with her prying neighbor, a woman also known for her fondness for gossip.

The place felt alien and no longer safe. With her pulse racing, she unlocked the front door and went inside. The scene that confronted her sent an icy shiver through her body. She owned nothing of value, nothing for a burglar to take, but the place had been turned over with her belongings tossed everywhere and the furniture overturned. A photograph with her husband on their wedding day had been destroyed.

Standing in the kitchen, Amelia stared at the glass on the floor, then at the broken window and the back door that had been left open. Realizing the intruder had stolen her spare key she decided to wait outside on the porch for the police to show up.

They seemed to be taking a long time. Were they too busy? She glared at the house next door and wondered if her neighbor had actually called them. Anxiety and fear was pushing her closer to tears. How had her life evolved into such a nightmare?

A couple of joggers ran by. She didn't know them but watched them until they reached the end of her street and disappeared from view. Mumbling with frustration, she stared at every passing car and repeatedly checked her watch. How naïve of her to think Laurel had reported the break-in. Amelia pulled out her cell phone and made the call herself.

Chapter 53

Doucette punched the names into the computer and found no previous convictions in the police database for Greg Grace. The criminal history for Steven Grace included traffic violations, theft, and armed robbery.

First arrested at the age of fourteen for stealing a car, Steven had failed to stay out of trouble and had spent most of the last ten years in prison. He was now forty years old and had been recently released on parole to live with his brother in the San Francisco area. Doucette thought about the connection to his victim and what this might mean.

Steven Grace's parole officer was Hugo Stamp. Doucette knew him as a power-tripping asshole and one of the worst to have to deal with.

When he called Stamp and informed him that his parolee was now a suspect in a murder, Stamp did not seem surprised, revealing that Steven had been reporting regularly and was undergoing treatment for drug use, but that going straight was not the kind of world he lived in.

"With his temper, it's only a matter of time before he winds up back in prison," he said.

It appeared so. "When did you last speak to him?" Doucette asked.

"A few days ago."

Stamp told Doucette he'd driven down on a couple of occasions to see Steven at the new gym after Steven got hired as a personal trainer there. Upon Doucette's request, he provided the last known address on Fell Street, which was the brother's residence to which Steven had access.

By leaving the county without permission and traveling to Las Vegas, Steven Grace had violated his parole, but the lazy parole officer didn't seem to care, just as long as the parolee continued reporting. That was a problem. The offender was a danger, willing to jeopardize his freedom by going against the legal constraints placed upon him, and possibly prepared to kill for bigger profit.

Doucette called the gym next and talked to someone named James, who seemed surprised by his questions.

James informed Doucette that Steven had been in attendance at the gym on the Friday evening in question, flirting with the girls at the front desk as he usually did, and working out with several new clients before going for a late night out in the city with James and a couple of the girls with whom he'd been flirting. James said he'd driven Steven home and dropped him off with one of the girls sometime during the early hours of Saturday morning.

"Mind telling me where you dropped him?" Doucette said.

James gave him the address.

Not surprised when it wasn't the one on Fell Street, but some single room occupancy hotel in the city, Doucette asked a few questions about Steven to see what else he could learn.

"Not everyone likes him, but he's a hardworking guy," James said. "He's a real sports nut and a big-time Raiders fan."

"You ever go gambling with the sports nut?"

"Nah, I'm not that much of a gambler, and I'm even less of a Raiders fan. I don't go to games."

"I'm with you there," Doucette said. "So the girl stayed with him at this place?"

"She was there when I left."

"Which was at what time?"

"Must have been around four in the morning. After I dropped him off, I went to get fuel and I ran into a friend of mine coming in for his early morning coffee. He's a trucker."

Although the timing provided a sound alibi, Doucette remained confident in his belief regarding Steven's involvement in the murder. Steven was local. He knew the victim. His record reflected his commitment to crime, and he'd violated his parole.

"I take it he's been showing up for work this week," he said.

"As far as I know, but I haven't seen him."

Doucette thanked James and ended the call, pissed off with Hugo Stamp, who appeared to be doing a crap job as a parole agent and little to monitor Steven Grace. If Steven was missing work, Stamp had no idea what he was up to.

Thirty minutes had passed without another call from the unknown person claiming a direct involvement in the murder. Steven Grace was mixed up in this, and so was his brother. Doucette felt it in his bones. Steven's criminal past gave him the type of connections to do the job, and clearly there were people who had helped him. The question bothering Doucette was how many.

With his partner out checking the latest leads on the case, Doucette decided to go have a chat with another colleague, Davis Douglas.

Davis Douglas was a junior colleague who'd been with the department for a couple of years. He'd returned to his job a few weeks ago following some time off sick due to a total breakdown after being dumped by his wife. Davis looked a lot better, but Doucette knew he still felt like shit.

He'd never taken a sick day before, and he believed he'd let his colleagues down.

Doucette strolled over to the younger man's desk and sat down across from him.

"Hey, Davis. You doing better?"

"Yeah." Davis gave him a strained smile, as if he believed smiling would make him feel happier. "It's always there in the background, but I've got it mostly under control."

"Takes time," Doucette said. "It won't always be so awful. Still exercising?"

"Only thing running is my mind. Probably still smoking and drinking too much, but each day a little less."

"Still love a bet?"

The smile disappeared. "I enjoy the odd punt. What do you care?"

"Thought you might be able to help me."

With a great memory, Davis played poker in his spare time and he knew more than the average player, going to Las Vegas whenever he could and getting good enough to win more than he lost.

"What d'you need?" he said.

"The murder victim was a conman with a crippling addiction. Got a suspect who's an ex-con and likes to gamble. I need a little information. Think you can help me with that?"

Davis nodded. "I know a guy who might be able to get you the information you want."

"Good."

Doucette's phone rang. He pulled it out of his pocket, answering in his usual manner, anticipating a call from the guy wanting to confess and hoping his case might be solved a little sooner than expected. Instead, it was Amelia Miller on the other end and she sounded distressed.

He listened as she told him about the break-in. The information about her husband's wallet retrieved from her driveway with his ID still inside it interested Doucette more.

"My neighbor reported it, but the police haven't arrived. She saw the intruder fleeing in a car. He got in through the back and he went through everything, but there's nothing to steal. It's bizarre."

This had to be connected to his case. "I'll be there as soon as I can," Doucette said.

Chapter 54

Doucette stopped by Cole Taylor's doorway and leaned in.

"I'm heading out, but I'm expecting a call about the Miller case. It could be significant, and if it comes in, I want it directed to my cell phone."

Frowning, Taylor motioned for him to step inside.

"What the hell is going on with the Miller case? Are you any closer to solving it?"

"Maybe closer than I was yesterday. I'm on my way to see the widow. Seems someone has paid her a little visit and it appears to be connected. Might be the lucky break I need."

"Well, damn, go, and try to find some evidence. We need this one off our books."

"You don't have to tell me. I know."

Doucette left the station and set out again, this time for Dolores Heights, which was where Amelia Miller lived. The drive took him through The Castro and forced him to remember the mother who lived there, still waiting for justice in the murder of her son, Isaac Rogers. Doucette wished he could find some answers.

Amelia Miller emerged from her porch and met him on the street. She was holding her husband's wallet in one hand and a leash in the other with a large barking dog attached to it. She looked frightened. The dog looked intimidating, but at least he wasn't snapping his teeth.

"Does he bite?"

"Not usually."

Doucette still felt uncomfortable.

"I only went out for a few minutes to walk him. The man must have been watching my house," she said, her eyes wide. She handed him the wallet. "My neighbor said he dropped it, but I think he left it intentionally for me."

"Why would he do that?"

"He wanted me to know he's been here before and he's going to come back." She burst into tears.

"Don't cry," Doucette said. "Try to take it easy. If he wanted to hurt you, he'd have waited for you to come home."

"I'm sorry, I'm a bit of an emotional wreck." She dried her tears on her sleeve. "I can't stop thinking about what's happened to Oliver, and what might have happened to me if I'd been home."

"I don't think he's going to hurt you." Doucette's eyes panned up and down the street and then back to the house. "How long have you lived here?"

"Four years."

"It's quite a place."

The exterior looked neglected with flaking paintwork, rotted areas of wood, and dry brown weeds in the driveway, rather unlike the tidy homes next to it. Thorny rosebushes planted beneath the windows looked like they needed maintenance.

"Is anything missing from the house?"

"It wasn't a burglar," she said. "I left my credit card on the table and he didn't take it."

"I'm going to go inside. You can come with me or you can wait out here."

"I don't want to go back in."

"After I take a look around, I'll come out and speak to

you."

Doucette moved beyond her and up the driveway to the back of the house, noting the small newly dug holes in the rear yard and the piles of soil beside some of them. Someone had spent a lot of time out here.

He picked out large footprints in the soft mud that appeared to have been made by at least two different sets of boots or shoes. Using a disposable film camera, he took pictures. Finding nothing else of interest in the yard, he switched his attention to the house.

The back door hadn't been forced, although the intruder appeared to have entered through the window. Doucette observed marks in the dust on the shelf below the window, on the outside and the inside.

He stepped through the open back door into the kitchen and walked around the broken glass lying on the floor, careful not to tread on any of the pieces, crouching to examine the bigger jagged shards, hoping to find certain trace evidence. He inspected the pair of muddy boots, the soles and heels of which looked like a match to one of the sets of prints. The size of them would fit an adult male, or an adult female with big feet.

Moving from the kitchen to the living room, he saw a variety of objects strewn across the floor, indicating the frantic search that had taken place. As he made his way through the home, he found the scene repeated in every room. There appeared to be no real malicious damage, except for one picture that had been destroyed with the frame left in splinters.

Finding only one possible clue, Doucette returned to the widow waiting for him on the driveway.

She remained where he'd left her, talking on her phone. "What do you make of it?" she said, putting the phone away when she saw him. "Do you think it's connected?"

He shrugged. "It's too soon to draw any conclusions."

"It's the only way that any of this makes sense."

"What's with all the holes in the backyard?"

"I was digging for answers."

"Mind explaining that to me?"

"Someone believes there's money here, so I tried to find it."

"You should have left it for us to conduct our own search."

"I didn't find anything."

He found himself wondering if she would tell him if she had. "I'm assuming you kept a spare house key," he said.

She nodded. "Behind a photograph. He must have taken it."

"Who else has a key to your house?"

"Penny Chapman." She rubbed her hand over her heart. "I can't stay here. I have to get to someplace safe."

"Okay, but I'll need to know where I can reach you."

She promised to call him with the details.

Other officers began to arrive, responding to the report of the break-in. Doucette walked over to confer with them, and then he went next door to have a chat with the neighbor.

Chapter 55

Laurel May opened her front door a crack and eyed him with an expression of distrust.

"Mrs. May? I'm Inspector Doucette. You reported a break-in next door."

After he showed her his badge, she removed the security chain and opened the front door wider.

"I understand you may have witnessed the intruder," Doucette said, pulling his black leather notebook from his pocket.

"That's right. I saw a man go in through the back and I watched him leave. He fled in his car right before she came home."

"Could you tell me what you remember?"

"I was in my kitchen and I noticed a man moving about in the backyard. It's not a very nice backyard. Something about it didn't look right. I heard glass break and I called the police, then a few minutes later I saw him coming down the driveway. He ran across the street to his car and escaped, but he dropped a wallet. I found it when I went outside to take a look."

"What can you tell me about the car he was driving?"

"Oh, not much, I'm afraid. It was dark, black, I think, and old. I don't remember anything else."

"May I see the wallet?"

She shook her head. "It belonged to Mr. Miller so I gave to his wife."

Good so far. "Perhaps you could tell me what you

remember about the man you saw."

"I know I'm an old woman, but my eyesight is still good," she said, sounding a little indignant.

Doucette smiled kindly. "I'm sure it is. I noticed you don't wear glasses."

"Like I told her, he had a hood pulled up over his head, so I couldn't see him."

Unable to give much of a description, she drew Doucette's attention to the fact that there had been several other recent break-ins in the area.

"We believe the person who broke in next door might be someone from around this area, so I'd like to ask you some more questions, if it's okay with you," Doucette said.

"Perhaps it's gangs. I've been watching the neighborhood."

"Great." This might be helpful. "Would you mind if I came in?"

"Not at all. I'm baking cakes today. They're just out of the oven if you would like to sample some, seeing as you're here."

"I would. That's very kind." Doucette was hungry. Cake sounded good. He followed her inside and closed the door. Her house was pleasantly warm, with an incredible aroma of sugar and spices filling the air.

She led the way to the kitchen where a couple of large homemade cakes sat cooling on a tray in the middle of the table. Laurel May put two cups and a pot of coffee in front of him.

"You pour while I cut the cake." She served him a slice and sat down. "Do you suppose he'll come here again? I live alone and I'm afraid for my safety."

"To tell you the truth, I don't know," he said. "I'm not actually here about the break-in. I'm investigating a murder and it seems it may be connected."

"Oh, I thought." The old woman looked at him for a minute and then shook her head.

"You seem confused," Doucette said. "What did you think?"

"She said her husband had been murdered, but I didn't believe her. I thought she was just being evil to an old woman. She's a spiteful sort."

"You mean your neighbor, Amelia Miller?"

Laurel May nodded. "Why would you want to talk to me about a murder?"

"I'm hoping you might be able to provide some information."

She shook her head again. "I don't know anything."

"You know the victim. You said you watch the neighborhood. Have you noticed any other unusual activity at the Miller home or seen any other strange vehicles that don't belong?"

"I have been seeing a lot of abnormal activity going on next door and a lot of different men coming to the house. They park their cars along the street and about an hour later they leave. If you ask me, it looks like they are going there for sex."

"Right. Well, we can talk about that if it seems relevant." Doucette didn't want her to lose focus. He took a big bite out of his piece of cake and gulped down a mouthful of coffee. "Now, that is delicious," he said.

"I'm so glad." She smiled and her eyes looked a little brighter.

"When did you last see your neighbor, Mr. Miller?"

"Oh, no, he doesn't live here anymore."

"I know, but I'm also aware that he recently visited the area, perhaps for a few days."

"I saw him last week," she said. "I remember because he helped me with my groceries."

"Who would he have been visiting here?"

"Perhaps a young woman. He's close to some young woman who lives in the city and he's mentioned her to me before, but I'm afraid I don't remember her name." She stopped eating. "This is terrible. He was a nice man."

Doucette softened his tone. "I'm sorry if it's upsetting you. It seems you knew him quite well."

"No, only as neighbors. Well, perhaps as friends, too."

"Do you have any idea who might have done this to him?"

She sipped her coffee slowly. "Have you talked to his wife?"

"Is there a particular reason you ask?"

"I heard that her husband got another woman pregnant. Maybe she paid to have him killed."

"Mrs. May, that's a strong accusation to make."

"It isn't an accusation." A faint smile flitted across her mouth. "It's only my opinion. If you want to find out anything, perhaps you should examine it more closely."

"Well, I certainly appreciate your opinion, but this time it should be based upon the facts and nothing else."

"Of course, although I would have thought that in your line of work, you would prefer to talk to someone who is prepared to be honest and direct."

Doucette closed his notebook. "You don't like your neighbor, do you?"

"I don't approve of all those young men."

"The crimes against the Millers appear to be personal and we're contacting everyone who knew them. We believe that Mr. Miller had a girlfriend with him at the time of his death and she is currently considered missing."

"He was alone when I saw him. I only talked to him for a few minutes when I went out to get some food," she said. "He helped me to put the bags in my car. Like I said, he's a nice man."

"Could you tell me which store?"

She gave him the name of a specialty market in the city. It told Doucette the victim had been in the shopping center near his old residence, and it raised a question of why he'd returned when he was supposed to be lying low in Oakland. Was he monitoring a situation, or was the old lady confused?

Doucette took another big bite of his cake. "This truly is excellent cake," he said, talking with his mouth full. "What did you talk to Oliver about?"

"I don't recall."

"I noticed you have a home security camera installed. Perhaps it caught some things on the tape. Would you mind if I have a look?"

"It was my husband's idea," she said. "He wanted the camera installed after a package went missing from the porch. The funny thing is the police never responded, so after he died I decided not to keep it running."

Realizing she would probably hinder him more than assist, Doucette finished his cake and thanked her for her hospitality. He put his card on the table. "I'm sorry to have bothered you," he said. "Please call me if you think of anything that might help."

On the way out to his car, he stopped beneath the palm tree at the foot of Amelia Miller's driveway and took a closer look at what remained of a chalk smudge on the curb. It looked like the kind of mark left by a criminal and he realized the property had been targeted.

He hung around the residence for another minute or

two, taking pictures of the chalk mark and of the vehicles on the street; then he got back into his car and headed out to get the film processed right away, knowing the friendly guy working at the shop would do it for him within the hour.

After he handed in the camera, he went next door to get a cup of coffee, already feeling overdosed on the stuff and wishing he could quit, but his brain seemed to work better when he drank the rotten stuff.

While he waited for his pictures, he finished writing his notes. Mrs. May's words repeated in his head, making him ask himself a question: had resentment put the words in her mouth or was this whole case all about sex? Was it possible that Amelia Miller had recruited one of her lovers to plot the murder of her husband? Perhaps rejection had pushed her to the edge of insanity.

Less than an hour later, Doucette collected his pictures and returned to the station to find his partner back at his desk.

Beaumont quickly updated Doucette on the result of his search following the tip they'd received from the anonymous caller admitting his involvement in the killing.

"Absolutely no hoax," Beaumont said, giving Doucette the details of the victim's vehicle that would now be towed in for forensics, hopefully to yield prints they could identify.

Doucette learned the vehicle had been abandoned behind an old building in a remote site in one of the few areas of the city that remained free from parking restrictions. It was probably not the killer's final destination, and it was over eight miles from the location of the body.

Externally, the vehicle appeared undamaged with no blood, leading both Doucette and his partner to believe the victim had not been abducted from the car and not murdered inside it.

Inside the vehicle, there were a few clues and a connection to a woman, probably the missing woman, including a promising explanation for her disappearance.

The first clue came in the form of a black nylon bag with a small amount of make up in it retrieved from the glove compartment, revealing a woman had been in the car. Emergency stash, Doucette thought. His girlfriend did the same thing.

The second clue was a ring that Beaumont had found trapped beneath the gas pedal. The band was small and so was the diamond. The ring interested Doucette more than the cosmetics, because it looked like an engagement ring that might have been thrown at the victim during an argument, and it indicated that the vehicle had been taken for only a short while before it was abandoned.

A scribbled note tucked behind the sun visor answered one of Doucette's questions. It raised another, and it told him who did not commit the murder. He read it silently and then passed it to his partner.

"You've got to be kidding me." Beaumont looked at him with raised eyebrows. "That's some grim kind of quirk or there's a link."

"Now we know why he came back to see her."

"If it's true. We'll obviously need to check it out."

"I'm satisfied," Doucette said. "I doubt he'd have come back without making sure." After he read the note again, he put it in his pocket. "Well, if the real Marcus Miller is dead, just who the hell is your guy working with, and why hasn't he called back?"

Chapter 56

Wilkes Smith headed north, his pace quick. Aware at least one man would be hunting him down, he kept to the busier streets, knowing that if he used the quieter ones he would be spotted more easily.

The anxiety built with each step and he almost wished the police would pick him up. He walked for a couple of miles before he tossed his cell phone into a trade waste bin, severing the connection to his family and to the maniac with the odd smile and the scar on his face.

He took deep breaths and talked to himself to drive back the panic. It might be too late for the woman in the basement, but Wilkes knew he had to do everything he could to protect his family. He'd made a devastating error and taken a life, but he would never allow anything to happen to his family because of it.

Late in the afternoon, when he returned to the old car he'd left parked on Castro Street, he felt strangely calm and focused, already detached from the world around him and ready to do what had to be done.

He drove the fastest route to the police station and stood outside it staring at the doors bearing the blue star and the letters SFPD. His heart started to pound. This was not going to be easy and this wasn't even the worst day of his life. Aware that each step was taking him farther away from everyone he loved, he walked slowly, like an old man.

Ready to trade his freedom for theirs, he continued moving forward, through the doors and up to the front desk where he spoke to a middle-aged man in uniform.

"I'm here about a homicide," he said, the words sounding bizarre as he said them. He gave the desk officer his name and told him which case. "I want to confess my involvement."

He refused to say any more until he could meet with the investigator in charge of the case. The desk clerk made a call. Wilkes took a seat to wait for someone to come out from deep within the building. He felt scared, yet relieved.

Within a couple of minutes, a tall and muscular officer, still with remnants of his youthful good looks, strode over and greeted him.

"I understand you want to talk to me."

"That's right."

He said nothing more.

"Okay. Do you want to tell me what it's about?"

Wilkes glanced around nervously. "I'm here to turn myself in for the murder of the man found in the bay."

"I see. Do you wish to confess?"

Wilkes swallowed. "Yeah."

"Then I should remind you of your rights."

"I know my rights and I don't want an attorney."

"I need to read them to you anyway."

The investigating officer took him to a small interrogation room with no windows and nothing to look at. Wilkes waited impatiently while his rights were read to him. His insides were twisting with pain.

"Your name hasn't even come up in the investigation," the investigator said. "We weren't looking for you."

"If I hadn't come here, it wouldn't have been long before you'd be looking for my body."

"Well, I appreciate you saving us some time."

"I'll keep it simple." Wilkes looked him deep in the

eyes. "I only wanted to recover the money that he stole from me. Killing him was never part of my plan."

"Why don't you tell me what happened?"

"I needed an address and that's how the other guy got involved. He calls himself Marcus, but I doubt it's his real name."

Using as few words as possible, Wilkes explained the events that led up to the killing, answering the questions fired at him in a calm voice, making clear the extent of his involvement and describing how Marcus tricked him.

"Let me make sure I understand what you're telling me." The investigator leaned back in his seat and regarded Wilkes through narrowed eyes. "You're saying the victim, Oliver Miller, robbed you some four months ago in Las Vegas."

"We were at work when he broke in. He raided the house."

"And you've spent the past four months tracking him down."

"I was desperate. I have a young child at home and he's dying. I need the money for his expenses."

"I'm curious. How do you know who robbed you?"

"That's why it took me four months. Eventually I got a tip and it brought me here."

"Four months is a long time. How did you plan to go about getting the money back? I'm sure there's barely any of it left."

"I planned to take whatever I could find."

"So this is about vengeance?"

"I suppose."

"Tell me about the murder."

"He used some kind of sedative and it worked fast. The guy stopped breathing." To back up his confession, Wilkes provided precise information and gave a detailed account of how the killing went down. It relieved none of the guilt or shame that he felt. "He put the needle right here." Wilkes touched two fingers to the side of his neck.

"You helped him?"

"No, but I couldn't stop it." Wilkes bowed his head. Feeling the investigator's eyes on him, he continued. "I followed his wife to the bar that night, and then we followed the target from the bar to a gas station. He got out of the car and went inside. Marcus got into the back of his car and waited for him to return."

"From what you're telling me, it sounds like you knew what he planned to do. It was your idea to hit back and this other guy went along with your plan."

"Yes, it's true, but it's not as simple as you make it sound. Marcus said he wanted his own revenge, but I didn't realize what he meant."

"Oh, come on," the investigator said with a smile. "I don't believe you're that stupid or naïve. I'm sure you could have worked out that he was a vicious type."

"Perhaps you're forgetting that I'm not from around here. I only got into town a few days ago. I'd never met the man before."

"How did you hook up?"

"I went into a couple of the local bars looking for Miller. That's how I met Marcus. He came up to me and made me an offer, said he could get me an address if I shared the money."

"I see. So you came to an arrangement? You promised to give this guy cash if he helped you take the man out."

"No." Wilkes shook his head. "I only wanted an address. Nothing more."

"How did you think this was going to play out?"

"I chose not to think about it." Wilkes met the investigator's gaze. "I only wanted to get my money back, but I got caught up in a bad situation and I couldn't get myself out of it."

"You need money that bad, yet you were willing to share it? You see why I'm having a hard time believing this?"

"I understand and I agree it sounds odd, but my life was already hell and it has been even worse since this happened." Wilkes looked away. "I'm not a criminal. I made a huge mistake and I wish I could go back and change things. Nobody was supposed to get hurt."

"How much money?"

"Sixteen thousand dollars. It was my entire savings, and he took my girlfriend's jewelry."

"You reported the theft?"

"Reporting it was a waste of time."

"Why were you keeping so much money in the house?"

"I didn't get around to buying a personal safe."

"Were you hiding it?"

"I'm not sure I understand."

The investigator rotated his pen between his fingers. "Is there a reason you couldn't keep it in a bank?"

"It was my personal preference to keep it in the house."

"Probably a bad idea."

"I realize that now."

"Is there anything else you want to tell me? Anything else you want to confess?"

"No."

"Where did you get all the mud on your feet?"

Wilkes gazed down at his right shoe and saw the mess. He was already in a lot of trouble. It couldn't hurt him any more to admit to a less serious crime, but he remembered the reason he'd come here.

"When Oliver stopped at the gas station, there was a woman in the car with him," he said. "I don't know if she's still alive."

Chapter 57

On the surface, this man's claim seemed to be true. He knew a lot of detail, and Doucette felt a buzz at the mention of the woman.

"I'd like to talk to you about the woman," he said. "Where is she?"

"He's keeping her in a basement."

"Where?"

"Somewhere in the city. I don't know the address."

"How do you get in contact with Marcus?"

The other man shook his head. "I can't risk it. He'll go after my family. You have to help them."

"Who is your partner?" Doucette wanted every bit of information he could gather on the man calling himself Marcus.

"He's not my partner. He's a maniac out for his own revenge and he used me to get what he wanted. That's all I know."

"You used him. You didn't know the man who robbed you and you needed someone to pick him out. That makes you equal. You were in this together."

"Look, you don't trust me and you don't have to believe me, but I'm not here to deceive you. I'm here to do the right thing, to try to save an innocent woman's life, and to ask for your help for my family."

Tears shone in the man's eyes. He sat shivering, as if a cold wind had hit him. Doucette had dealt with enough cranks to know when someone was playing him for a fool, and his gut told him to take this man seriously.

"You can answer this for me," he said. "Does Marcus have a scar on his face?"

"Yes. Running down the left side."

"Is he working with anyone else?" Doucette was thinking of Greg and Steven Grace, the brothers he suspected of the actual killing.

"It's possible that I've been talking to two different men on the phone."

Without another word, Doucette got up and left the room. He spent a few minutes discussing the situation with his partner and his boss, and then returned to the interrogation room. He spread his hands on the table.

"Do you have any other information about Marcus? If you do, you need to tell me now."

"He only told me what he wanted me to know."

"Yet he made you trust him."

"I've been fucked over more than once in my life. I never trusted him."

"You need to tell me everything you know about this guy, otherwise I can't do a thing to protect your family."

The man sitting in the chair opposite eyed him for a long time. "How did you know about the scar?"

"I've seen it before," Doucette said.

"If you know him, you're aware of what he might do, what he's capable of."

"It sounds to me like you know, too."

"I should have, but I didn't understand until he said something by mistake and I figured it out. When Miller robbed me last September, he had a partner. Marcus was involved. Something must have gone bad between them."

"At what point did you become aware he intended to kill the man who robbed you?"

"Until he got out of the car at the gas station, I had no idea…my head was spinning. By the time I realized the connection it was too late to stop it." Wilkes shot a glance at the clock on the wall. "You're wasting time."

"She's been missing for five days. You could have called for help."

"She might still have a chance. Marcus is expecting me to bring him the money. He's keeping her alive until he has it."

"Where is the money?"

"Marcus believes it's hidden in Miller's house. I searched the whole fucking place and I didn't find it."

"How do I know you're not lying to me?"

Wilkes let out a heavy sigh. "It's up to you whether or not you believe me, but you'll be making a huge mistake if you don't."

"How long do we have?"

"Thirty minutes, probably less."

Dressed all in dark clothing, the young man looked wretched. Blood pulsed through Doucette's veins. Convinced the man was telling him the truth, he did something he normally wouldn't and asked Wilkes Smith to make a phone call to the man waiting for the money.

"Tell him you have the money. Tell him you want proof the woman is still alive before you deliver it and get him to meet you at the basement apartment. We'll have men following you and we'll get him when he shows up."

"He'll know something is wrong. If I make the call, he will kill her, and after he kills her, he'll go after my family."

"I'll do what I can to help your family, but my priority is saving an innocent woman's life."

"My priority is my family."

"Make the call."

"I can't. I tossed my phone and I don't know the number."

Doucette's shoulders tensed with frustration. "Where did you arrange to meet him?"

Wilkes shook his head. "Not until I know my family is safe. They're innocent. You have to promise me."

"I don't make promises."

"Then I can't tell you."

"If what you say is true and this accomplice of yours also helped rob you, then he knows where you live. What do you suppose will happen to your family if you don't show up with the money?"

Wilkes blew out his breath and clasped his hands behind his neck, clearly tormented. His eyes searched Doucette's and he seemed to be struggling.

"He'll know you're cops. He'll sense it."

"So, you're going to let him get away with it?"

"It's too risky."

"Yeah, it's risky, but you've already put them in danger."

It took the man a moment to make up his mind. His shoulders slumped. "What do you want me to do?"

"I want you to stick to the plan. Do whatever he asks, but get him to agree to meet you at the basement."

Chapter 58

Wilkes Smith revved the engine and reentered the flow of afternoon commuters, thinking about his family and realizing that he and Marcus were not much different. For both, revenge was an obsession and they'd reacted with the same seething anger, neither of them able to resist it. Killing brought him no satisfaction and it had cost him far more than he'd lost.

Deep in his heart, he still believed he was a good man, better than the fool who'd allowed his anger to control him. All he'd done was try to fight for his family. He was no criminal, but he was not innocent. He was broken.

He turned left and then right, noticing that at the junction up ahead the lights were turning red. He tapped the brakes and slowed, fighting the sudden impulse to drive straight through it. The woman might already be dead and this senseless police plan would jeopardize his family if Marcus caught onto him.

He stopped and stared at the lights, concentrating hard and realizing there was nothing he could do. Marcus had killed his own friend. He was crazy and unpredictable.

The light changed from red to green. Wilkes drove through the junction, propelled by his own guilt. His whole body buzzed. As he drove, his heart hammered in his chest and his nerves tingled with a weird rush of energy. To have any chance of succeeding in fooling Marcus, he had to believe in what he was trying to do.

He drove straight for about a mile, the usual traffic on

Leavenworth Street impeding his progress. The police stayed right behind. Unable to clock up any speed, Wilkes honked his horn, upset with the slow pace, knowing he now had only a couple of minutes to get to the meeting place. No one seemed to be in a hurry. He glanced around for gaps to cut through the traffic but could see none. The roads were choked. He took several turns along the route. The traffic crawled along.

Growing more frustrated, Wilkes tried to control his breathing, forcing himself to stay calm, telling himself he had time. The uneasiness increased when he got within a block of the sports bar on Lombard Street where he'd arranged to meet Marcus. If Marcus had been watching the traffic, he'd know Wilkes was here and he would have noticed the unmarked car still behind him. A glance in the rearview mirror confirmed it was still there, too close.

Wilkes swore, unsure whether to keep driving or to stop. His fingers tapped the steering wheel as his stomach churned with nerves. The police should have dropped farther behind. He could feel himself panicking and wiped his sweaty palms dry on his thigh.

As the destination came into sight, he sat straighter in his seat and again checked the mirror, relieved to see the unmarked car pull over. He took a couple of quick breaths of air and drove into the parking lot next to the bar, reluctant to get out of the car.

The parking lot seemed quiet and no other cars turned into it. The building looked dark. Wilkes cut the engine and glanced around. His mind went back over the details. He felt certain he hadn't gotten it wrong.

He stared at the voodoo doll hanging on the outside wall. This was definitely the right place and the bar should have been open. It made no sense. He could not understand what had gone wrong. Tormented by the thoughts of his family, he closed his eyes and rubbed a hand over his face. He wished he could reach them, but he'd tossed away his phone. He would go crazy if Marcus hurt them.

Chapter 59

For a few minutes, nothing appeared to be happening and Doucette wondered if this was a mistake or a waste of his time, and possibly an attempt by Wilkes Smith to mislead him.

Then a black truck entered the bar parking lot and circled it slowly.

Parked on the street and farther away than he would have liked, Doucette watched. The dark windows of the truck made it hard to see the driver. He picked up his radio and talked to a detective on his team, sitting inside another unmarked unit nearby.

"Who the fuck is this?" Doucette asked.

"Don't know," came the reply.

"Think he knows we're here?"

"We'll find out in a few minutes."

Another officer was leaning against a street sign, observing the meeting place and trying to blend in. The whole setup made Doucette uneasy. If they got this wrong, it would be on him.

He glanced at his partner, who was staring across the street, too tense to speak.

"Are we moving?" he said into the radio.

"Not yet."

The driver of the black truck stopped. The passenger door opened and a woman got out. She crossed the street and walked in the opposite direction of the bar, passing Doucette's vehicle without looking back. No one followed her. With her short stature and long dark hair, she did not fit the physical description of the missing woman.

Seconds later, the driver of the black truck pulled out of his parking space and got back onto the road. It all seemed normal and Doucette got no inkling in his consciousness that the driver was aware of them. He settled back into his seat and waited for another minute, observing Wilkes Smith sitting behind the wheel of his car, his head down.

"Whoever he's meeting is watching us. He knows we're here," Doucette said.

"I don't think so." Beaumont adjusted his position. "The place is shut down today and it's not opening for a week. He knows it and he knows his partner is not here."

"Are you suggesting he's not coming or that no one else is involved?"

"I'm telling you that this guy is making us look like bigger fucking chumps. We gave it a shot, but it's time to end this."

Doucette thought about it for a minute. "Yeah, you're right," he said, his face taut. He started the engine of his car, drove across the street into the small parking lot, pulled up close to Smith's vehicle, and got out, motioning for Smith to do the same.

The man did as instructed. He appeared frightened and confused. "Is my family okay?"

"That's not my concern." Doucette caught him by the arm. "You've wasted enough of my time and I'm onto you. I know your accomplice isn't coming."

"He'll be here." Wilkes Smith tried to shake his arm free. "I swear to you he'll come. He won't leave without the money."

"Shut up and get in the car."

Doucette put one hand on the top of the man's head and shoved him into the back seat, then climbed into the front and radioed his colleagues.

"I'm not trying to trick you," Smith said. "Why would I turn myself in and then lie to you?"

"I guess only you know the answer to that."

"I've risked everything."

"Yeah, and I've heard enough of the bullshit."

"You have to believe me," Wilkes said. "This is the place where I'm supposed to meet him. Maybe he got held up."

"And maybe he's getting away."

Smith appeared stricken and remorseful. He had no previous criminal record. Doucette believed he had not intended murder, and that his crimes were an act of desperation, but it didn't matter. A thief robbing another thief had ended in murder, both men willing to risk it all.

In case he was making another mistake, Doucette waited in the parking lot for a couple of minutes, listening to Smith repeating the same story about the threat to kill his family. It was obvious to Doucette that he believed it.

The man in the back seat pleaded. "He wants the money that was taken from him and he'll do anything to get it. Let me go back."

"I can't do that," Doucette said.

"He'll show. Give my family a chance. Please."

"I gave them a chance." Doucette started the engine, exiting the parking lot and heading back out onto the road with two police cars following him. "Perhaps it's time you told me the truth."

"You think I made it up?" Smith began shouting. "I knew you fucking cops would never believe me. What's the fucking point, when nothing I say seems to make a fucking difference. So now what are you going to do? Let him kill my family?"

He let out a strange guttural noise as if trying to inhale through an obstructed airway. He complained of chest pain. It sounded like a panic attack. Familiar with it, Doucette told him to breathe in through his nose and blow it out through his mouth.

Beaumont leaned around to check on the man.

"Is he okay?" Doucette said.

"No, he's not, but it can wait."

Hands locked on the wheel, eyes fixed straight ahead, Doucette drove to a hookah bar in the middle of the city. It was the place where Smith said he'd first encountered the man who used him to kill. In his current flustered state, perhaps Smith had made an error and mixed up the meeting point.

Chapter 60

Two teenagers entered the Bootkam hookah lounge at the same time as Doucette and were asked by the owner to leave for being under the legal age.

Four male smokers of Middle Eastern descent sat together drinking coffee. At least thirty people could fit inside the place without making it feel crowded.

Soft music played in the background. The air inside felt cool. Staff appeared friendly and the whole vibe seemed relaxed, a fine place to hang out.

A short man with an expressive face introduced himself as the owner and asked to see the private club membership.

Doucette's identification satisfied his request.

"How can I help?"

"I'm investigating a murder."

As it usually did, that put an end to any friendly conversation.

"The killing happened sometime late Friday night or early Saturday morning," Doucette said. "We've received a tip that the suspect showed up here on the night of the murder and met with an accomplice, an out-of-towner."

"I see." The owner's forehead puckered with a frown. "I'm not sure I can provide any information."

"One of the men was quite distinctive. You wouldn't easily forget him. He's a tall man with deep and jagged scars on his face."

"You're sure he came here?"

"Maybe it was his first time."

The owner shrugged. "It's busy all the time, especially on the weekend. As you can see, it's quite dark in here. It's possible, but I don't recall a man with scars."

"His name is Greg Grace."

"The name's not familiar."

"But you were in the bar around the time in question?"

"I'm here every night."

Doucette got out his notebook. "We picked up the accomplice—the out-of-towner—this morning and he pointed us here."

"I'd be glad to help, but I have no idea who this man is," the lounge owner said gently with a glance at the door. "If there was any dirty work going on here, I'm not aware of it."

"Tall, with a long facial scar. We believe he's still in the area. In fact, he was planning to meet his accomplice here right around now."

"Fuck. Give me a minute."

With the lounge owner in the backroom checking his records, Doucette sat in the bar and talked to a bartender making coffee. Having already made eye contact with Doucette a couple of times, which Doucette interpreted as a signal that he'd like a minute alone to chat, Doucette was interested in hearing what he wanted to say and granted him the time.

"A man with facial scars came in last week, but he's not a regular," the bartender said. "He sat over there with another dude, a much shorter guy around the same age, early forties, maybe a little younger." The bartender indicated a cozy corner table. "They drank a lot of coffee and stayed for about two hours. When I switched out the coals, a third man had joined them."

"About what time was this?"

"Couldn't say. To be honest with you, I don't remember much more than the scars."

"Would you recognize any of these men if you saw them again?"

"I'd remember the one with the scar."

"Please call me immediately if he shows up here." Doucette pulled a card from his pocket and wrote his number on the back.

The bartender moved away, almost guiltily Doucette thought, as the owner returned to the lounge area, his face looking a little flushed, clearly uncomfortable with being drawn into the murder investigation. He confirmed, with noticeable relief, that the suspect named in this case was not listed under the club memberships, frustrating Doucette's efforts to find him.

"Sorry I couldn't be of more help."

"Thanks for your time. I'll be in touch."

Doucette gave a quick nod to the bartender and slowly made his way back to his car. He needed a few minutes alone to think.

Neither Smith nor the Grace brothers could have known when the victim would be back in the city unless someone had informed them, either intentionally or by accident. Keith Sigmund had been in Oakland at the same time as the victim. As Doucette tried to piece it together in his head, how Sigmund came to be connected to the crime, he realized that Sigmund must have some kind of relationship with the killers and had passed them the information. In return, the killers had used Sigmund's history with the victim to betray him.

Chapter 61

By the time he reached his car, it had started to rain. With thoughts of Keith Sigmund and the missing woman rattling around in his brain, Doucette felt he had no choice but to head back to the station and admit to his superior that he'd again failed to find any new reliable information to help solve his case.

He already knew that Wilkes Smith had been the third man in the lounge, but Wilkes had left it rather late to mention the second man involved and his failure to do it sooner harmed his credibility. Doucette turned his head, about to speak to the young man still sitting nervously in the backseat of his car, when his cell phone rang and diverted his attention.

He hesitated, and then got out of the car to answer it. The call was from the junior colleague he'd asked for help.

Davis Douglas said he had managed to get his teeth into some information. Within the past few minutes he'd received a tip passed along by a reliable informant who'd explained the source had had a recent falling out with Steven Grace and was only willing to reveal what he knew on the condition of anonymity.

Doucette pressed his colleague for the details.

As Davis described the small-scale gambling setup in the city involving the Grace brothers, Doucette considered the set of connections and asked who else might be mixed up in it, hoping Davis could draw in Keith Sigmund.

While the operators did not include Sigmund, Doucette

learned that Steven Grace played card games for significant sums of money. Davis passed on the name of one of the other players with a private address and details of the bookie happy to take his business.

"He was there at that address with his brother about an hour ago," Davis said. "They were heard arguing and they got into a furious fight before they left."

"I want to find Miller's girlfriend," Doucette said. "Where is she?"

"I have no idea, but I'm working on it. I have some more news," Davis said, with a hint of excitement in his voice. "The girl is what they were arguing about. That tells me they're both involved, and it also tells me she might still be alive."

The information got Doucette's blood pumping.

Davis told him he had someone from the homicide team already talking to the bookie and had put someone else on the other card player with the private address. "If either of the brothers head back there, we'll be ready to pick 'em up," he said.

Doucette thanked his colleague and put away his phone.

Climbing back into the car, he leaned across to his partner. "Greg Grace is the one who found the body. I believe it was his brother who killed him and it's Greg who's been keeping the girl alive."

"Which brother is meant to be meeting him?" Beaumont motioned with his head to the guy in the back seat. "Whichever one it is, he's no longer controlling the situation so it's unlikely they'll keep her alive now."

From the back seat, the quiet voice of Wilkes Smith entered the conversation.

"You may think you know the man you're dealing

with, but you don't know anything about him. Marcus is smart and dangerous, pure evil. If the girl is still alive, he's only keeping it that way for his own personal gratification."

"You don't know anything about him either," Doucette replied sharply. "The real Marcus is dead."

Chapter 62

Doucette spent the rest of the afternoon collecting more data and comparing it, trying to find pieces to fit. He checked with the residential hotel that rented the single room to the female from the gym where Steven worked, and talked to the young woman to determine that Steven did not actually live with her.

The woman struggled to answer his questions, claiming she remembered little from that night because she drank a lot more than usual and passed out. She admitted to waking up alone and realizing she'd had sex with the man who took her home, confirming it had been Steven.

"He must have put something in my drink," she said, her voice breaking. "I don't even remember getting home."

Doucette asked her for a phone number for Steven, which she was unable to provide. Under the conditions of his parole, he'd not been allowed to have a cell phone, or so she'd been told. Doucette pressed her for an address.

She told him she believed Steven lived with his brother, but didn't know for sure and could not say where. The only useful piece of information Doucette obtained from their conversation was that Steven had not been seen in the gym since Friday. He seemed impossible to locate.

Still mulling over the conversation an hour later, Doucette arrived at the Fell Street address, where Steven Grace was supposed to be living with his brother, to discover the condo was vacant and on the market with the elderly seller living next door.

After a brief conversation, Doucette realized the seller knew nothing about the brothers or the murder; however, upon learning of the investigation and hearing about the missing woman connected to the murder, the seller showed Doucette through the empty property, including the partial basement. He informed Doucette that his property had been vacant for a month after his long-term tenant, a single woman in her fifties who'd occupied the condo for the past fifteen years, decided to move out.

If anyone had been using the basement, Doucette found no evidence of it.

He inquired about the white BMW parked next to the property. The owner confirmed the vehicle belonged to his daughter. Irritated by the inconvenience of another wasted journey and regretting the time expended, Doucette handed out another of his cards with a request that the seller call if he heard or saw anything unusual.

That evening, working late at his desk, he made a couple of phone calls and then sat back to ponder the significance of the Fell Street address, wondering if it had been picked at random by Steven Grace for his probation officer because it was in close proximity to his actual residence. If Hugo Stamp had been doing a thorough job and monitoring his probationer rather than allowing things to slide, the woman might have been found by now, he thought. The lack of supervision made him angry.

He checked his cell phone repeatedly, waiting impatiently for a return phone call to come in. Keith Sigmund did not appear to be the type to kill, but he was connected to this case and not by coincidence. Doucette knew that Sigmund had been in the same area as Miller on the night of Miller's murder, and years of experience had trained him not to believe in coincidences.

When he couldn't take it anymore and thought Sigmund wouldn't answer his phone, Doucette tried the number again. This time, he got a busy signal. He wondered if Sigmund could be blocking numbers or diverting his calls, giving himself time to come up with some more well-thought-out answers, or perhaps he had simply reached the point where he didn't want to talk anymore.

After hearing his story for the first time, Doucette had accepted it as the truth, but a few details now left him inclined to reconsider his earlier conclusion.

Some considerable time later, Doucette's cell phone buzzed on his desk. He answered it quickly.

"Homicide, Doucette."

"Sigmund."

"Thanks for returning my call."

"Are you still fishing for information or have you arrested someone?"

"Something like that," Doucette said. "I checked out your alibi this morning. The hotel manager verified you were there."

"Of course he did. That's because I was there."

He sounded contemptuous. Doucette continued. "I want to talk to you again about your recent visit to Oakland, the real reason behind it. I believe you were not…"

The other man cut in. "I explained all of this to you the last time we talked. I spent the night with an old girlfriend who happens to live in Oakland."

"The last time we talked, you left out a few details," Doucette said.

"I have no idea what you're talking about."

"Well, it's been a few days so let me see if I can assist your memory. While I was in Oakland checking out your alibi, I went into a couple of places to ask questions, see what shook loose, and I talked to someone who witnessed an argument between two men. It took place outside his restaurant. Sound familiar?"

"Should it?"

"The restaurant was a block away from the hotel you used. One of the men was Oliver Miller and the other man fits your description. Perhaps you forgot to mention it before, but I'd appreciate it now if you'd tell me what you argued about."

It was a partial deceit, but Doucette knew he was close to the truth when, for the second time, Sigmund became flustered.

"Yeah, okay, so it's true. I saw Miller that night and yeah, there was a confrontation, but I had no idea he was going to be in the area. I couldn't believe it when I saw him."

"And you didn't think you should have brought it up the last time we spoke?"

"I panicked. I knew with my history it would look bad."

"You're damn right it looks bad," Doucette said. "Real bad. This is serious. From what I'm told, the situation became unsavory."

"It never even got close to being physical."

"I'd love to believe you."

Sigmund snapped. "I see what you're doing, and it won't work."

"What is it you think I'm doing?"

"You're no closer to finding this guy so you're trying to pin the murder on me. I might be a good fit for it, but it's not me."

"You expect me to believe you suddenly showed up in the same place?"

"Sure I do, because that's exactly what happened."

"Bet it was a shock. Must have really opened up those old wounds."

"I won't deny it got heated, but I'm telling you, I never touched him." Sigmund paused. "I'd been holding on to my anger for too long. I let it go when I saw him, and then I went back to the hotel. He was alive when I left him."

"You were the last person to see him alive."

"No. Whoever killed him is the last person to see him alive."

"How heated did it get?"

Gripping the phone in his hand and realizing he was getting desperate, Doucette listened to the story, trying to decide whether to believe it or keep pushing. What if, for the second time, he let the wrong man get away? Sigmund had motive, opportunity, and a connection to the victim.

"I'm going to be honest with you," Doucette said. "The timing is causing me some serious concern."

"I can understand that, but I've already told you where I was and what I was doing. I'm not guilty and yet you're still harassing me."

"Well, I'm sure you can see the problem. You were overheard having an intense argument with the victim on the night of the murder."

"Yeah, but I didn't kill him."

"Then who did?"

"Someone who saw us and figured they could set me up for the crime."

"From my position, you're still looking pretty good for it."

"I get it that you want to solve your case, but you know I didn't do it." Sigmund said it without any anger. "I was with my ex all night."

"Which could make her an accomplice."

Sigmund sighed. "Think about it," he said. "It's too easy. With my name cropping up, I would have known you'd be looking for me and I'd have tried to hide my involvement or at least hide myself, but I didn't. I disclosed my connection to Miller. His relationship with my sister is the only reason my name came up and it's the only reason for your interest in me."

"Maybe that's true." Doucette rolled his pen between his fingers, some lingering doubt in his head.

During their earlier conversation, Keith Sigmund had presented himself as a resentful person, unable to internalize his anger. Remembering this, Doucette expected a sudden face-off with his old enemy would have left the social worker in a flood of rage that would have overwhelmed him unless he released it, and there'd been no signs of a violent struggle. Sigmund made a good suspect, yet with the history that existed between him and Oliver Miller, Doucette realized that he would have killed the victim in a fit of rage where he saw him.

"I didn't do it," Sigmund said again. "I have an alibi."

"I'm aware of your alibi."

"Then you know there's someone else with motive."

"I still believe you're acquainted with the murderer. He didn't use your name by chance."

"No, I guess not."

"I've made a few more inquiries and if you want me to believe your story then I need to identify how you know him, plus understand his motive for implicating you."

"I've been thinking about it since you first showed up," Sigmund said. "It's obvious that it's someone who's been tracking my movements."

The social worker sounded almost confident for a

moment, as though he was going through a mental checklist. Encouraged, Doucette waited patiently, anticipating the reply, but it never came.

He asked another question to try and get at the information that would help him find the two men he wanted to talk to.

"Who have you spoken to about your confrontation with Miller?"

"Blackie. Bill Blackwell. He's a good friend and he's always trying to talk to me about stupid stuff like tolerance and forgiveness. Blackie never holds onto his anger."

Chapter 63

After the police finished processing the break-in they left, and then the fear mounted quickly. Amelia Miller was more scared now than when she'd first arrived home and found the place had been ransacked. It was starting to get dark outside, which heightened her fear.

She pressed her fingers against the throbbing pain in her head. The house was tainted, no longer secure. The intruder had stolen her spare key, which meant he planned to come back. She couldn't face staying here.

Snatching up a bag, she picked up a few of her things, whatever she thought she might need, and then headed downstairs, banging her hip against the misplaced desk on her way out of her bedroom. She swore and rubbed her hand over the sharp pain, then broke down again, furious with the police for the lack of sympathy and progress. She was alone and vulnerable, and it felt like they weren't even trying.

Taking her dog, she left her home for her friend's apartment.

Penny Chapman lived in The Mission District, a working-class area pulsating with street art and street life, a diverse variety of bars, live-music clubs, and stores catering to a wide range of sexual fetishes and fantasies.

Amelia liked coming here. She found the beaten-down gritty character of the place appealing and the people friendly, not fake and superficial like those in the trendier cities filled with expensive boutiques and luxurious apartment buildings.

The apartment complex Penny lived in was gated, with parking and a private patrol. The added layer of security helped Amelia manage her own fear. She parked on the street and called her friend.

Penny didn't answer, and Amelia couldn't see her friend's car.

Parked a little farther down on the opposite side of the street from her was an unfamiliar brown sedan with the interior light on revealing a man sitting in the driver's seat. He appeared to be watching her, but then he pulled out of his spot and drove away. As she got out of her truck, the anxiety stayed with her.

She entered the building through the pedestrian gate, gaining access by typing in the code on the keypad, and making sure the gate closed behind her. Keeping her dog close to her body, she tensed as she walked past a man talking on a cell phone. He made eye contact and she looked away quickly. His voice followed her all the way to Penny's apartment. Convinced he was following her, she hurried her step and used the front door key code Penny had given her.

Since their last conversation, Amelia didn't like letting herself in; however, she welcomed the cool, fresh air, was surprised by the neatness, and wondered how Penny kept such a tiny place so tidy. She glanced around for a place to drop her bag. Everything looked so precise and clean that she worried about bringing in her dog, afraid that her presence and her addictions would leave a permanent stain on this spotlessly clean home. The dog was already pulling on the lead, clearly ready to start snooping.

Amelia removed her shoes and left them by the front door, then proceeded to the kitchen, keeping her dog close to her heels. Glad to have the place to herself for a while, she opened the refrigerator to find it empty, and then remembered with her friend's schedule that the apartment was hardly ever lived in.

In the bathroom, she stared quietly at her reflection in the mirror, certain that the image gazing back at her could not be her own. The pale face looked plain and old, with dark circles and heavy lines beneath the tired brown eyes, and an inch of dark roots showing in the dirty dyed blonde hair. Disgusted with what she saw, she turned away.

A soft sigh escaped her. She felt uncomfortable here, convinced her host would try to do her best, but would raise issues Amelia did not want to talk about. After waiting for almost an hour, she realized she needed to leave, but as she went to retrieve her shoes, the dog started barking, and the front door opened. Penny Chapman walked in with a bag in each hand.

"Hi," she said, closing the door with her backside. "So, you decided to come."

"I was about to leave and go to a hotel. Here, let me help you." Amelia shouted at the dog to shut up, then took one of the bags from her friend and carried it into the kitchen.

"You can stay a little while. I just got all this extra food."

"I don't want to get in your way, and you don't like dogs."

"You won't be in my way and I do like dogs. At least, I like yours. Have you eaten?"

"No."

"Dinner, or all day?"

"My mind isn't on food."

"I'll make us something." Penny patted the dog's head and began unpacking one of the bags. "What made you change your mind?"

Amelia pulled out a chair and sat down. "Someone broke into my place this afternoon."

"What? Are you kidding me?"

"No, I'm not. He tossed the place and he took my spare key. I'm afraid to go back there."

"You must be terrified. Do you think it has something to do with Oliver's murder?"

"Of course, and he wanted me to know it." Amelia watched her friend crossing from the table to the cupboards to put stuff away, the dog following his new friend. "He must have been looking for the money."

"How do you know it was a man?"

"My neighbor saw him. He had Oliver's wallet, which contained his ID, and he left it on the driveway for me to find."

Penny stopped unpacking. Her shoulders dropped and she seemed lost for a few minutes. Amelia wanted to go to her friend, but held back, afraid to move, unsure what Penny wanted.

"Why would he leave evidence? It doesn't make sense."

"Nothing makes sense." Amelia rubbed her eyes, the weariness threatening to overpower her. "I see it as a taunt. He's telling me that he can get to me any time he wants to. He thinks he's smarter than the police and he might be right."

"I tipped them off about the Grace brothers, and I'll keep on it until they link them to the murder," Penny said, as she finished unpacking groceries.

"It's not enough. How can we be so sure about their involvement? I mean, what physical evidence do we have?"

"I could try talking to Greg. He's a bit odd, but he's not a monster. He used to be a good friend to Oliver and maybe I can get him to confide in me and tell me what happened."

Amelia shook her head. "That would be stupid, and it could be seriously dangerous."

"You're right, but the police don't have the resources. They're still no closer to figuring it out and it's frustrating when I know who the murderer is."

"But you're not the police and talking to Greg might make it worse."

"It can't get any more fucked up than it already is."

Amelia laughed.

Penny changed the subject. "What are you going to do about the funeral?" Before Amelia could answer, her cell phone rang. She snatched it up. "Hello."

She listened without speaking. Amelia couldn't hear what the other person said, but from her friend's expression she sensed it was important.

"Hang on," Penny said to the caller. She apologized to Amelia and took the phone into her bedroom to continue her conversation privately.

For a moment, Amelia stayed in the kitchen with her dog, wondering what the problem was. A mixture of hope and irritation washed over her.

Chapter 64

As Penny continued her private conversation, Amelia wandered through the apartment and looked at the numerous photographs on the walls, pausing by one that showed her with Oliver on their wedding day. It was one she hadn't seen before and the picture captured her joy. It had been a beautiful summer day. She remembered the happiness she'd felt. She also remembered the moment she knew that her marriage was over, the first time she realized Oliver no longer loved her.

The next photograph was also of Oliver, this time with his arm wrapped around the slender waist of a woman Amelia recognized. Also in the picture were two women standing with two other men. All six stood beneath the legendary Las Vegas sign.

The women were not important. Amelia's interest lay only in the men. One was short, dark, and powerfully built. He stood staring at the camera with parted lips and a predatory look in his eyes. He seemed to be holding her gaze and his features seemed twisted with passion, or with a violent uncontrollable anger. It made her so uncomfortable she found it difficult to look at. The taller man's long hair and beard concealed part of his face, though not enough to hide the vivid scars. Amelia had never seen either of the men before, yet instinctively felt she knew who they were.

She took down the photograph from the nail on the wall and went back to the kitchen to wait for her friend to finish her conversation.

When Penny returned, Amelia pushed the photograph across the table. "Who are the two men with Oliver?"

"Where did you get this?" Penny said. Her brow furrowed.

"It was hanging on your wall."

"This was taken in Las Vegas. I'd completely forgotten about it."

"I didn't ask where it was taken. I can see that for myself."

"It's the brothers, Greg and Steven Grace. I took the photograph on the first day, before anything happened."

"This shows that they knew Oliver and it puts them with the woman who is missing. We should show this to the police."

"Yeah, I'll give it to them in the morning. I'm hoping I might be able to provide more information." Penny explained. "That phone call was from a good friend of mine. He's a lawyer. I discussed our situation with him and asked him to help us."

"Help us, how?"

"He has access to resources and he can gain information to help us find things out about the brothers, or figure out who's helping them. He's good. He said to come by his office in the morning."

"I'm not sure that's such a good idea," Amelia said. "If we tip off the wrong person, we could make it worse. I think we should leave it to the police."

Penny snorted. "We don't have to tell them what we did. Anyway, the police aren't going to crack this case. I'm not even convinced they believed me, and if they don't have any leads they won't investigate." Her expression changed. "One or both of the brothers killed Oliver and I'm not going to let them get away with it. I don't think you would want that either."

"Of course not." Amelia picked up the photograph and gazed at it with another jolt of emotion. "What do you think has happened to Eve?"

"She's probably dead."

"If she's not, they might do something stupid if they think we're getting too close. I don't want to be responsible for that."

"Well, you can do nothing, but I'm not going to be talked out of it."

Amelia didn't like the direction of the conversation or the weird look in her friend's eyes. Sensing any further argument would be a waste of her energy, she asked her friend for a pen and a piece of paper.

"What do you want them for?" Penny said.

"To make a list of everyone that Oliver knew. Someone might know where the brothers are or where they're hiding out with Eve."

"Glad you're starting to see it differently."

The pen and paper arrived. "Let's start with his family." Amelia wrote Marcus's name at the top of the page. "We can't forget about him," she said.

"I haven't, although I'm not sure anymore that he had anything to do with it."

"I'm not ready to eliminate him." Amelia remembered he'd been released and she could imagine him going after her friend again. If he'd already found her, he might be targeting them both. Perhaps coming here was mistake. "Tell you what," she said, putting the pen down on the table. "Why don't we eat first and finish this later?"

Penny fixed a plate of instant spaghetti and meat sauce. Amelia took small bites of it. She wasn't hungry and it didn't taste that good, but it was nice to eat a meal with her friend.

Late that evening, when she settled down on the sofa, there was no doubt in her mind that she would not sleep all night. She got up and went to the window to take a peek through the blinds, thinking of her dead husband's cold body, and of Marcus Miller and the Grace brothers out there somewhere in the darkness. Staying awake might be better than going to sleep. When she did finally doze off, a nightmare woke her. She sat up and switched on a lamp, and then made her way quietly into the kitchen, pulling the door closed behind her.

It took her a few minutes to locate the card with the investigator's number.

Chapter 65

Doucette's partner had gone home to take a shower and change his clothes. It was late in the evening and Doucette was still sitting at his desk with a fixed determination and no inclination to go home or take a shower. Jack was at a friend's house for the night and he decided Isabelle must be too busy to answer her phone.

Doucette called the number again that he'd been given for Bill Blackwell. His first call had gone directly to voicemail, but he hadn't left a message. This time someone answered but didn't speak.

"Hello," Doucette said.

Nothing.

"Is this Blackie? Bill Blackwell?"

"Who wants to know?"

Doucette recognized the voice and realized he'd met the man before. "It's Inspector Doucette."

"Right. I'm screening my calls."

"I remember you," Doucette said. "You're with the running club, the one with good judgment, dispensing sound advice."

"Yep, that's me, and you're the detective pretending to be an athlete."

It seemed Blackie had remembered him, too.

Doucette apologized for the lateness of his call.

"What can I do for you?" Blackie said.

"It's about your buddy, Keith Sigmund."

"You figured out he didn't do it?"

"Not yet."

"Then go find the asshole instead of wasting your time."

"I know about the rift and the sudden confrontation with his old enemy," Doucette said, still believing there might be a bit more to it than Sigmund was telling.

"What confrontation? Who you been talking to?"

"A couple of witnesses and your good buddy Sigmund. Or should I call him Freud? I know he got pretty upset and I also know that he discussed it with you. He told me what happened and now I want to hear it from you."

"It was nothing."

"I don't believe that. The other guy is dead and there's been bad blood between him and your buddy for a long time."

Blackie snorted loudly. "What do you really want?"

"I want you to think back over what you said after he talked to you and I want to know what information you passed on."

"You got a problem with him talking to me?"

"I'm pretty sure it has some vital bearing on this case," Doucette said, wondering why the man seemed so defensive. "I only want to know whom you told."

"I mentioned it to my wife and she probably told at least a dozen people. She's like that. She doesn't mean any harm."

"Well, the word got around."

"If someone heard something, he heard it from somebody who heard it from somebody else. Everyone talks."

"Tell me something," Doucette said. "You believe your buddy Freud and his old enemy just happened to be on the same street?"

"Yeah." Blackie paused. "I remember the day his sister died. Freud wanted revenge and he got his chance, but he never took it."

"Oh yeah? What chance is that?"

"I hate funerals," Blackie said. "I can't handle the grief. Anyway, I was worried because I thought Miller might show up at the sister's, and when he did I thought Freud was going to try to fix him."

"Fix him?"

"I knew he was packing some heat and it wasn't to protect himself. He was losing it. After everybody left, I saw Miller on the ground. I thought he was dead. His nose was crushed and his face was bleeding, but he was otherwise unharmed."

"Sigmund attacked him?"

"I never said that. Looked to me like Miller had too much to drink and tripped."

"Interesting. Your buddy never mentioned it." Doucette pulled open the file on his desk. "The guy I'm looking for knows his old address. He put me onto the running club. There has to be a connection."

"He could have found the information."

"He didn't hunt down his old enemy without help."

"Well, sorry to disappoint, but you're wasting your time looking at Freud. Now, if you don't mind, I have another problem," Blackie said.

"Maybe I can help?"

"Doubt it, but seeing as you're offering. Got to do with some snake at the gym. Seems he's with a different woman every day and now he's pestering my wife. Time for me to crawl up his ass and turn his life upside down."

"Hey, hang on a minute." Doucette glanced at the paper in the file on his desk. A sudden rush of adrenaline made his head pound. "What gym are you talking about?"

When Blackie mentioned the name of the place, Doucette recognized it as the one where the parolee Steven Grace worked, at least until he'd disappeared.

"Blackie, how much do you know about the guy that's been pestering your wife?"

"Not much. Why? You think he's caught up in this? I heard he's done some time."

"This is a complicated case," Doucette said. "Just tell me what you know."

"His name is Steven Grace and he's about my wife's age, so somewhere around forty."

"Have you ever met him?"

"Yeah, once. He's short and he looks mean. He's weird, the way he just stares at you like half his face is frozen."

"When did the harassment start?"

"Couple weeks back when he asked for her number and followed her home, as creepy as fuck. I went outside to talk to him, but he never spoke a word, so I called some useless dude passing himself off as a manager at the gym to complain."

"What else?"

"They did nothing about it, so I finally went there to sort it out, except no one has seen him for a few days. When he comes back, I'm going to go after him."

"I need to know where I can find Steven Grace."

"Here we go again, you can't determine the connection. Seems to be a recurring theme."

"We've heard that he rents a basement out of a house," Doucette said, ignoring the taunt. "It's local and it's probably not a legal dwelling."

"I don't know anything about that, but I'll talk to my

wife. Maybe one of her friends has been invited inside."

"Steven Grace might have been the last person to see the victim alive. It's important that I find him."

"I get it. When she gets home, I'll have her call you," Blackie said.

"Thanks."

Doucette had another call coming in on his phone. It appeared to be from Amelia Miller and he wanted to take it. At this late hour, it must be important. He picked it up on the third ring.

Chapter 66

"Homicide, Doucette."

He listened to a few seconds of silence before she spoke in a soft voice.

"It's Amelia Miller."

"Hello, Amelia. Is everything okay?"

"I'm staying at Penny Chapman's apartment for a few days," she said, and gave him the address. "I thought you should know."

"I appreciate you telling me." He glanced at his watch. "You know, tomorrow would have been just fine."

"It's not the reason I'm calling."

"Oh? What is?"

"What if I told you that there might be someone who can help you with your case?"

Shit, Doucette thought. He already didn't like the sound of this. He didn't need anyone poking around and jeopardizing his case or making him look worse than he already did. Even Sigmund was minding his own business and he was the one being framed.

"I'd say you'd better tell me what it is that you've been getting into," he said, with a warning in his tone.

"There's this friend of Penny's, a lawyer. She says he can find anyone."

Doucette shut her down. "Listen to me," he said. "I know you're only trying to help, but I don't want you or any of your friends interfering in my investigation. Do you understand me?"

"Yeah. I told her not to involve him in case he accidentally said something to the wrong person."

It was precisely what Doucette was worried about. "I want to be clear. If you interfere or obstruct my case, I will have you arrested."

"I'm not trying to get in the way. I'm telling you this because Penny has already reached out to him. She's supposed to be meeting him at his office in the morning."

Damn. With his boss already displeased with the way he was handling this case, Doucette couldn't afford for it to take another wrong turn.

"Who is this lawyer?" he said. "I need his name and a number."

Amelia told him she couldn't give it to him.

"I'm warning you for the last time," he said. "You and your friend had better not get in my way."

She responded with indignation.

"We won't, but it's not too difficult to see that you've hit a snag. You still don't know who did this, do you?"

"I'm sorry, Amelia, but this is police business. Please stay out of it. I can't have anything jeopardizing my case." It irked him when she persisted.

"What's happening with the lead that Penny gave you?"

"As I said…"

"Have you tried to contact the Grace brothers or is Penny going to have to do it for you?"

He could tell she was being sarcastic, but the question raised an issue in his mind that had been of some previous concern. The Grace brothers may have already tried to make contact with Penny if only to figure out what she knew. If they thought she'd given them up, they might strike again.

"Look, Oliver was killed because of something he

did," Amelia said. "It happened during the week in Las Vegas and I'm certain it involved the Grace brothers. Penny told me they got into some kind of conflict."

"Yeah, I'm aware of it." Doucette hesitated and let the flare of irritation die away. "We believe the Grace brothers are behind Oliver's murder, and we're getting close to figuring it out. In fact, I'm waiting for a call with some information on one of the brothers and then I'm going to pick him up."

She then asked him about Marcus.

He decided to tell her. "The real Marcus Miller, your husband's brother, is dead. He was shot in his car a week before Oliver's murder."

Amelia stayed silent for a brief time. "Do you think Marcus's killer is responsible for what happened to Oliver?"

"It's doubtful. Marcus's body was discovered in San Diego."

"Does Penny know?"

"We only just learned of it and we haven't yet verified all of the information."

"From what I've been told, his brother was a monster. He got what he deserved." She paused. "Perhaps this is the reason Oliver came back."

"It is. We've located his vehicle and we found a note. It seems someone had already made him aware of his brother's murder and we've been trying to figure out who that someone might have been."

"I don't know," she said, leaving the nagging question in Doucette's mind.

He wasn't sure why, but his instincts told him he might be missing something vital. He wondered if one or both of the Grace brothers had traveled to San Diego and killed Marcus, but it didn't answer the question of how Oliver had known, unless Marcus's killer made sure word got back to him.

"I don't understand," Amelia said. "If Marcus is dead, why is someone using his name?"

Doucette could think of several possible reasons and chose not to provide an answer. He shut it out of his mind, focusing his attention instead on a question of his own. The information about Penny meeting with her lawyer could also have waited until morning.

"Is there another reason you called me this late?" he asked.

"I found a picture taken in Las Vegas and I couldn't stop thinking about it. It puts Oliver and the brothers together with Eve. Perhaps it holds some new clues. I can drop it by tomorrow."

The photograph would place the suspected killers with the murder victim during the week the alleged robbery occurred, and Doucette needed to see it. He could also use it to see if Wilkes Smith recognized either of the men as Marcus.

Doucette thanked her. He had barely ended the call when another call came in. It wasn't Bill Blackwell, but a call from Davis Douglas that he wasn't expecting.

"How's it going this evening, John? I have some new data on your guy," Davis said, not giving him a chance to answer. "You ready?"

"Sure." Doucette grabbed his pen.

Davis spoke for two minutes. Doucette scribbled down the details.

Steven Grace had just come out of a new session, wrecked and more than a few hundred dollars down. As he left, he threatened another player with a gun. In response, a couple of homeboys followed him, driving the ten miles to his home and making him realize his mistake.

"Thanks," Doucette said. "Good work."

"Easy enough."

"I believe the woman is almost certainly there."

"I hope it's not too late."

"Me, too. It's been nice to talk to you."

"Same. Let me know if I can do anything else."

Satisfied that he was after the right men, Doucette grabbed his jacket and his keys. In the car, he radioed his partner and told him he was heading out to an address on Page Street and would wait for him there.

Chapter 67

With his night ruined and all of his money gone—taken by the two thugs who'd jumped him outside the basement, then driven him to a deserted area, beaten him up, and taken off in his car—Steven Grace kept his head down and limped home.

Fuming from the attack, he stumbled along, bloodied and seriously shocked, until he finally reached the apartment building in a murderous mood and entered through the unlocked front door. He knew his left hand, probably his nose, and several of his ribs were broken, and he couldn't see anything out of his right eye.

Steep wooden steps led to the basement. He descended them slowly, the gloom making them even harder to navigate. Desperate for a drink, he continued along a dark and narrow hall, groping his way until his hand touched a door. It took a great effort to open it. He staggered inside and leaned heavily against the wall, then switched on the light and released a long string of curses, believing he would go mad from the pain.

This was his brother's fault, but Greg would never accept the blame. As the elder of the two, Greg believed he had power over his brother. He led the way and he always expected Steven to follow. Greg wanted control. He had little interest in hearing what others thought and he made stupid decisions. Using Wilkes Smith was a mistake. The man had too much to lose, but Greg would not be told.

Close to passing out, Steven went to the sink and

turned on the tap. When the cold water touched his face, it hurt, snapping him out of his trance. He scooped some of the water in his palm, held it to his split lips and swallowed. Revived enough to focus, he remembered the woman lying drugged and asleep on the floor a few feet away.

He gazed down at her prone figure and wondered if she was dead. He stared for a while, speculating about what his brother planned to do with her. He wanted to kill her, but he knew his brother wouldn't let him. She was of no use to them and keeping her alive was another mistake. The woman had seen his face. She knew his name. Steven had no intention of going back to prison.

Her dirty long hair covered most of her face. As he looked down at her, she moved the locks from her mouth and began muttering.

"About time you fucking woke up."

She said something he couldn't understand.

He stepped closer and cocked his head to one side until he could make out the words.

She was begging for her life.

"Don't bother to scream," he said. "No one will hear you."

A sudden chill ran through him. There was no doubt that his injuries required medical attention, but he was not about to see the doctor. He hobbled over to a chair by the door and sat down. Pain shot from his ribs to his shoulder. It made him want to weep.

Clenching his jaw, he examined his injuries, trying to assess the bones in his left hand to see if more than one was broken. Man, it fucking hurt. Blood had dripped down the front of his shirt and his breathing was becoming more labored. Worried that a rib might have pierced a lung, he found his phone in his pocket and called his brother, telling him in as few words as possible what had happened to him.

The conversation lasted less than a minute, with his brother erupting in anger over the loss of the car.

"You fucking idiot," he screamed.

The sharp response cut deep. "It's not that big of a deal," Steven said, the exhaustion spreading through him. He didn't want to argue.

"It's a major fucking problem. The car contains evidence."

"Then you should have taken care of it." The criticism triggered Steven's resentment. He hated being made to feel incompetent. "This was all your idea so it's your fault."

"Wait there," Greg said. "I'm coming to meet you." He hung up.

As Steven waited for his brother to arrive, the antagonism festered. When Greg got angry he could turn violent, but Steven was not afraid of him.

Chapter 68

Despite the late hour, there was traffic. Even though Doucette chose the best route, the three-mile journey to the Page Street address took him twenty minutes.

He was close to Kezar Stadium when another vehicle pulled up and he saw his partner inside it. Doucette parked a short distance from the apartment building and got out of his car.

Under the lights from the street, the front of the old house looked okay. There was a garage space, a ground floor, and a unit above it. He decided there must be a basement below grade at the rear. Wondering what awaited them inside, he ran up the front steps and approached the main door. He got no answer when he knocked.

His partner came up the steps behind him. "Who are we confronting here?"

"Steven Grace. Just checking him out." Doucette knocked again. "The sooner we do this, the sooner we can go home."

The front door yielded when he pushed it.

"Don't we need a warrant?" Beaumont said.

"We can get it later. I believe he has the woman here."

Doucette drew his gun. As he entered the house, he motioned for his partner to follow. In the dimly lit entrance hall, Doucette shone his flashlight and noted numbers on the various doors. It appeared to be a rundown rental building operating with four or five units.

"There's fresh blood on the floor," Beaumont said.

"Yeah, I got it. I'm heading over there." Doucette pointed to the stairs leading down. He made his way over and shone his light into the darkness. It looked like the steps led to a cellar, or more of a dank cave with a cold, rank smell rising up.

There was more blood on the railing. "Someone has recently gone down there," he said. With what he now knew, it was pretty easy to figure out what had probably happened.

Beaumont also drew his gun. "I'll wait up here in case anyone else shows up."

"If I'm not back up in five..."

"No problem. I know what to do."

Doucette descended the stairs without making a sound. At the bottom step, he checked behind him, and then crept down the narrow corridor until he stood before a door. A thin line of light could be seen beneath it.

What the hell do I do? He hadn't stopped to consider how many people might be in the basement.

A voice moaned, though not in protest.

Doucette heard a male voice yell, "Shut up."

Then there was silence.

With Beaumont covering him, he banged once on the door.

Quite a few seconds passed before it opened.

The man who appeared before him looked as if he had been seriously messed up. He was conscious, though barely, and he looked like someone Doucette had seen someplace before. The situation felt too familiar and he could not ignore what looked like a corpse in the middle of the floor.

"Steven Grace?"

"Yeah. Who the hell are you?"

"Police."

"Oh, fuck."

As Steven tried to close the heavy door, Doucette pushed him inside the room and shoved him against the wall, checking the injured man's pockets for a weapon and ignoring his angry protests.

Doucette pressed his gun to the man's temple. "If you move one inch, I'll pull the fucking trigger and put a bullet in your head." He glanced at the half-naked body slumped on the floor, about five feet from where he stood. "Is she dead?"

The woman moaned.

Steven Grace stared at Doucette through his one good eye. "Doesn't look like it, does it?"

"Is there anyone else here?"

"Why don't you take a look around?"

The unfinished basement, lit by a single bulb hanging from a short chain in the ceiling, appeared to consist of one small, windowless room with a low ceiling and barely enough space for Doucette to stand up in. There was a sink in one corner with a pee bucket next to it, a mattress on the floor, a table with what appeared to be scraps of old food on it, and a chair by the door. There was also a knife and a cell phone on the table. The room was bare of any other furniture.

The woman lay on her side on the cold concrete. Doucette called out to her and asked her if she could tell him her name.

"Eve." She coughed and tried to push herself up into a sitting position. "My name is Eve Powell and I want to get out of here."

"I don't blame you." The room reeked of urine and he could see that one of her legs was shackled and chained to a hook in the wall. "Can you tell me what happened to you?"

"There's two of them, and they've been keeping me here. They killed my boyfriend."

"Well, this is disturbing." Steven Grace sighed. "With all the sedation, she should be dead."

Doucette knocked him down and used his handcuffs on the man's wrists. Then he put his face close to Steven's left ear, so close he could smell the blood, and asked him, "Where is your brother?"

Slumped on the floor with his hands behind his back, Steven Grace remained silent.

Before Doucette could ask the question again, the cell phone on the table rang once, shut off, and then immediately rang again. No number had appeared on the display. Instinct told him the answer to his next question.

"Is your brother coming here?"

Steven Grace refused to answer.

Chapter 69

People remembered a face like his with the deep and jagged scar that ran down the left side of it from the corner of his eye to his mouth. Some people stared at him in disgust. They already thought he was a criminal.

Greg Grace pulled out his phone and called his brother to let him know he was stuck in traffic. Steven didn't answer.

"Fuck," he said, thinking for a moment and putting away his phone, furious that his brother had put him in this position again where he had to clean up his mess. Half the money belonged to him and he'd already been screwed over it twice.

Why couldn't Steven keep his cool? What didn't he understand about boundaries? Greg was mad at his brother for a lot of things, but right now for letting the two fuckers get the better of him and take his car. Greg knew the two cunning shits and especially their crimes, and if they found anything incriminating in the car he expected them to keep their mouths shut.

Greg preferred to work alone and he regretted involving his younger brother in this, but he'd needed his help to pull it off because of the scar that made him so easily recognizable. Steven was an amateur, the brutal smash-and-grab type, but he was good at blending in, and it was mostly because of Steven that they'd been able to get even with Oliver Miller for stealing their money.

It still amazed Greg that his brother had been right.

After the coward betrayed them and took all the money, he fled; however, he left behind his wife, and a close friend for whom he still had a lot of affection. Oliver Miller was shrewd and cunning, but not sadistic. His brother Marcus had been the opposite: vicious, murderous, but not clever. Greg considered his own brother to be like Marcus, except for a few odd occasions when Steven got a sudden clever idea.

The hit on Marcus Miller had been Steven's idea, and once he'd found someone in San Diego to do the job, the rest had worked out like a dream, far better than Greg could have hoped. If the cops figured things out, they might suspect that one killer was connected to both murders, but they'd find no DNA match. It didn't matter who'd spilled Marcus's blood, but Greg wanted the satisfaction of killing Oliver Miller.

Greg wanted his enemy to know who'd caused his death and he would have preferred it to end violently, make Miller feel the pain, but he knew the fat son of a bitch would fight hard and probably defeat him. They'd been in a public place after all, and he could not afford to create a scene, so he'd done it without too much of a struggle, surprising him in his car and thrusting the syringe deep into his neck.

It was also Steven's idea to use Marcus's name to spook the girls. From what they'd learned in Las Vegas, Steven believed that only something significant would bring Oliver Miller back into the city to see his close friend, and that was why Marcus was murdered; not because of what he'd done, but to flush out his brother.

Then, most unexpectedly, Wilkes Smith had come along also looking for revenge. Funny to think about the kinds of conversations one could strike up with total strangers in a bar. They'd met without planning to and Smith had been useful, right up until the killing, which freaked him out and turned him all honorable and principled.

Bitterness flooded through Greg at the thought of the man's name. After the effort Smith had put in to track his man down, Greg hadn't counted on him to give up. With Smith no longer cooperating, he assumed the idiot had turned himself in to the police. He would never understand the stupidity.

Now that things had gone wrong, Greg felt it was his duty to stick by his brother. His hands clenched around the steering wheel. It must be bad for Steven not to answer his phone. He wondered if his brother had passed out as a result of the head injury he sustained in the beating.

"Fuck," he said again, muttering to himself. "This is worse than I thought."

Anxious to get to the apartment, he drove as fast as the damn traffic would allow and tried not to attract too much attention, constantly scanning his surroundings and checking for cops. He saw none and drove on toward his destination.

When he reached Page Street, he placed his hand on his gun.

Chapter 70

Damn it, I don't need this shit, Doucette thought.

The stench made him want to gag, but the intense desire to keep the woman safe kept him down in the basement. He could feel his heart pumping and his blood getting hot.

Even with Steven Grace injured and restrained, Doucette knew that he should have called for backup before he entered the house instead of following his hunch and rushing ahead to check this out alone. In doing so, he had placed himself and his partner in danger. He knew better. He'd known it would be bad from the moment Wilkes Smith mentioned the basement.

Doucette snapped his head at the sudden noise.

The woman had lost consciousness and fallen backwards, hitting her head on the concrete floor. She was helpless. He knew he had to get her out of the building, but it would take more time than he had, convinced, as he now was, that the other Grace brother was on his way.

Doucette only had his handgun. He expected Greg Grace would be armed. From what he knew, both brothers lived in the neighborhood and Greg could be closer than he thought, maybe only a few minutes away. There was no emergency exit from the basement, no other way out than the way he'd come in. He should have noticed that before. It was at this moment he realized how badly he'd screwed up.

Keeping his gun trained on Steven Grace, watching him with close attention, Doucette moved first to the woman to check on her breathing, and then made his way back across the room.

The heavy basement door stood open; outside it, the dark hallway that led to the stairs. Doucette listened. He heard nothing. Absolute quiet. He could feel his heart beating, and almost hear it.

He trusted Beaumont and understood him well enough from the years they'd worked together to know how his partner would react. Still, he wanted to stop this from ending violently, and he wanted to warn his partner that the other brother was probably on his way and give him time to prepare.

He was about to step into the hall when a soft noise from inside the basement attracted his attention. He turned his head and saw Steven Grace halfway to his feet. The man faltered.

"Stop," Doucette shouted loudly.

Steven looked up, then lurched and made a sudden charge.

As Doucette leaped to the side, the other man's head slammed into the wall. For a second, he seemed surprised. Then his body slumped to the ground, unconscious and no longer a threat.

This gave Doucette some time. He ran fast along the hall and started up the steps, yelling to his partner to let him know the status and warn him that they might not be alone for long and that Greg might already be in the vicinity.

Leaving his partner to radio for backup, Doucette raced back along the hall to help the woman, reluctant to leave her down in the basement. He couldn't let anything else happen to her. When he reached her, she was beginning to regain consciousness

The unresponsive man was still lying on the floor,

making a low moaning sound. He needed medical attention, but he was not Doucette's primary concern.

Using the knife that had been left out on the table, Doucette managed to unscrew the hook where the woman was chained and wrench it out of the wall. As he picked her up, he tried not to hurt her.

Her lips moved, but no sound came out. He remembered there was a possibility she might be pregnant, and she'd begun to have trouble breathing. She must have been down here for three or four days, he thought. What the hell were they going to do with her?

"I'm going to get you out of here," he said.

When he had her in his arms, he saw the fear and the tears in her eyes, but she refused to cry.

Chapter 71

Greg Grace was driving an uninteresting old silver Honda Accord, a car not likely to attract police attention. He continued along Page Street with a strong sense that something was wrong. As soon as he got within two blocks of the apartment building, he knew what it was.

The vehicle parked on the left side of the street looked similar to the one the cop drove last week, the investigator he'd first met at the pier. Returning both hands to the wheel, he immediately slowed and moved cautiously past it, staring straight at the red brake lights up ahead, certain the cops would be out looking for him.

Farther down the road, he spotted a white sedan with a heavy tint on all the windows. It was parked improperly at the side of the road and gave him a weird feeling in his gut. He looked carefully, noting the mean, blacked-out front end and some odd equipment attached to the hood, checking in his rearview mirror as he drove past. With the daylight gone, he could not see if anyone was inside it, so he didn't know if the police were monitoring the building. Though there was no lease or documentation to tie him to the building, if someone had witnessed and reported the attack on his brother, the cops could be in the area. They could already be in the basement.

When he glimpsed the sedan pull out behind him, he started to worry. He couldn't see a plate. Unsure if he was being followed, he kept his speed the same, continuing in the direction of the apartment building, and kept looking in the mirror, watching with eager attention, and then he pulled into a space big enough for only one vehicle and waited to see what would happen.

The sedan passed by him and didn't stop.

Greg veered back out into the road, telling himself not to panic. It was obvious the cops knew nothing. If they'd discovered the basement, there would be a heightened response.

He made a slight adjustment to his mirror, still watchful. His head ached. He'd been through a lot with his brother and had spent most of his early years protecting him from a father who'd turned violent after his mother died giving birth to him. They weren't always close, but they were brothers. They shared the same addictions and traits, except Greg had learned to control his emotions and Steven had grown up to be more violent than their father.

As he approached the apartment building he grew warier and ran a hand through his dark hair. This still didn't feel right and there were a lot of people on the street, which was unusual for this area at this time of night. Some were standing together in groups and talking on their cell phones. It all seemed a little crazy and he didn't like the look of the situation, couldn't shake the strong sense of foreboding or ignore the nauseating dread that had crept into his stomach.

A man saw him draw near and stepped out into the road. Greg tried to drive past, but another man stopped him by getting out of his car. Greg slammed his foot on the brake. The second man jumped back. They locked eyes for a second. Greg cursed, anxious to know what was unfolding at the apartment building.

Deep in his gut, he knew. He stretched his neck to see a tall man in the doorway. It was the cop from the pier and he was holding a woman in his arms. Greg could see she was in bad shape. She had to be the reason for the cops, and he regretted abducting her, or maybe he now regretted letting her live. She was the only link to the murder. He couldn't see his brother.

Wrapped up in his guilt and fearing the cops might cut off his escape route, Greg found a gap big enough to drive through and, gripping the wheel tightly, quickly passed the building, leaving his brother behind.

The sound of a distant police siren made it through the jumble of noise in his head.

Chapter 72

Steven Grace remained unconscious, but alive.

With backup on the way, Doucette exited the apartment building carrying the abducted woman in his arms. She appeared to be going downhill so fast that he decided not to wait and put her in his car. He didn't know what drugs were in her system, or how much, or if she'd survive whatever else they'd done to her, but he hoped she would be okay.

As he drove with her through the still heavy traffic toward the hospital, he stole glances at her unmoving form to see if she was still breathing. She looked a pitiful mess and she smelled sour. He figured she'd probably been raped.

When he swung the car into the hospital grounds, he headed straight to the emergency department. The doctor who'd been waiting for him came out and met him.

The doctor gazed at the unresponsive woman. "Do we have a name?'

"Eve Powell."

"What has she ingested?"

Doucette shook his head. "Not sure, some combination of tranquilizers or sedatives, more than enough to keep her quiet."

The doctor nodded, checking her pulse. "How long was she sedated?"

"She's been held for around five days. There's something else. She might be pregnant."

"We'll do all we can for her," the doctor said, placing his hand upon Doucette's shoulder.

"Appreciate it. I want to know how she is."

"Of course."

"Thank you for your help."

As Doucette drove through the city again back to the basement apartment, his thoughts returned to his suspects, and more specifically to Greg Grace's whereabouts. With Wilkes Smith in a cell and Steven Grace under arrest, he needed to catch one more suspect and he expected the third man to be somewhere nearby. Greg Grace was the one he considered to be the mastermind, more dangerous than the other two.

Greg Grace posed a threat to anyone in his way. Pretty certain he'd have a gun and would be prepared to fight hard, Doucette wanted this man taken off the street before he could hurt anyone else or take another hostage. If he was here, he was coming for the woman. Why else would he take such a huge risk?

He saw additional units had arrived and begun to put up tape. Eager to locate his partner and find out who was running the apartment building, knowing he was not going to find the Grace brothers named on any lease, Doucette pulled into the nearest parking space. His partner met him as he got out of his car.

"We've got a witness who says he saw a man carrying a woman into the building a few days ago, but thought she was drunk," Beaumont said. "Also says he reported the behavior to the management company and never heard back."

"Did he see the man's face? We need to link it to Greg Grace."

"He could only describe him as a middle-aged man in a

black jacket."

Beaumont said he'd also talked to a second witness who'd claimed the driver of a car almost hit him in the moments before Doucette left. "Said it looked like he was fleeing the scene."

As soon as he heard this, Doucette felt certain the driver had been the third suspect, the one he'd first met on the pier.

Chapter 73

Despite the powerful urge to get away, Greg Grace drove carefully, slightly below the speed limit. With nowhere to go, he continued to check in his mirror for anyone following, putting more distance between him and the apartment.

He wondered if his brother would betray him? He knew he wouldn't mean to, but Steven could be dumb, though he would never give up easily. Deserting his brother left him conflicted, but what would he accomplish by going back for him? He'd been planning this for months, obsessing over it and allowing the dark and hostile anger to twist inside and turn him into a murderer. His plan had not gone well. In fact, it had turned out to be a disaster, but he wouldn't admit defeat without waging one last war.

For the next mile he drove a little distracted, going over in his mind his brother's voice in their last conversation, trying to work out if Steven had been forced to make the call. It seemed to Greg like minutes before the cops were there on the scene, and there had been more people than usual on the street. He believed he knew why.

Greg figured the cops must have rousted all the residents from their apartments trying to find him. He also believed the police had used his brother as bait to deceive him. He wondered if Steven had actually been beaten up or was even injured. What about the dude who almost got himself run over? Was he part of it, assisting the cops, put there to signal a murder suspect's approach? It appeared to

Greg as though they might have been expecting him, but he refused to believe he'd been deceived by his own brother, because recognizing it stirred up more anger than he could deal with.

The cops would probably be setting up a perimeter. They would be expecting a fight. Greg recognized the reality of his situation. With no backup plan and no money, he saw no way out of this. He would wind up in prison with some real uncivilized badass fuckers doing twenty-five-to-life.

Though the desire to escape remained strong, it was time to end this. If he had to go, he'd go out kicking ass and make sure he took somebody else with him.

He hadn't seen Penny Chapman since the week in Las Vegas. He recalled her as quiet and aloof, a judgmental bitch with an average level of intelligence, but he realized now that he might have underestimated her. She must have figured it out and gone to the cops, put them on his trail. How else would they know to look in the basement? This fuckup had her name all over it and he blamed her for the failure of his little operation. It was easier than blaming his brother.

His miscalculation created a vortex of bitter hatred. As he progressed through the city, he reached into his pocket for the folded piece of paper that he'd taken from Oliver Miller's wallet. On it was a handwritten name and address.

Penny Chapman lived about two miles away on the 600 block of Minna Street in The Mission, a neighborhood known for theft and assault crimes. A lot of the people living there kept their eyes closed, worrying about their safety and staying inside their apartments, but as a six-foot, muscular male, this sort of area never much bothered Greg.

Eager to get there, he kept going along Oak Street and

then changed his mind and used the city side streets instead of the most direct route, partly due to traffic, but mostly because he was hoping to make it harder for police to pin down his location. It was a risk, seeing as he was not trying to get outside their perimeter.

Watching carefully for authority figures, or anyone who looked like they might cause him trouble, he made his way closer to the address Miller had noted.

Turning left onto her block, he pulled into a vacant space at the curb and got out of the car, leaving the keys in it and the engine running, hoping for some low life to steal it.

Then, tucking his gun into the waistband so it sat against his lower back, he continued the rest of the way on foot, until he stood directly across the street from a parking garage gated at ground level beneath the block of apartments that included her unit.

Damn.

It appeared that he needed a gate code and he didn't have one.

Chapter 74

Adrenaline pumped inside him. Doucette took a deep breath and filled his lungs with the damp evening air. He wanted to get out a description and the last known direction of travel before the man he was after could send a text to a friend to come get him.

"He couldn't have made it far," Beaumont said. "He's in the general area."

"I think I know where he might go."

Doucette was relying on negative gut instinct. He'd remembered the chalk mark on the curb outside Amelia Miller's Dolores Heights home, and he was thinking about the last time he talked to her. She'd mentioned a photograph and she'd spoken in a low whisper as if she didn't want anyone to overhear her.

"You drive," he said to his partner, tossing him the keys. "I don't have time to explain."

Penny Chapman lived about three miles away. Doucette estimated that Greg Grace had only a few minutes head start, but it might be all he needed.

He tried to reach Penny Chapman on her cell phone. His call went directly to voicemail. He tried calling her friend. Amelia Miller answered. Despite the hour, she sounded energized and fully awake.

"Where are you?" he said.

"I'm still at Penny's apartment. Why? Is something wrong?"

"It seems you were right," he said. "We just picked up

Steven Grace, but his brother got away."

"What do you mean, he got away? How? Where is he?"

She sounded angry. He couldn't blame her. "I'm on my way over to you now," he said, aware of the steady rise in his pulse. "Are you alone?"

"No. Penny's here, but she's in bed."

"I'm about fifteen minutes away. I want you to stay inside and keep your door locked until I get there. Call me if you notice anything unusual, anyone waiting around."

"Do you think he's going to come here?"

"I don't know, but I want you to understand the risks. It may not only be money that he wants." Doucette felt certain that Greg Grace had remembered the photograph and planned to take away the piece of evidence that could be used to solve the case and identify him as Wilkes Smith's accomplice.

"It's a gated community." Amelia gave him a four-digit code. "I have my dog with me. He can be vicious with strangers."

"Good." A dog would be beneficial, though possibly not enough.

The roads were still busy. Doucette directed his partner to take Clayton Street to Oak Street and continue along Oak for a couple of miles. He radioed his superior to let him know where they were heading.

"We believe he's going to the apartment."

"All right. Follow him, and make sure he doesn't leave there."

"Yes, sir."

Doucette put away his phone, still struggling to reconcile with the mistake he'd made in letting the man go. Guilt flowed over him like an itch, making him uncomfortable in his own skin.

"You sure you're not miscalculating this?" Beaumont said.

"I'm still thinking about it."

If Greg Grace thought the police had discovered his identity, he could be ruthless and more dangerous than his brother. Doucette believed he would kill anyone who got in his way. Nothing made him more certain than the knowledge that this man had murdered his own friend.

Chapter 75

The piece of paper he took from his pocket did not include a code for the large metal gate. Greg swore loudly. He tried punching in various four-digit number combinations, cursing each time they failed. Nothing he tried got him in and no one was driving up to the gate. It drove him mad. He hit every damn button on the intercom, and then checked around for another way in.

He noticed a small gate box at the entrance. It was located in a separate area used by visitors and it listed the names of the residents. Unable to find Penny Chapman, he selected a name at random, pressed a button, and waited while it auto-dialed the resident's phone.

She answered.

"Pizza delivery," he said, thinking fast.

"Didn't order any." The woman didn't press the buzzer and the gate didn't move.

Greg tried the same ruse with a different resident, this time pretending to be a cab driver. The second effort also failed. He swore, looked around, and then checked his watch, surprised to see it was almost eleven o'clock at night. Then he realized what might get him in.

The next female resident he tried to trick sounded sleepy, or perhaps drunk. "Honey," he said, making sure he didn't sound mean or angry. "I forgot the code and I've left my key at your place."

"Not too clever, are you?"

"Are you going to leave me outside?"

"Course not."

He stepped back and waited. As the warning buzz sounded and the black gate slowly started to open, he let out a short laugh.

As the gate opened, a vehicle pulled up behind him. Expecting to see cops, Greg stood a little straighter and strode inside the complex without turning his head, attempting to give the impression that he belonged here. A truck passed him without stopping, spewing obnoxious fumes into the air.

Having never been here before, Greg started off through the complex following in the same direction as the truck, and looking for the apartment number he wanted. He got closer and closer, and finally found Penny Chapman's apartment located on the ground floor all the way at the back of the building. The quiet location pleased him. It thrilled him to see the interior lights and movement inside.

Someone was home.

Breathing hard, he put on a black mask intended to terrorize her and withdrew his gun from his waistband. With thoughts of killing her swimming inside his head, he rapped once on the front door with his knuckles, a solid hard knock, and shouted out, "It's the police. Would you mind opening the door?"

He heard the deep bark of a dog from inside the apartment. It sounded fierce. Greg took a step back.

"Fuck," he muttered under his breath. He'd forgotten all about the friend and her dog and he hoped that he wouldn't have to shoot it.

No one answered the door.

He knocked a second time and called out, "Police. We need to talk to you for a minute."

Chapter 76

Doucette was about a mile from Penny Chapman's apartment when his cell phone rang. The display showed Penny Chapman's number.

He answered, asking himself why she was calling.

"Penny?"

"Yes."

"Are you okay?"

"Where are you?"

She sounded tense and a sudden suspicion hit him. He experienced a wave of anger and a burning sensation in his gut. "I'm about a mile away," he said.

"Did you send someone else?"

"No. I did not."

"There's someone at the door. He says he's a police officer. I don't believe him."

It confirmed Doucette's suspicion. "Stay inside," he said. "Do not open the door. You do not have to speak to him."

"How do I get him to leave?"

"Tell him you don't want to talk. You're within your rights to say no."

"What if he won't leave?"

Doucette instructed his partner to make a left turn at the second cross street. "If you feel comfortable you can talk to him through the door," he said into the phone. "Ask him his name. Find out what he wants."

"But, if you didn't send anyone, why is he here?"

"I think I know who he might be and he's trying to trick

you."

"What do I do?"

"Tell him you've called the police. We're almost there," he said. "Less than half a mile away."

"Please hurry." She reminded him of the location of her ground-floor apartment within the complex.

"It's only a couple more blocks." Doucette spoke calmly despite a surge of adrenaline that made his heart race. "We're close. Whatever you do, do not open the door."

Greg Grace was a cunning and intelligent individual. He must know the police would be looking for him and it didn't worry him because he believed he could outwit them. By going to the apartment, he was making either a bold or a stupid move.

Doucette viewed it as a taunt, a killer mocking the police and daring them to catch him, and it was exactly this kind of crazy shit he didn't like. He glanced across at his partner's face, knowing Beaumont was probably thinking the same thought.

Why wasn't this man giving them more trouble? If he'd given up, it made him more dangerous; however, Doucette doubted that this killer had given up. He expected Greg Grace to fight to the end.

It was up to him to stop this now, before anyone else got hurt. The two women had nothing to do with this, but criminals like the Grace brothers would not care.

As they approached her block, located between Seventh Street and Eighth Street, he noted an old man standing with his dog on the sidewalk. The area appeared calm. Nothing alerted him to a disturbance of any kind, but he felt it.

Chapter 77

The dog continued to bark, but there were no footsteps moving through the house and no one came to the door.

Greg knocked again. "If you don't open the door, I'll come back with a warrant. It will be easier for you if you talk to me now."

He knew the two women were inside. If he couldn't trick his way in, then he would force his way in and kill them both. He'd considered the possibility that at least one of the women would have a firearm, and maybe she had even learned to shoot it, but he doubted she'd be quick enough or precise with her aim.

The apartment had an average quality wooden door with a lock that appeared to be old, the typical inexpensive type that he'd picked before, but it would take too much time. The window had bars installed and a thorny rosebush beneath it. He took a good look at the front of the apartment for the best point of entry, and decided he would have to use brute force. Without wasting any more time, he drew a sharp breath and then rushed at the door, pitching his full weight against it.

The wood cracked, but the door held.

"Open the fucking door," he ordered, stepping back and then ramming it again with his shoulder. It gave a little.

On the third try, he crashed his way into her apartment.

No security alarm went off and no big dog charged, though he could hear it going crazy inside one of the rooms.

He glanced around.

The apartment was small, consisting of a short and narrow hallway and three rooms. Knowing the two women could be hiding behind any of the three doors, he checked the room closest to him first, a small and bare room with a single bed and a closet.

Next, he checked the kitchen with its tiny diner booth.

On the kitchen table he saw the photograph that had been taken in Las Vegas. It showed him standing with his brother, Oliver Miller, and the woman in his basement. With his hair now cut short and no beard, the image barely resembled him, except for the betraying scar.

Turning away from it, he tried the bathroom door and couldn't get in. Unless the women were in the process of escaping through a window, they were locked inside the bathroom with the dog to protect them, terrified and cowering behind the door. Apartments like this one had no rear entrance.

"Did you think you could beat me?" He banged on the bathroom door repeatedly and twisted the knob. "Come out of there," he yelled. "If you don't I'll kick down the door and I'll shoot you and the damn dog."

His threat was met with an empty silence and it was really starting to annoy him.

The door had an easy push-button lock, the type designed for privacy and not security, and a simple paperclip would get him in. He ran his hand along the top of the doorframe but didn't find one.

He heard the scrambling sound of someone trying to escape, and then the dog stopped barking.

Greg rammed the door with his shoulder. The flimsy thing held, adding to his frustration. As he raised his leg to kick a hole in it, he heard another noise.

The lock clicked, the knob turned, and the bathroom

door opened. Penny Chapman stood facing him. "Please don't shoot me."

"Shut up."

"If I tell you where the money is, will you take it and go?"

"You don't know where the money is. For you, it's too late."

"It's a lot of money, Greg. Are you sure you want to leave without it?"

He pushed her back inside the bathroom and continued holding the gun on her while he checked out the tub and the big closet. There was no sign of the dog or of the other bitch with the dyed blonde hair. He assumed they'd both gone out through the open window.

"Your friend's a coward, like her husband." He waved the gun in her face. "Why didn't you try to get away?"

"Because I know you, and I'm not afraid of you," she said. "If you came here to kill me, you would have already taken a shot at me."

"So you figured it out. Took you a little longer than I expected."

"The police know you're coming here."

"Yeah, I realize that."

She stared at him. "What are you going to do?"

He stared back. "I'm going to ruin your life before they get here, and it's going to be a whole hell of a lot worse for you now that you're alone."

"You want the money. I can see that you're desperate."

"Shut the fuck up."

"Why did you come here if you don't want the money?"

"I never said I didn't want it." Her courage surprised him, and then he noticed the chef's knife in her hand. "Drop it," he said.

She ignored him. "If I give you the money, you can go on your way."

"Yeah? How much?"

"Five thousand. You can still get out of here. You're sharp."

"And you're easy to deceive. I said drop the knife."

"No. You'll have to shoot me."

He pointed the gun at her face, astonished when she didn't flinch.

"Wait a minute," she said. "You called Amelia a coward, yet you're the one who's hiding behind the mask. Are you afraid to show me your ugly face?"

"Trust me, you don't need to try and provoke me." In anger, he pulled off the black mask and tossed it aside. "If you don't drop the knife, I'll shoot you and I'd be well within my rights. You've caused a lot of problems."

"Did you really come here to kill me, Greg?"

He shoved her into the hallway, itching to place his hands on her neck. "Move," he said.

"Where?"

He motioned to the kitchen, out of sight of the broken front door. "Make it quick. I'm about to be arrested for murder so I don't have much time."

"Tell me why you killed Oliver."

"The man deserved to die for his greed."

"His greed? What about yours? You stole that money."

"We stole it, and then Oliver betrayed me."

"So, I was right."

"About what?"

"You robbed someone in Las Vegas."

"No comment." He grinned. "You know what they say."

"It's in my bedroom," she said. "Some of the money is hidden under the mattress in my bedroom. Oliver was coming back to collect it, but it's yours, so just take it and go."

"We are way beyond the money." Despite the gun he held in his hand, he was not used to this situation. Unlike his brother, he didn't enjoy killing.

Her eyes met his. The challenge he saw in them triggered a familiar unease in him. She was a strong unemotional woman competing with him intellectually and it made him feel unsure.

"You came here for the money or to kill me," she said. " Maybe both. If you don't want the money, then why don't you pull the trigger?"

"You think I won't?"

"I'm not sure, but if you do, it will make you less of a man."

"That's true; however, I don't see any other option." He thrust the gun into her abdomen, but found he couldn't pull the trigger.

She gasped. For a second, they stared at each other. He saw the incredulity in her eyes.

"I knew you wouldn't be able to do it," she said.

Then she went wild, lunging for him and swinging at him with the knife, knocking the gun from his hand to the floor and forcing him to step back out into the hallway. Out of control and trying to slash at his neck, she sliced him across the face instead, the sharp blade ripping open the old scar.

He screamed with the hot pain. His face felt like it had exploded. Blood ran between his fingers as he tried to hold the gaping wound together.

When she came at him again, he wrestled the knife

from her hand. With a snarl and a surge of pure hatred, he punched her, giving her a bloody nose. It was the first time he'd ever hit a woman and it felt good to hurt her.

He held her head tight in the crook of his arm so he could hit her a second time, and a third time. He continued hitting her, pumping his fist into her face, hell-bent on showing her that he possessed the capacity to kill her. She fought back, and for a small woman she put up a respectable struggle.

The burst of negative energy was like a bomb going off inside him and he couldn't let go, could not stop hitting her, even after she'd stopped responding. He wanted her to get a taste of four months of rage.

A noise came from behind. Then, without any warning, his legs crumbled beneath him. He dropped abruptly and slid to the ground.

Chapter 78

The small square-shaped apartment complex had one common access point shared by all residents and visitors. This should make it easier for Doucette to trap his suspect.

Penny Chapman's residence was located in a quiet corner at the back of the complex. Because of her past, it surprised Doucette. He followed the numbers. Nobody seemed to be about.

Then, out of the darkness, he saw a woman running and a dog without a leash. Caught in the glare of his lights, she stopped and raised her hand.

He recognized her and pulled up close. "Mrs. Miller. Are you hurt?"

"No, but he's still inside the apartment."

Her voice sounded strange, although her words were straightforward. Doucette got out of his car.

"Is he alone?"

"I don't know."

"Where's Penny?"

"She couldn't get away. We were hiding in the bathroom. I managed to get out. He said he would shoot us."

"I want you to wait here. Do you understand?" Doucette put her and the dog in the back seat of his car.

"I'm not sure if I've killed him," she said. "I smashed him in the head with a hammer."

Doucette approached the building with his gun drawn, listening for the sounds of erratic breathing and running footsteps.

As he entered the apartment through the broken front door, he saw two bodies on the floor in the hallway, lying in a small puddle of blood. It was obvious that they were both unconscious and possibly dead.

His partner followed him inside and moved past the bodies, returning and holstering his gun when he'd cleared the rest of the apartment.

"She's hurt pretty bad," Doucette said, checking for a pulse. She'd been beaten so badly he hardly recognized her.

The condition of the hallway indicated the struggle that had taken place. There was also blood on the walls.

The man was lying on his side on the floor with blood in his hair and the red and raw wound visible on his left cheek. There was no doubt in Doucette's mind that this was the same man he'd first met at the pier claiming he'd found the body, the runner trying to frame Keith Sigmund.

He'd been struck from behind. A bloodied knife and a bloodied hammer lay on the floor beside the bodies. Doucette shook his head. "I could have prevented this."

"Give yourself a break." Beaumont did not have his police radio with him and called in to report it from his cell phone. Then he returned to the car and brought Amelia to the apartment.

"You'll find the gun in a garbage bin," she said from the doorway. "I had to get it away from him in case he woke up."

Doucette nodded. "Pretty good nerve you have there."

"Thank you for getting here so soon. I thought he was going to kill us."

"You can thank your friend," Doucette said. "She made an intelligent decision to call me. I don't think he was expecting that."

"Will she be okay?"

"She needs a trip to the hospital."

"What about him? Is he dead?"

Doucette shook his head. "No. He'll probably make it."

"So much for security," Amelia hugged her dog close. "These are supposed to be safe premises."

Chapter 79

On an overcast morning, her disguise drew more attention than it deflected. She wore a brown knitted cap with most of her hair tucked inside it, and a large pair of sunglasses covering half her face. She strode across the hospital parking lot with urgency in her step.

Doucette caught up with her as she unlocked her car door.

"Can I have a minute to talk to you?"

Penny Chapman didn't say anything. She removed her sunglasses to reveal ugly, swollen black eyes.

Doucette winced. "How do you feel?"

"I feel terrible," she said. "I've spent two nights in the hospital. Have you tried sleeping in a hospital?"

"Anything else keeping you awake?"

"I'm not sure I know what you mean."

"I can always sense when someone is afraid," he said.

"It's true. I am afraid." She fiddled with her sunglasses. "I'm still scared that Marcus isn't dead and that he's going to send someone else to kill me."

"Marcus is dead. So far, we've found no evidence linking his murder to our investigation. We believe his death may be drug related." Though Doucette suspected the Grace brothers, he lacked proof.

"Why did they use his name?"

"It suited their situation. They'd learned of your past and they wanted you to think he was coming after you again."

"Bastards." She pressed her hand against her forehead.

He saw tears well in her bruised eyes. "I wanted to thank you," he said. "You were right about the robbery. Without your help, we wouldn't have made the connection to the Grace brothers so soon, and maybe not at all."

"Is it over?"

"Not quite, but it's all going to end soon. I wanted to let you know that Eve will survive. She's strong, and she'll be able to help us put the brothers away."

"Good."

"We're confident we'll be able to identify Greg Grace as the accomplice from the photograph you took."

"That was because of Amelia, not me."

"I also brought a letter we found in Oliver's car. It's intended for you."

"I don't understand. Why did he write me a letter?"

"To ensure he got the chance to say goodbye." Doucette put the note in her hand. "You wanted to know the reason he came back? Well, this will explain it."

"Goodbye?" She gazed at the note in her hand and then shook her head. "Thank you, but I don't think I want to read it, at least not yet. I can't help thinking that it's because of me that he's dead."

"It isn't. He was relocating across the country to start his life again. I guess he didn't know how to put all those years of friendship into a phone call."

Doucette left her in the hospital parking lot and went inside to talk to Eve Powell, who'd been too incoherent to tell them much.

After a test for drugs, Eve had been found clean except for the sedatives. The last thing she said she remembered was returning to the car and finding her boyfriend unresponsive. Doucette's questions were now starting to awaken other memories.

She told him that she recalled music had been playing on the car radio before her boyfriend turned it off.

"We were arguing. I threw my engagement ring at him and told him I didn't love him and that I never wanted to wear it again," she said. "I didn't mean we should break up. I just blurted it out because I was hurt and now I'm horrified that my last words to him were so hateful."

It answered Doucette's question about the ring found on the floor of Oliver Miller's car. He wondered what words or actions had wounded her, but he didn't have to ask or wait long to find out.

"I couldn't understand why he kept a picture of his ex-wife in his wallet. When I asked him why he hadn't filed for divorce, he refused to answer. He said he didn't want to get into it, but we were engaged and we're having a baby. We had a pretty nasty fight a few days ago and I'm afraid I really laid into him. Now I'm never going to see him again."

It would probably have explained the chest bandage, but Doucette didn't ask. She had so much pain in her blue eyes that he found them hard to look at. "What happened after you threw the ring?"

"We were at some nasty gas station in Oakland. I had to pee, so I got out of the car. As I came out of the restroom, this man approached me." She bit down on her lip and pressed a hand to her belly. "He had a gun and he told me I had to go with him or they were going to kill my boyfriend. I didn't know it then, but they had already killed him."

Doucette waited while she took a small sip of water. He noticed the wrinkles around her eyes, and the dry, dull skin of her face looked less than healthy. The young woman wiped a hand across her eyes. Damp hair stuck to her forehead. Doucette felt sorry for her.

"Are you all right?" he said.

"I'm fine."

She appeared exhausted, yet agreed to continue. He showed her the photograph he'd taken from Penny Chapman's apartment and asked her if she had seen any of the men that night at the gas station.

She didn't hesitate. When she saw Steven Grace in the photo, she identified him as the man who'd approached her with the gun. She also recognized his brother and confirmed he had been there in the car.

"I can't believe Oliver was murdered by his friends."

"Sometimes, it's easier to forgive an enemy than a friend," Doucette said. Someone at the gym had given Steven an alibi. Doucette wondered if they'd been paid to do it or had offered it up to return a favor. He intended to go back there and find out.

He rubbed a hand over his chin, the skin rough, reminding him he needed to shave. "One thing's been bothering me. You were in the area for three days leading up to the murder. What were you doing?"

"Seeing the sights," she said, shifting her gaze.

"What did you visit?"

"Nothing really."

"Seriously?"

She shrugged. "I don't know what else to say."

"I want you to think hard," Doucette said, getting the sense that she no longer wanted to talk to him. "Your boyfriend was seen in the neighborhood and it seemed like he might have been heading back to his old home. Why would he go there?"

"I'm afraid only Oliver can answer that."

"Well, he can't now, can he?" He waited for her to say

something. When she didn't, he decided she must be lying and felt something inside him harden. "I've derived the opinion that the two of you returned for the money. How much of it did he hide in his old house?"

She shook her head. "It doesn't make any sense. Why would he leave money in his old house?"

Her response convinced him. She hadn't asked what money he was talking about. "Thank you for your help, Miss Powell," he said, getting up to leave. "I'll be in touch."

Chapter 80

After Doucette left the hospital, he met with his superior to go over the case.

Prepared to get his ass chewed out in Lieutenant Cole Taylor's office, Doucette declined to take a chair, preferring to stand and be addressed at eye level.

Taylor also stayed standing.

"Okay, give me the latest," Taylor said, ignoring the phone ringing on his desk.

Expecting criticism, Doucette obliged. "The Las Vegas robbery provided the motive. One brother, Steven Grace, devised the plan and the other brother, Greg Grace, acquired and administered the drug that killed Oliver Miller. They dumped him in the water after he died."

"The lure of easy money. What about Smith?"

"Wilkes Smith got tricked from the start. He must feel absolutely cursed."

Cole Taylor snorted. "What Miller stole from Smith measured up to be a lot more than money, but Smith is equally guilty. He was involved in the plan and he admitted to making the phone calls meant to intimidate Miller's wife."

"The brothers never intended to let him out of the agreement alive. It was a dangerous plan and Smith knew it."

"You're assuming Smith intended to deliver the money."

"Yeah, he's as guilty as they are, but as a parent I

understand why he did it. Some might say he had good reason."

"I don't. They share the same primal instinct, men willing to hit back, savage, weak, and barbaric. They raped and almost killed an innocent woman."

"Guiltless of murder anyway."

"What's that supposed to mean?"

Doucette smiled. "She denies it of course, but his girlfriend knew about the robbery. I believe the money is the primary reason for Miller's return, not to say goodbye. He left a note in case anything happened to him."

A frown darkened Cole Taylor's features. "Have the brothers asked for a lawyer?"

"Not yet."

"Then make them talk and get them to confess. I don't care how low you have to go."

"We'll do our best," Doucette said.

"I expect nothing less. What about the landlord, or is he another piece of shit?"

"He doesn't appear to know a lot about his tenants." Doucette explained. "The original tenant lives in one of the apartments and the lease is still in place, but he's been out of the country for six months. He was using the basement for storage, and Greg Grace simply answered an ad."

"Are you saying he's been planning this for at least six months? That's before the Vegas robbery even took place."

"Yeah, I realize that. Probably intended to use it for some other criminal purpose." The timing posed a lingering question for which Doucette could not summon an immediate answer. It was obvious that Greg Grace was not going to live down there.

"You're not looking for anyone else?"

"We've got the guys we want."

"What about Keith Sigmund? I mean the real Sigmund, not the dude you let go. What's the reason for his connection?"

"He's easy to exploit, single man with no family and no one to go after him if he's in jail. Grace took advantage."

"You could have saved us a lot of time," Taylor said, shaking his head. "I have to tell you, I don't like the way you handled this case."

"I followed my gut."

"You made a lot of mistakes."

"I know." Doucette lowered his gaze slightly, understanding the situation for what it was. He'd screwed up. He knew that without the help of the two women, the brothers might never have been caught and another case might have gone unsolved. Eve Powell would have died.

"You look like shit," Taylor said.

"I feel like shit," Doucette replied. "Deprived of sleep and food and water."

Taylor's expression changed. "So, you believe some of this money is hidden at the old address, am I right?"

"Yeah, and there was enough of it to bring the original thief back. It's also my belief that he was planning to pay his wife a visit and never got the chance."

"Smith said he ransacked the place."

"Maybe he didn't know where to look."

"Or someone else found it." Taylor raised a single eyebrow. "Maybe you should go have another chat with Mrs. Miller, see if you can figure out what happened to it."

Doucette said nothing. He waited for what he knew would come next.

The lieutenant continued. "You know you're one of my best. That's why I put you on the Roger's case."

"Yes, sir."

"His mother has been calling. I want her to know that we are still looking for her son's murderer. I don't want to have to take you off the case."

That hit Doucette where it hurt. He matched Taylor's stare, trying to control the silent anger building inside him. "I've never stopped being committed to the case."

"I've never doubted your determination." Cole Taylor exhaled loudly. "I want a daily update on your progress."

"You'll have it."

Chapter 81

Echoes of Ireland and the strident tones of her mother's voice found their way inside her head.

You're no different. You're exactly like me.

Amelia glanced in the rearview mirror and stroked her hair back from her face. Half an hour ago, she'd been lying naked in the arms of a man she had just met, breathing in his fresh scent mixed with slight traces of disinfectant in the motel room. She didn't even know his name, but the sex had been good. She could feel soreness where his rough hands had grabbed her hips and a burn from his faint stubble that had rubbed against her skin.

As she parked the blue truck outside her home, it seemed natural to wait and see if anyone had followed. With a sigh, she glanced at the lonely apartment. She'd become used to arriving home to an empty place with nobody opening the front door.

She inhaled. Glad to see no sign of Laurel May, she used her new key to let herself in, leaving the dark shadows outside.

In a strange way, Oliver's murder made it easier for her to deal with what needed to be done. She'd been mourning his loss for four months, unable to move on when a small part of her refused to give up the hope that he would come back. His death left her feeling the distance and it paved the way for her to let go of her grief and put her life back together.

Moving on meant parting with the few possessions

he'd left behind. His things in her home no longer brought her comfort. It was not necessary to keep them.

First, she tackled the boxes in the basement, finding the task much easier to face than she'd anticipated. It was only a couple of dusty boxes, a few random items, and some old furniture that held no memories. She carried the boxes upstairs, took out the photographs she wanted, and dumped everything else outside for trash. The furniture would be donated.

Then she went upstairs to clean out the clothes he'd left behind in the tiny closet they'd once shared. Previously reassured by their presence, she found the removal of them a rather more difficult undertaking. As her hands moved through the dozen dark suits and white shirts that he'd worn, she remembered the impact they'd had on her.

Oliver Miller had known how to dress. He'd looked successful, intellectual, like someone who might be going somewhere in the world, and she'd been drawn to the smart and professional appearance. How incredibly naïve she'd been, she thought, to conclude an opinion of a man based on what he wore. Now, lifting the hangers from the rail and extracting her dead husband's clothes from her closet, she wondered why she'd wanted to keep them and why they still meant something to her.

As she carried an armful of his suits to pile up on the bed, a fat brown envelope fell from a side pocket. Amelia picked it up. It was sealed and not addressed to anyone. She tore it open. Inside, she found a large number of loose bills, mostly hundreds and fifties. There was no note. With shaking hands, she pulled the cash out and counted it.

Three thousand dollars was a lot of money and it almost left her speechless. She held it in her hands and stared at it, almost certain she knew where it had come from. She stuffed it back inside the envelope and nervously placed the envelope on the bed, thoughts of easy sex and booze flitting through her brain. Sex and booze always made her feel way better than a session with Dr. Butt, and it cost a lot less. It was too late for her to change.

She started to make a phone call, and then stopped.

The money wasn't hers. It wasn't Oliver's. It belonged to someone else's family. She thought about the man following it and hounding her, threatening her. Perhaps he could still get to her.

Filled with contempt for herself, for her contemplations, she called the investigator on the case and asked him if he could come over to her home.

"Sure," he said. "But what's it about?"

"Change." It was all she could think of to say.

About The Author

A British author of mysteries and thrillers, Jenny Hilborne divides her time between California and England. Her background is in real estate and the finance industry, elements of which often find their way into her novels.

Jenny enjoys reading, cycling, and traveling. She is an avid fan of puzzle books and crosswords.

Jenny's other works include: *MADNESS AND MURDER, NO ALIBI, HIDE AND SEEK, STONE COLD, THE BLACKEST NIGHT,* and *EASY TARGET.*

———••———

For more information about Jenny:

www.facebook.com/pages/Jenny-Hilborne-Author-Page/1393637564216420

www.jfhilborne.com

www.amazon.com/Jenny-Hilborne/e/B003YYF5F4